The Touchstone

By the same author

The Love Spoon

The Touchstone

Pamela Kavanagh

ROBERT HALE · LONDON

© Pamela Kavanagh 2005, 2008
This edition 2008

ISBN 978-0-7090-8467-9

Robert Hale Limited
Clerkenwell House
Clerkenwell Green
London EC1R 0HT

www.halebooks.com

2 4 6 8 10 9 7 5 3 1

Typeset in 11/16 pt Palatino
Printed and bound in Great Britain by
Biddles Limited, King's Lynn, Norfolk

Chapter One

Catrin Jenkins paused on the humpy stone bridge and cast a look around, her heart bumping with excitement. Bright April sunshine sparkled on the water that gushed under the bridge and glanced off the new blue-slated roofs of the old stone-walled mill, the low-roofed mill house, outbuildings and tearooms ahead. It brought smiles to the faces of the gatherers who were setting up their stalls in the cobbled courtyard, and created a pool of warmth for Tabs, the little mill cat, whose rumbling purrs as she sat washing herself by the entrance had to be heard to be believed.

Everything promised well for the official re-opening of Capel Mair Woollen Mill.

All winter the valley had echoed to the clamour and banter of workman as the long-standing ruin was being brought to working order. But yesterday, when Catrin had called by for a last-minute check of the preparations, all had been quiet. It was a waiting quiet. Inside the mill, the weaving room with its raftered ceiling and white-painted stone walls stood with loom at the ready, set up for the morrow when the carefully-restored wooden water wheel would be set in motion once more.

For the first time in over a hundred and fifty years, the original machinery that carded, spun and wove would again function. Though not, Catrin reflected, in quite the same capacity as before. They all hoped that the present-day mill would draw custom of a different type to the valley. This remote and beautiful corner of the country where the River Teifi had its source was an ideal tourist pull, and together with canoeing, outward bound holidays, walking and horse riding, the mill venture with workshops and guest accommodation would be an added attraction.

'Fingers crossed we're a hit,' said Greg Marriott, the newly appointed manager of the mill. Greg spoke with feeling, having uprooted his wife Beth and two small boys from their comfortable four-bedroomed Ludlow home to settle in the centuries-old mill house in the depths of rural Wales. Catrin could see Beth's corn-gold head now, bobbing about amongst the stalls that displayed an amazing variety of goods for sale in honour of the event. Beth, in charge of the tearooms, the mill shop and the self-contained hostel where the guests who came on Catrin's weaving courses would stay, already seemed run off her feet.

Catching sight of Catrin on the bridge, Beth waved vigorously. 'Hey, Catrin! Your mother's arrived with the cheeses and stuff. She wants you to help her with the display,' she shouted above the general bustle and the busy gush of the millrace.

'Coming!'

Tossing back her mane of waving black hair, Catrin forded the bridge and entered the courtyard, which now swarmed with people, mostly locals, here to do their best to make the day a success. Extra trestles were being set up along the pink-washed wall of the mill. Catrin dodged a trolley loaded with plants and arrived at the first stall.

'Hi, Tracey,' she said to the youngish woman behind the counter, who owned the gift shop in nearby Llandysul and had sacrificed precious working hours to be here. 'Love those Celtic knot brooches. Might just be tempted myself.'

'I'll put one aside for you,' Tracey said at once.

'Thanks.' Smiling gratefully, Catrin pressed on, passing the WI stall with its mouth-watering display of cakes, fruit tarts and homemade sweets, and then the Animal Sanctuary selling notebooks, pencils, toys and other tempting fund-raisers. Finally she came to her mother, Bronwen, who with her healthy cheeks and determined expression looked every bit the farmer's wife she was.

'Thought you'd got lost!' Bron parried, shooting her daughter an exasperated look. 'What do you think of the stall so far? I've put the eggs in these baskets of straw, see. Nicer that way, more countrified. And the jam and marmalade on the other side. Pity the daffodils in the orchard are over. I've had to make do with bunches of primroses instead, but there you are.'

'It looks great, Mam.'

'If you could just fetch the tray of cheeses from the car, please Catrin? Oh, and Dad put in some crocks of honey as well. Took a bit of persuading, mind.'

'I can well believe it!' To make Llew Jenkins part with a single jar of his precious honey took some doing. 'Wow!'

'Said he'd best do his bit,' Bron said out of loyalty to her husband. 'You know Dad. All grumbles, but comes up trumps in the end. Is Will here?'

'You're joking! Some sort of delay at the farm. Ministry business, Will said. He promised to come over as soon as he could,' Catrin added hastily. 'Kate sent some of her home-made wine over. Elderberry, I think. Lovely.'

Will Meredith was her intended. Catrin had really wanted to wait and get her career off the ground before making the engagement official, but Will could be very persuasive. His ring gleamed on her finger; a small solitaire diamond. Will's and his mother Kate's sparse little hill farm, Ty Coch, bordered the Jenkins's valley farm where Llew had dairy cattle and crops, and from which Bron ran her pony trekking business.

Bron was regarding her daughter shrewdly. 'Be naming the day soon, you and Will, now you've got this job close to home. Nice and convenient for Ty Coch.'

'Mmm,' Catrin replied non-committedly.

'Don't leave it too long, *cariad*,' her mother cautioned. 'You know how Dad and I feel about Will. One of the family, he is, always has been. Doesn't seem fair to keep him waiting.' Catrin made no response and Bron came back to the task in hand. 'Now, where did I put those gooseberries? Ah, here they are, under the table. Goodness, only half an hour to go and Greg will be opening up. Catrin, the cheeses!'

'OK, Mam, no need to panic.'

Laughing, Catrin hurried away to the parking ground, passing the other side of the mill where a rustic bridge had been erected for visitors to cross the stream. Having delivered the cheese – cut neatly into affordable sections – she spied the Marriott boys, Sam and Oliver, aged six and four respectively, sneaking off towards her own department – the weaving-room.

'Hey, you guys! What are you up to?'

'Nothing,' Sam said. 'Nothing much. Ollie wants to copy the dragon on the wall.'

Both boys had sketchbooks and, horror of horrors, packs of felt-tip pens clutched in their fists. Catrin could just imagine the potential havoc wrought by the two small artists on her precious designs.

'Go on, Catrin,' Oliver said. 'Let us in. Please.'

Two pairs of clear blue eyes, legacy of their mother, met Catrin's dark brown gaze beseechingly, and her heart softened.

'Bit pushed at the moment,' she said. 'Tell you what. When I've a spare minute, I'll sketch you a dragon to put on your bedroom wall. Then you can copy him any time you want. Fair enough?'

Sam nodded. 'Guess so. You won't forget? Mum often forgets things.'

'Only because she's a bit busy just now.'

'Could you make lots of flame coming out of its nose? And really shiny scales and big claws?' Oliver said.

'Sure I will. It'll be the fiercest dragon ever. Want an ice cream?'

Two straw-coloured heads nodded eagerly. 'Yes please,' the boys said in unison. Dipping into her black sack-bag, Catrin handed them each a pound coin and watched, smiling, as they went running off towards the ice-cream van that had parked in the shade of a stand of ash trees that were just coming into new leaf. Satisfaction fizzed through her. Once she would not have been able to treat the children so affluently. Now, with her first month's salary in the bank, she felt flush for the first time since getting her degree in textiles and design, four long years ago.

She couldn't resist a peep into her new domain, where general assistant Glenys Jones was putting the finishing touches to the range of coloured wools on the traditional weaving loom. 'Everything all right?' Catrin asked.

'Fine. Love this mix of purples and pinks, threaded with gold. You wouldn't have thought gold would blend but it does, very well indeed.'

'Yes. It's taken from a traditional Celtic motif I cooked up for my finals – the wedding ring design.'

Glenys, a busy housewife and mother, trilled a laugh. 'Wishful thinking?'

'Not just yet.' Why was everyone so keen to marry her off? 'I'm going all out for a career. Can't believe my luck. A job at a working exhibit in the mill right here in my own valley! And the workshops to run as well.'

'Great to be in on the start of a new thing too. D'you feel jittery?'

'A bit. What about you?'

'Terrified! What if the loom breaks down on us?'

'After all the hours Ewan's put in on it? Get a grip, Glenys!'

Ewan McInnes was the architect in charge of the reconstruction of the mill and the workings. His tall, craggy figure in working cords and all-weather coat had become a familiar sight in and around the village over the winter months. Ewan lodged with the Marriotts and had a makeshift studio in one of the spare rooms in the mill. Many times had Catrin watched him at his drawing board, thrusting his fingers in grim contemplation through his tousled sandy hair, his dark-grey eyes narrowed on the complex blueprints in front of him.

'All we've got to do is please CADW, and we're in!' he'd comment in his pleasing Highland voice. CADW, the Welsh Heritage Department, enjoyed a reputation for strict attention to detail. Since the mill was a listed building, every single nail and stone had to be authentic, and every single move that was made had to be checked out at least ten times over, or so it seemed to Catrin.

'Fussy lot!' she muttered.

Ewan had shaken his head. 'Not really. Someone's got to be in control, and these folks sure know their stuff. Just keep your fingers crossed they'll accept my modification of the old loom, or else we're stumped.'

In the event not only had the powers that be accepted the blueprint, but Ewan had received an additional word of praise from the department on his ingenuity, and work had gone ahead on the rusted, worm-riddled piece of apparatus that anyone less dedicated might have thought fit only for the scrap-heap.

Suddenly Catrin could not wait to get started, to feel the coloured threads against her fingers and see her design come to life, section after intricate section of it, to the steady clank and whirr of the shuttles. In the shop below, an assortment of woven goods were displayed for sale. Skirts, capes, waistcoats. Rugs and bed-throws, and smaller, less expensive items too; purses, wallets and bookmarks. Woven on modern looms in a less historic mill than this, and made up by skilled machinists, the display represented the sort of wares that Catrin hoped in time to produce with her students.

Moving to the window that overlooked the courtyard, she glanced at her watch. 'Almost twelve. Time we went outside, I guess. Grief, see all those people! Half the village has turned out.'

'Half the county, you mean,' Glenys said. 'There's Dr Hughes from Pencader. Wouldn't have thought he'd have been interested.'

'Think he's a member of the local history society. There's Greg getting his speech together. Let's go.'

The mill, tearooms, mill house and the barn conversion used as holiday accommodation ranged the courtyard on three sides. Already the three self-contained apartments were booked up for the weaving course, the first influx of guests due to arrive over the weekend. As she left the mill, Catrin chanced to glance up. Someone at the window of the first apartment was looking down at her – a girl with bobbed dark hair framing an oval face. Something about her struck a chord and Catrin stared, eyes squinting against the sun, quite unable to tear her gaze away even though the dazzle was intense. She felt a surge of elation and put it down to the thrill of the day. At last it was all happening. Here was a member of her very first group and

Catrin raised her hand in a cheerful salute. The girl waved back. And then the tannoy started up with an ear-piercing shriek and Greg's voice boomed out, welcoming visitors and inmates alike to the celebrations. Beaming, Catrin went with Glenys to join the throng.

'There, I think that's all,' Beth said to her first guest of the season, a curvy young woman in denims and chambray over-shirt, who had signed in as Rissa Birch. 'You'll find towels in the bathroom and the bed's made up, Miss Birch.'

'It's Rissa,' the girl said, smiling. She had very even white teeth and her highlighted black hair was cut in a trendy bob that swung over her cheeks as she moved.

'Rissa it is. And I'm Beth. Meals can be taken across in the tearooms, or you can cater for yourself, whichever you prefer.'

'Bit of both, I expect,' Rissa said. 'Is there a supermarket close by? Village shop even?'

'Shop's a good two-mile walk down the lane, and the nearest supermarket's Carmarthen. Llandysul's fine for supplies – that's about six miles away.'

'Good thing I came in my car. Almost didn't. It's a wreck!'

'Oh well, so long as it goes, that's what I always say. If you have trouble, Dewi, the chap in charge of the mill machinery, is a good mechanic. His brother owns the garage you passed on the way up, so between them they'll sort you out.'

'That's handy to know – thanks.'

Beth glanced at her watch. 'Better go and finish the sand-wiches. Will you excuse me? There's such a lot to do today, I don't seem to have enough pairs of hands! We've taken on a girl from the village to help, but she's only a youngster so she's bound to need a bit of direction. If you want anything, Rissa, I'll be in the tearooms. Feel free to come across and ask.'

'I will, and thanks again.'

'No problem. Oh, just look down there at those two scamps! Mine, of course. Looks like they've bullied someone into buying them ice cream. That's the second today that I know of! Well, I'll leave you to settle in. Bye for now, Rissa.'

With a harassed chuckle she left, closing the pitch pine door behind her with a decisive click. Rissa listened to her footsteps descending the wooden staircase to the open garage below, where Rissa had left her car. A minute later Beth was crossing the courtyard, dodging between the listening groups of visitors, seizing her two little sons by the hands and hustling them into the tearooms under her watchful eye.

Breathing in the freshness of new plaster and paint, Rissa went through to the compact galley kitchen to make herself a cup of coffee. As she waited for the kettle to boil she made another tour of the small sitting room furnished in white and blue, and the pine-clad bedroom with shower room off. Both main rooms were kitted out with a television set and radio and the solid fuel central heating, run from a vast boiler downstairs, rendered everywhere cosy and warm. Rissa, who felt the cold, was glad to see the brand-new radiators everywhere, for it was early yet and the weather could easily take a dip for the worse. As it stood, the holiday flat, her base for the next three weeks, couldn't have been more comfortable.

Making the coffee strong and black, she took it through to the sitting-room and stationed herself at the window, sipping, and gazing down at the bustling scene below. The enviably slim young woman in the cream slacks and fitted red jacket coming out of the mill had to be her future instructor, Catrin Jenkins. Bet she didn't have to watch her weight, the way Rissa did! Suddenly the woman halted and looked up, her long hair lifting in the slight breeze, and as their gaze locked Rissa experienced a jolt. It was as if they had met up before, though Rissa was pretty sure they had not. The woman waved and automatically Rissa returned the greeting. Curious, she watched her walk on. Beth had let slip that Catrin was local. Lucky creature, to have landed a job here. Rissa, more into lacemaking than textiles but keen to learn the ins and outs of weaving, would have given anything for such a chance. The plumpish woman with her was probably an assistant.

Rissa's large dark eyes ranged the rest of the company. Making the opening speech was Greg, Beth's husband, a good-looking Englishman with a ready smile that no doubt won him many friends. The two men leaning against the tearoom's wall, both wearing forest-green sweatshirts sporting the mill logo, were obviously staff as well. One of them was probably Dewi that Beth had mentioned. And the rangy, sandy-haired guy in grey slacks and navy blue guernsey had to be Ewan McInnes – she recognized him from the photos in the brochure. He seemed OK too. Had a look of Mike about him, though Mike was younger and maybe not quite as tall.

She sighed. Missing Mike was all part of the course, she supposed. Not that she'd had much time to miss him, yet. If she hadn't lost her job in the cutbacks at the museum, she reflected a bit sourly, she'd be in the canteen now, sharing a tea-break cuppa with him. At a loose end, despondent, she had mooched around the house, too deflated even to think of looking for another job. It was Dad who had suggested a working holiday and ferreted out the brochure for the Capel Mair Weaving Course, from the travel agent's on Ealing High Street.

'You even get a qualification at the end of it, Rissa. It'd be another string to your bow. That, with your other assets, in all likelihood might get you a place at art college. It's what you've always wanted. Go on, Riss, go for it!'

He had smiled encouragingly at her, his dear, rather sad face crinkling up with anxious affection.

In fact for Rissa, the very location of the course had clinched it.

Capel Mair, south-west Wales. Rissa's heart had turned over. Now, she fingered the heavy locket of chased silver she wore on a silver-link chain around her neck under her clothes. Was it fate that had brought her here, to the very place she had spent the past twelve months since her mother's death wondering about? It had to be something more than coincidence and Rissa, who recognized in herself an uncanny sixth sense, was all too ready to believe in the hand of destiny.

The stallholders were probably local tradesmen and women, here to boost the event, and making a splendid job of it they were too. Clearly the speech was coming to an end. The two men had taken themselves off into the mill, ready for the cue to switch on the controls that started up the mechanism. Taking another sustaining gulp of coffee, Rissa's gaze went back to Ewan. The architect stood seemingly relaxed, his eyes fixed on the varnished buckets and gleaming black metalwork of the wheel, as with a clatter and churning of white water and a jubilant roar from the crowd, the newly restored mill works swung into action.

Inwardly, Ewan was triumphant. Twelve months almost to the day since he had begun the deskwork, and now the fruits of his labours and abilities were there for all to see.

'Isn't it wonderful?' said a voice at his side.

Ewan looked down to find Catrin's trim figure standing beside him. 'It sure is,' he replied. 'Look at that wheel! Look at her cutting through the water! Not bad, eh?'

A smile crossed his normally solemn face and the grey eyes

that could be stormy took on a gleam. He'd enjoyed the work, found it a challenge. Certainly, it had helped to take his mind off Tracey and all the unhappiness and trauma of their broken marriage. Broken business too – damn Alistair and his conniving mind! Ewan's expression tightened. Losing your wife and your business to your best friend was no easy obstacle to overcome.

'Yes, it's great,' Catrin said. 'Just think. This is the first time the wheel has turned in a hundred and … how many years is it? When did the mill close down?'

'In 1843 or thereabouts. The last miller here was a man called Hywel Rees. The mill went on fire. No one knows what happened to the miller. Maybe he perished in the flames.'

'Ugh!' For the second time in an hour Catrin shivered. She didn't want to think about dying. 'Was he a bachelor, or what? Dire, isn't it? Born and bred here and I don't know my local history!' She gave a faintly embarrassed little laugh. 'The mill's always been just an old ruin and that was that. As children we were warned to keep away because the building was dangerous, and of course there's the water as well, it's very deep. When I was older—'

'Yes?'

'Well, you're going to think me a perfect wimp. There's an ancient grove just along the stream. Don't know if you've seen it.'

'A druid's grove? Yes, I read something about it. Meant to look it up but there's never been time.'

'It's small, you could easily miss it. There's a copse of old beech trees and a spring that never, ever runs dry, even during the worst drought. At the head of the pool is a stone known round here as the touchstone. Oh, there's lots of stories about it, probably all fabrication. Legend has it that the stone has magic powers. Mam said when she was a child, people used to go up there and leave little offerings. Coins, ribbons and so on.'

Ewan's brows shot up in mock surprise. 'Wouldn't have thought that would have gone down well with the cleric!'

'Doesn't make any difference. Faith's one thing, superstition's another. I never went near the place. Well, I did once but … to be honest it always gave me the creeps!' Catrin swallowed and went for a change of subject. 'So what about you, Ewan? Are you stopping on for a while? Hope so. You've become part of the community.'

'Glad to hear it. My contract doesn't end for another six months, so I'm a fixture till October. Have to get the place up and running and make sure there are no hiccups – heaven forbid! Then, who knows?'

'Maybe the Heritage people will find you another mill to restore. You'll make a name for yourself and become famous.'

'And go down in posterity as the man who saved the woollen mills!' Ewan chuckled. 'It's a thought!' They edged back as a laughing crowd of teenagers pushed past, all of them black-clad, the girls with impossibly-coloured hair, the lads' locks flowing, earrings and ankle bracelets glinting in the sun. 'Those were the days,' Ewan commented. 'Your life before you, not a care in the world. Grief, if they only knew!'

'Cynic! That's Dad's line. Talking of Dad, there he is.' Catrin nodded towards her mother's stall, which was now empty of produce. Llew Jenkins, stocky, a shock of greying black hair framing a square, wind-reddened face, had for once shed his everyday farmers' gear of navy boiler suit and army fatigue boots and looked spruce and unfamiliar in lightweight summer slacks and fine-knit jumper. 'There's smart he looks. Better go and tell him.'

'Right.' Ewan smiled at her. 'I'm off to check the workings. See you later, Catrin.'

He went striding away, an upright, rather solitary figure, his mind clearly full of the job in hand. Catrin strolled over to join her parents.

'Hi Mam. See you're stall's cleared out. Honey's gone as well!'

'What d'you expect?' Llew cut in, affronted.

Catrin affected surprise. 'Mam. Do I know this handsome guy with you?'

'You ought to,' Bron said. 'He's been around all your life.'

They all laughed.

'Where's Will?' Llew asked.

'Still up at Ty Coch. An official visit by a Ministry vet, he said. Something to do with checking out the sheep. Must say Will's taking his time getting over here. You know farmers!'

'Yeh, yeh, we're all the same!' Llew grinned at his daughter.

'Pity he missed the start,' Bron said. 'Greg's speech was terrific. Not too long, lots of humour. He got it just right. Wasn't it great when the wheel started up?'

'You bet,' Catrin said. 'Think Ewan was keeping his fingers crossed, mentally at least. When I think of all those hours he must have sat up, sometimes far into the nights, puzzling out first this problem, then that.'

'He's a clever chap,' Llew said.

'True.'

Bron said, 'Have you seen your first guest? Rissa, she's called. Beth told me when she came over to buy some jam. That's her car in the parking space.'

'The red Metro?' Catrin said. 'Right. Think I remember one of them was due today. To be honest, there's been so much going on my mind hasn't taken it all in. I'll give her chance to settle in, and then go and introduce myself.'

'Tell her if she fancies a bit of fresh air, we'll always find something for her to do at Brynteg,' Llew put in, grinning.

'Yeh – mucking out and carting straw! Some holiday that would be! Isn't the wheel noisy? This was always such a quiet place. Bit ... well, desolate, somehow.'

'Ruins always are,' her mother said. 'Not any more though, not this one anyway. Ponies are in for a shock when we bring them down.'

The pony trekking season began on the first of May. Bron's stock of twenty or so sturdy Welsh ponies and cobs ranged the hills all winter, their grazing supplemented by regular feeds of hay when the weather closed in. Any time now, Bron and whoever else she could rustle up, usually Catrin, fetched the ponies down to the farm and started the strenuous task of getting them groomed, shod and generally tidied up and schooled for the first influx of trekkers.

'Hi there!'

They looked round to see Will striding towards them.

'Hi Cattie.' He put his arm round her shoulders and kissed her cheek, and then he greeted his neighbours. 'Bron. Llew. How's it going?'

'You should ask!' Catrin said, chidingly. 'Trust someone to turn up when the show's all but over. Farmers!'

'Go on. Where would everyone be without us?' Will quipped.

'Heard you've had the white-coats round, Will,' Llew said. 'How did it go?'

'Fine. No problem.' He glanced around. 'Good turnout, yeh? Nice set-up as well. Look at the water wheel. Great.'

Catrin said to Will, 'If you want to see where I'll be working, I'll show you round now, before they let the public in.'

'Right-oh then. See you, Llew. Fancy a jar tonight?'

'Wouldn't say no.'

'Drovers, around eight?'

'But Will, it's Saturday,' Bron said. 'You and Catrin always go into town on Saturday night.'

'Can't make it tonight, Mam. I'm a bit busy.' Catrin avoided Will's decidedly reproachful look. When she had worked for the soft furnishing firm in Carmarthen, having taken the only fairly suitable job that had come her way, her free time had been just that – free. Now, things were different. The mill she regarded a crucial starting point to her career, a long and successful career, she hoped. But could she make Will see that? No! 'Got some notes to write up for Monday. And I want to check the loom. Glenys is stopping behind to run off a few sections of the pattern, just to see how it looks.'

Will's good-looking face had darkened. 'There's dedication for you!'

'Well, you farmers aren't the only ones to work overtime,' Catrin said lightly. She took his hand, smiling up at him. 'Come on. I can't wait to show you my designs. Just think, my artwork might be the very thing that puts Capel Mair on track. Imagine!'

Will allowed himself a tight smile and was immediately dragged off to the weaving room, into the mingled smell of newly-varnished timber, treated wools and yarns and the yeasty aroma of the coconut matting that covered the stone-flagged floor.

'Wow!' Will stopped in the doorway in obvious surprise. 'Posh, eh?'

'Functional, too. Soon as I was taken on the payroll Ewan had me map out a working area. Well, it's not the same as an ordinary working museum. Having students in on a holiday basis, the place has to be attractive and comfortable to work in.'

'Guess so. Tell you one thing. The old miller who once toiled here wouldn't recognize the place. That your design?'

'The wedding ring, yes. It's from a traditional Celtic theme.'

'Thought it seemed familiar. Mam's got some quilts and shawls back home. Think they came from her side of the family. They're pretty old. I remember I once nicked one to put down in the dog's bed. Mam nearly threw a fit.'

'I should think so! Honestly, Will. Those things are precious.'

'They're relics. I'm not one for history. It's the future I'm into. Especially our future.'

He made to put his arms around her but Catrin slipped away and went to open the pine-fronted store area that held her yarns. 'These haven't been made up here, of course. But in the future most of our wool will be spun and dyed here. Those are natural fibres.' She pointed to a shelf stacked with cones of cream, brown and soft-gold wool.

'Some Jacob there,' Will said, surprisingly. 'Foleys over at Cenarth kept Jacobs for the fleeces. Don't think they paid, though. He went over to a more commercial breed of sheep afterwards. That yellow's probably Suffolk. Not a bad colour, that.'

'It's beautiful,' Catrin told him. 'All the natural colours are. And they blend so well together. Want to see the spinning room?'

'Might as well while I'm here.'

Biting back a swift retort that he could try and make an effort to show more enthusiasm for her future employment, Catrin led the way and patiently showed him round. No way was she going to spoil the day with argument. If Will wanted to behave like a spoilt brat, then fine. She, Catrin, would do her utmost to give Capel Mair the best possible start, and if that meant humouring chauvinistic farmers with huge chips on their shoulders, then so be it.

She gave him a full tour of the spinning room, the workshops and the ground floor where the bulk of the machinery was based. To give him his due, Will showed genuine interest here. They came across Ewan, examining the complex array of cogs, wheels and braces that worked in tune with the rhythm of the water wheel beyond the walls. The two men enjoyed a brief chat about the workings.

'Incredible, to think that someone cooked all this up, all those years ago,' Will said.

Ewan nodded. 'Aye, it's a rare piece of engineering all right.'

'And you've restored everything exactly as it used to be?'

'Give or take a few modifications, and those mainly in the interests of safety. We've had to put rails up on the stairs and in the upper chambers. Can't risk an accident, not in this day and age!'

'True.' Will laughed. 'Insurance must be pretty high on a place like this.'

'Yes, it is. Not my worry though, that. Well, think I'll go and sample some of Beth's fare. I'm feeling quite peckish after all the excitement. You coming?'

Catrin made to accept but Will forestalled her. 'Got a picnic in the car, actually. It was Mam's idea. She thought we'd like a bit of time together, seeing as you're all too busy here for us to go out on our usual binge tonight.'

'Fine. See you later then, Catrin.' Giving them a genial nod, Ewan left the building.

As soon as the door shut on him, Catrin rounded on Will fiercely. 'Did you have to put it so bluntly? No one's *making* me work this evening. I'm doing it out of my own choice. For goodness sake, Will. How many times have I waited, all dressed up to go out, and you haven't turned up? Always an excuse. Lambing. A ewe fallen sick, or something's gone wrong with the tractor and you've had to stop and fix it.'

'That's different. It's the farm.'

'And this is work. My work. My chosen path, that I spent three years at university studying for.' Catrin sighed, feeling the usual twist of conflicting emotions. She loved Will, yes. It was just his attitude. Or did she love him? Was it a case of familiarity? Will, always there, ever ready to talk, to take her out to places. Will and Kate who had been widowed young, good neighbours and on the best of terms with her parents.

As quickly as it had arisen, her antagonism faded. She held out her hand. 'Come on, don't let's quarrel, not today. What's Kate done for lunch? If it's her home-raised chicken and salad and slices of her own bara brith' – a bun loaf rich in fruit and nuts – 'then you're on!'

Will smiled, a bit shamefaced. 'Add a bottle of wine, and you've got the menu right down to a tee. Salad's all yours, as usual. Healthy stuff doesn't do me any good at all!'

'Oh, Will!'

Laughing, they left the mill, recovered the picnic hamper from the boot of the battered Fourtrak and found a spot a little way downstream, away from the crowds of people. Will spread the car rug on the rocks and they sat down to enjoy the picnic, while the millstream gushed merrily by at their feet and the clank and churn of the mill wheel sounded in the distance.

On the opposite bank and a little way along, no more than a stone's throw, was the druid's grove known locally as The Well. Glancing that way, Catrin could not help a little shiver.

'Cold?' Will said. 'Here, have my jacket.'

'No, I'm fine, thanks. It's sheltered here and the sun's warm for April. It's not that. I was ... well, to be honest it's The Well. It always freaks me out.'

Will's brown eyes regarded her steadily. 'You're not alone in that. I've known grown men avoid the place. Mam says her dad, a toughie if ever there was one, wouldn't go near.'

'I know it's got a bit of a reputation. Shame, because it's such a lovely spot. When I was small we used to make up ghost stories about it. Wasn't that that's put me off, though. I once sneaked up there to play. Oh, I couldn't have been more than five or six. I saw – things, or thought I did. It gave me such a fright I ran home. Left my Barbie doll behind. Dad had to go and fetch it.'

'The pool's deep. It's not the safest of places for children. Bet you got the telling off of your life!'

'I did. Mam told me never to go there again. She needn't have bothered because I had no intention of going.' She shivered again. 'Spooky place.'

'Here, have some more wine,' Will said. 'Or d'you want coffee? There's a thermos flask.'

'Cup of coffee would be great.'

Between them they drained the flask, chatting easily, totally at peace with one another. This is how it should be, Catrin thought drowsily. No prickly talk, no petty jealousies. Just happy and content to be together.

Inevitably, it was Will who broke the spell.

'Have to be pushing off, Cattie. Got to take those ewes back up to the grazings and feed the dogs. You know how it is.'

'Yes, I know.'

She spoke matter-of-factly, no hint of accusation, but Will threw her a sharply questioning look. She met it with a smile, and then started deftly to pack up the leftovers of the picnic.

'There. My thanks to Kate. Tell her it was the best picnic ever.'

'I won't forget. It'll buck Mam up no end.'

'Why, isn't she well? I thought she looked pale last week when I saw her in the village. Sort of drained looking.'

'Mam complains of being tired all the time. Must be something in it because she went to the surgery for a blood test. That's not Mam.'

'No.' Catrin looked worried. 'Give her my love. Tell her I'll pop up to see her in the morning.'

'Shall do.' Will dropped her a kiss and stood up. 'Coming?'

'Might stop here a few more minutes. It's so peaceful after the panic of the past few days. 'Bye Will. See you tomorrow.'

She watched his sturdy figure retreating along the path, walking with the steady, easy lope of one raised on rugged mountain slopes, the picnic hamper on his shoulder. Reaching the bend, Will paused and waved, then he was gone.

Catrin leaned her back to the sun-warmed rocks, turned her face to the sun and closed her eyes. Bliss, after all the organizing, the rushing around and ticking off lists, just to relax and not to have to make any effort at all. Funny, she thought, how quickly you became used to the noise of the wheel. It was there and yet not there, a steady throbbing in the distance. A fish leaped with a splash and her eyes opened to see the myriad drops of spray, transformed into rainbow colours by the refracted light of the sun through the budding rowans. Light glistened on the water, hurting her eyes, and she closed them again, the throb, clank, throb, of the distant wheel a lullaby that calmed the senses — and soon she slept.

'Here you are, John. Here's Mam's old skirt and blouse and I've found a shawl too. She'll not miss them. There's a couple of pins here as well, just in case. That skirt will never fasten round your waist. Quickly now, put them on. Mam and Da have gone to chapel but they'll be back soon. Da's the same as your father, hasn't any truck with rioters. Load of trouble-making scum, he called them only last night. If he but knew!'

'Ah well, depends which side you're on, don't it?' John struggled awkwardly into the long brown woollen skirt and dark-blue blouse. 'Damned buttons. Why do women have to wear such fiddly clothes?'

'Here, let me.' Deftly she fastened the two rows of buttons on the blouse, and then pinned together the skirt. 'Good thing Mam's tall. You'd look a treat if your trouser bottoms showed!' She giggled deliciously.

John threw her an admonishing look. 'Be serious, Elin.'

Elin? In her dream Catrin wanted to say her own name, but found she could not.

She looked up into John's darkly handsome face. 'I am serious. Now, what shall we do about your hair. I know. You can wear my sunbonnet. It's nice and floppy with a wide brim, so it will hide your face. Just a moment, I'll fetch it.'

She hurried to the mill house and went under the low lintel of the doorway. It was dark inside and a steep flight of stairs led directly up to her bedroom. She was back directly, a sunbonnet of coarse cream-coloured linen in her hand. In the background the water wheel creaked, clanked and thrashed, churning the waters of the pool.

'Here,' Elin said, standing on tiptoe to arrange the bonnet over John's head of black curls. She fastened the ribbons in a bow under his chin. 'There. There's a lovely girl you'd make, John Caradoc – I don't think!'

Bubbles of laughter escaped her lips yet again and John frowned. 'I've told you, Elin. Be serious. This is important work we're doing. Dangerous too.'

'Dangerous?' Her laughter fled. 'What d'you mean, John?'

'Getting rid of the toll gates, aren't we? Destroying them.

Anyone found vandalizing public property … well, don't have to go on, do I? Ah, don't worry, *cariad*. It'll be fine.' He took her in his arms, rocking her like a child. 'It's getting late. Have to go, the others'll be waiting. Look, I'll leave these things by here under the bushes. 'Bye now, *cariad*. Wish me luck.'

Firm lips came down crushingly on hers. He hugged her roughly, released her reluctantly and left, soon to be swallowed up by the shrubby undergrowth of the darkening hillside.

The scene blurred, fragmenting. The wheel thrashed and churned, getting louder. A face appeared, blood oozing from an ugly gash on the forehead – John's face. There was shouting, rough, fierce.

'Caradoc! Caradoc!'

In her dream Catrin tried to cry out a warning, but no sound would come past her lips.

Rissa shrugged on her quilted jacket and left the flat, running lightly down the wooden staircase. She'd unpacked, eaten – well, briefly, more coffee and a cheese sandwich – and now she needed some fresh air.

Woodland scents of wild thyme and early bluebells teased her nostrils as she wove through the groups of chattering people on the still bustling courtyard, heading for the path along the millstream that she had seen from her window. Spring sunlight sparkled on the water and the roar of the mill wheel grew louder as she approached the wooden bridge that spanned the wide, deep waters of the mill leet. Crossing the bridge, Rissa gained the path and headed uphill, her cheeks fanned by a cooling breeze fresh off the mountains and smelling of upland grass and sheep. High above, a buzzard traced lazy circles in the blue. She heard its cry, high, plaintive, and the answering call of its mate.

And then, above the gush of water over big brown boulders, the distant clanking of the wheel and the lonely call of the bird, came another sound – a sort of high-pitched whimpering. Rissa stopped short, looking around, her heart thumping and her throat suddenly gone dry. On the other side of the stream was a stand of trees. Not willows. Beeches? Born and bred in the city as she was, identifying plants and trees was not one of her strengths. Making a mental note to purchase a pocket book on flora and fauna, she pressed on, more cautiously now, approaching a bed in the stream.

The noise had stopped and Rissa was beginning to think she had imagined it, when rounding the bend she came across someone curled up asleep on the bank. She recognized the cream slacks and red jacket immediately. It was her weaving tutor, Catrin Jenkins. Clearly her slumber was not restful, for even as Rissa made to tiptoe past, she started to thrash about and mutter.

'Caradoc! John! It's John! Oh no, no!'

Without thinking twice Rissa darted forward and subsided to her knees beside the slumberer. Lost in the thrall of the nightmare, Catrin's face was contorted, the eyes behind the closed lids rolling and troubled, little whimpers sounding in her throat.

'Wake up!' Rissa said sharply, seizing the slim shoulders and shaking hard. 'Miss Jenkins – Catrin! Come on, wake up. Please!'

Someone was urging her to wake up, but the past held her in its grip and the voice seemed to come from far away. Strident, insistent.

Catrin eventually felt herself being drawn out of the horror of the dream. Heart thumping wildly, her skin slick with sweat, she flicked open her eyes – and blinked in shock.

The face she was looking into was slightly fuller than her own, the smooth skin over the high cheekbones more rose-brown. But the bright-black eyes were hers, as were the small straight nose and full lips. Catrin might have been looking in a mirror and she choked back a little cry of surprise. And to judge by the startled expression on the face of her rescuer, she was obviously possessed of the same thought!

Chapter Two

'I ... what is it?' Catrin mumbled, still gripped by the power of the dream. Confused, disorientated, she stared up into the face before her. Of course it wasn't her own. This girl was fuller-cheeked and her eyes were darker, almost black. Catrin forced her concentration, struggling to focus on the present, to drive away the strange disconcerting forces that had all but overtaken her. The girl's hair was not the deep blue-black of her own either, it had russet tints, though to judge by its expert cut it could have been professionally high-lighted. She was probably older by two or three years as well.

'Sorry to wake you up,' the girl said. 'I think you must have been having a nightmare. I heard you cry out, thought I'd better see what was wrong.' She smiled, rueful. 'That must have been some dream!'

'Yes, it was.' Shakily, Catrin rubbed her hand across her fore-head. The shreds of it were still there, playing themselves before her eyes. It had been more than a dream. It was real. What her gran would have called a waking dream. The girl was watching her, hesitant, sympathy in her eyes. Catrin said, stumblingly, 'Who are ... where did ... oh, listen to me! Gabbling away as if I've totally lost it! I'm sorry. What must you think of me? You must be one of the first intake.'

'That's right. My name's Rissa Birch,' the girl said.

'I'm Catrin Jenkins.' Thankfully her head was clearing at last. Catrin struggled to her feet and brushed the grass from her clothes. 'Rissa. Of course. If my memory serves me right, you're one of my weaving group. What a way to meet!'

They looked at each other, smiled. 'Sure you're OK?' Rissa said. 'You still seem a bit wobbly to me. I'll walk back with you if you like.'

'I'm fine now, but thanks.'

The two girls fell into step, heading back to the mill, the water wheel getting painfully louder with every stride. As they walked, Rissa kept up a steady chatter.

'Love your red jacket,' she said with an admiring glance at her companion's trim shape. 'You're so slim! Don't know how you manage it. Don't think I've seen my cheekbones ever!'

'Go on, you're not fat.' Catrin forced herself to respond, part of her mind still raking over that baffling episode from the past. She had felt herself at one with the incident. It was as if she had actually been that girl – Elin, was she called? She had felt the unaccustomed stiffness of starched petticoats and heavy woollen skirts against her limbs, felt the itchy rough-ness of the coarse woollen shawl through her cotton blouse and shift. And the injured boy … there had been the sharpness of mingled blood and sweat in her nostrils. So chillingly real it had been.

'Well, I have to work on it!' Rissa replied with a wry little laugh that suggested a far more streetwise background than Catrin's. 'Funny, how people come in types. Some plump, some skinny. When I was little I used to play a game, putting jobs of work to the people walking past. You get all sorts in London. I live in Richmond. Dad's converted the attic into a bedsit for me, so I've got my independence. We're just opposite the park so I do look out on trees. Nothing like here of course.' She prattled brightly on, not seeming to expect a response, and Catrin was glad of the chance to gather her scattered wits. 'This is my first visit to this part of Wales. The scenery's just breathtaking, isn't it? I kept stopping the car on the way over to take shots of the views.'

'Yes, it is lovely,' Catrin managed to say. Rissa caught her eye and smiled, and Catrin realized with a rush of liking that the chatter was for her own benefit, covering up an awkward few moments. She said, more confidently, 'So you're a photographer then.'

'Oh, I wouldn't say that. Dad gave me a camera for my birthday – a Nikon F3.'

'Wow!'

'I know. Dad spoils me rotten – he's such a love! Actually Dad's in the trade so I expect he got a discount. Dad owns a fleet of photography shops – well, he's retired now. His heart, you know. He's had to put a manager in charge but he still goes into the base shop most mornings – just can't keep away!'

'I expect it keeps him going, the interest.'

'True. Especially since Mum died. Life's funny, isn't it. She was much younger than Dad and she went first. Mum died last year.'

'Oh, I'm so sorry.' Catrin flashed a look of quick sympathy. She was warming to this girl with the direct gaze and open way of talking.

'Thanks,' Rissa said. 'What about you? Are you from round here?'

'Oh yes. We've got a farm the other side of the village. It's called Brynteg. Dad sees to it, mostly. Mum runs a pony trekking centre from there as well.'

'You've got horses? I'd love to go riding. Does your mother hire them out?'

Catrin nodded. 'Sometimes. I expect she could find you something reliable. I'll ask her if you like. Have you ridden much?'

'Oh yes. I was one of those pony-mad little girls who dreamed of nothing but having her own animal. It never happened, of course. You need to live in the country for that, and Dad liked to be near his work. I had to make do with rides at our local centre – still go for hacks in the park.'

'Not a novice, then. I'll see what Mum can rustle up. Lucky the weaving course is in the mornings. You'll have all the rest of the day to yourself.'

'Great. I'm really looking forward to learning how to weave. I'm more into lacemaking. It was Mum's hobby and she sort of fired me off.'

'Wonderful.'

At that moment the wheel, which had been turning noisily, came to a sudden stop. The silence was sweet and Catrin felt an inexplicable wave of relief. Silly, she admonished herself. To have waited all these months to have the wheel operating, and then to be glad when it stills. Silly!

She said, 'I didn't realize it was so late. Better hurry. I've got things to sort out before Ewan locks up. Has Beth shown you round? Where to eat and everything?'

'Oh, yes. Beth was great – very efficient and friendly. Looks like the other residents have arrived, the parking area's full. I'd best go and introduce myself. Nice meeting you, Catrin. I'll look forward to seeing you on Monday. What time about?'

'Tennish? Just a get-together for the first session and I'll show you the designs and so on. Then I've got workshops in the afternoon. It's all go! 'Bye then, Rissa.'

They went their separate ways, Rissa to the holiday accommodation, Catrin to the weaving-room. She still felt vaguely shaken and out of sorts. It had been so compelling, that dream. A little shiver touched her. She hoped Ewan had the kettle on. Cup of coffee and a chat might be no bad thing. Ewan's staunch matter-of-fact attitude spiced with dry humour would be blessedly reassuring. Then she must catch Greg to check if he'd put in that order for the extra raw wool she needed. Angora was great, but you couldn't beat Jacob for natural colour.

'Right then, Cattie. I'll see you sometime. Take care. 'Bye!'

Will put down the phone with a frown. Damn! He'd looked forward to a night out with Catrin and now it was all off. Again!

'You there, Will? I thought I heard the phone?'

Will swung round to find his mother descending the backstairs. 'It was Catrin.'

'Anything wrong?'

'No. Well, some.'

Kate Meredith came down into the narrow, low-beamed kitchen and went to warm herself by the old-fashioned black-iron stove in which a fire crackled cheerfully despite the warmth of the May day. Kate was a slight, pale woman with gentle brown eyes and a tired smile. She had never really recovered from the loss of her husband in a farm accident five years before. Now her health was suffering and an afternoon nap had become necessary.

Automatically, Will went to fill the kettle for tea. 'You all right, Mam?'

'I'm fine. It's you I'm concerned about. What is it?'

Will shrugged. 'Oh, I'd booked a table at the Fenice in Swansea – Cattie loves eating Italian. Thought we'd take in a movie afterwards. She's just rung to say she can't make it. To be fair she didn't know I'd made special arrangements.'

'I see. Did she say why?'

'Too shattered to go out, apparently. She's finding the new job exhausting and isn't sleeping too well either. Brain too active, I guess. Damned mill! She'll wear herself out if she goes on like this.' Will stared bleakly out of the window. ''Tisn't the first time Cattie's cancelled, Mam,' he muttered, more to himself.

'Oh dear.' Kate bit her lip. 'I'd noticed you were a bit at a loose end. I suppose … everything is all right between you and Catrin?'

Will turned to face his mother. 'Oh, I guess so.'

The kettle boiled and Kate went to make the tea. Pouring her son a steaming mugful, she watched him spoon in sugar and stir broodingly, then took her own tea to the table and sat down. Will, leaning his back to the blue melamine unit his father had put in years ago, took a scalding gulp of tea. It was Catrin's joke that he had a cast-iron gullet, to which Will usually responded it was mind over matter. You told yourself it wouldn't burn and that was it. Will wished his powers of persuasion extended to convincing himself that all was as it should be between himself and Catrin.

'Cattie's changed lately,' he admitted, cradling the mug between his big, work-roughened hands. 'She's been so … distracted.'

'That's hardly surprising, Will. Like you've just said, Catrin's got a lot on with this job. Can't be easy, being part of a team. Lots of responsibility. New venture, too.'

'Mm. I'm trying to see it her way but … oh, I don't know. I always come round to the fact that once we're married Cattie's going to be needed here at Ty Coch, not down the valley slogging away doing workshops for local Heritage.'

Kate sipped tea. 'But it's her career, Will,' she pointed out. 'You can't expect a girl to give everything up to be a farmer's wife. Girls these days like and value their independence and you can't blame them. Catrin's worked hard to get where she is. She needs your support. Later, once she's got into her stride, things will be easier. Most women manage to juggle a career and home. Catrin will be fine.'

'Just hope you're right. My big worry is Ty Coch. We're only a small concern and farming's in a bad way at present – I don't need to tell you that. First the BSE, then foot-and-mouth—'

'We didn't get it, Will. Look on the bright side.'

Will threw her a frowning glance. At the moment, to him there didn't seem to be a bright side. 'Farmers going out of business left, right and centre,' he continued. 'It'd better not happen to us. Then there's all this red tape. There's days when I spend more time in the office than out on the hills with my stock where I belong. Forms for this and that, everything to be recorded in triplicate. Paperwork always did defeat me but Catrin can do it blindfold. I know you'd tackle the office readily enough, Mam, but it tires you out and I don't like that.'

'I'm coping. These new tablets the doctor prescribed are suiting me. Catrin—'

'Oh, to blazes with it!' Irritably Will shoved his empty mug down on the worktop with a clatter. 'I'd best cancel that table, then I'm going down to the pub. Cheers, Mam. Don't wait up.'

He rustled up a brief smile for his mother and stalked out.

The Drovers was stone-built, dark-beamed and crowded. Rissa sat in the bar lounge with four of the other residents, a jolly middle-aged couple from Lancaster and a rather serious pair of schoolteachers from the Midlands who spent every holiday in Wales, and thus considered themselves experts on the area.

'Of course,' Henry was saying, pint of best bitter in hand, 'if you want really spectacular scenery you need to go down to Pembrokeshire. Isn't that right, Fliss?'

His wife tossed back her long pale hair and nodded. 'Absolutely.'

'Pretty good round here, I thought,' Rissa remarked.

'Beautiful, isn't it love?' put in Beth. 'Fred and I went to Cardigan Bay earlier to see the dolphins.'

'Oh, and did you?' Rissa asked.

'Not a whisker.' Fred winked at her over his glass. 'Grand excuse to go again though, isn't it?'

Everyone laughed. The door opened to admit Will. He was scowling.

'Isn't that Catrin's young man?' Beth observed. She waved her hand wildly. 'Over here, Will.'

Rissa, having a strong feeling that Will would rather have kept his own company, sent him an encouraging smile as he approached.

'Hello everyone. Nice evening,' Will said.

Fred said affably, 'Grand, isn't it. Nice and fresh after that drop of rain we had earlier.' He pulled to his feet. 'Another round, folks? Same again, is it? What're you drinking, Will?'

'Half of bitter, thanks.'

Fred went off to the bar and Will sat down next to Rissa. 'Hi there. How's the course going?'

'Wonderfully well. How's the farm?'

'So-so. Soon be dipping time then shearing, then the sheep can be turned out in the hills for the summer.' Will cast her an appraising glance. She wore yellow shorts and a brief white top and had fastened her hair back with slides. 'See you've caught the sun. Suits you, bit of a tan.'

'Oh, I always catch the sun easily. But thanks for the compliment. Nice to know you're appreciated!' Rissa laughed and drained her glass – diet coke, since she had already exceeded her calorie intake for that day. 'Mike says I look like a glorified daisy in this outfit.' She wrinkled her nose. 'Beast!'

'Mike?'

'My chap. Well, sort of. We've been going out forever.'

Fred came back with the drinks and there was a pause while they were passed around.

'What's Mike doing letting you come down here on your own for the summer, then?' Will asked.

She shrugged. 'Oh, the usual, you know. We needed a break from one another, then Dad saw the ad for the course in the travel agent's and here I am! I can't believe it's been two whole weeks. Another month to go yet though, thank goodness. I've been so absorbed with the weaving and exploring the local beaches, I haven't had time for much else.' She'd managed a trip to Aberystwyth, though, to scour the archives for some information she wanted. So far she had come up with nothing. Will took a long swig at his beer and began to chat to the others. Rissa leaned back in her chair, sipping her drink, her mind ranging back. The weaving course was not her sole reason for coming here. During these last months, ever since Mum had died, Rissa had harboured a mission that had grown stronger with every passing week.

It had come as a shock to learn from her mother that Dad – dear, generous, warm-hearted Dad – was not her true father at all. Her natural father, it turned out, had been a sailor Mum had met when she was a girl in Malta.

'I'm not trying to make excuses,' her mother had said in her new, strangely weakened voice as Rissa sat at her bedside at the hospice. There was the smell of the freesias she had brought, the brightness of sunshine falling across the room with its pretty curtains and pastel walls. 'But you need to know the truth. He was a good man, one of the best. I was terribly young and foolish. Naïve. We all were in those days. The thing is I really loved Taff and he loved me.'

'Taff?' Rissa had questioned shakily, feeling very much as if her whole world had been pulled from under her feet. Her father, a sailor? Surely this wasn't true.

'He was from Wales,' her mother went on with a remorseless surety. 'On the boats all Welshmen were dubbed Taffy. My Taff had joined up with two friends. They'd grown up together at this village called Capel Mair. When they were children, they'd made some sort of pact that they would all join the navy together and see the world. It must have seemed credible, because that's exactly what happened. After they'd trained for their different positions, they got separated. Then they met up quite by chance in Malta.'

She paused, swallowing, and licked her dry, cracked lips. At once Rissa offered a sip of water.

'Thanks, love.' The sick woman smiled faintly and continued. 'Malta was on the verge of being closed down as a dockyard by then, though we still had quite a few ships coming into port. I met Taff and that was it. Wildfire! I never told him when I suspected I was pregnant. Didn't really get the chance. My mother found out first and all hell broke loose. We were a Catholic family, much respected in the neighbourhood. I was kept bound to the house and never saw Taff again. I remember seeing his ship leaving the harbour and thinking my life was at an end.' She paused again, memories drifting across her tired black eyes. 'A marriage was arranged for me. He was a well-to-do man in England. Older than me of course. A businessman, someone my father had known for years.'

'Dad,' Rissa said flatly. She felt shocked, confused, trembly. Nothing would ever be the same again.

'Yes. Don't think I wasn't happy. I was – eventually. I never regretted marrying him. Geoff's been a thoughtful, loving husband to me and a wonderful father to you. We've had a strong marriage. You can't hope for more than that.'

'No. And … my true father? You didn't ever try to find him?'

'No, I didn't. What good would it have done? Anyway, he may not even be still alive. Oh, he was a splendid fellow. So handsome with his black curly hair and laughing dark eyes. Brooding too – they are, the Celts. He had a rather good singing voice, I recall, a clear tenor. His family were farmers. I don't know what backgrounds his friends had. Maybe they were farming stock too. Wales is largely agricultural, particularly the south-west.'

'And you've nothing else to go on? No reminders?'

'Just a silver-chased locket that Taff gave me. I wore it often, you'll know the one. And I had you, of course.'

Again the sad, sweet smile, laced this time with deep affection. She indicated the bedside cabinet, where Rissa located the treasured locket. Inside were two portraits. Mum as a girl and a young man in naval uniform, smiling into the camera, his dark hair ruffled by the breeze. Her father.

'All these years and I never knew. I thought the locket had wedding pictures of you and Dad. Or me as a baby, or something.' Rissa's voice trailed away.

Her mother had said, 'You'll find more photos in a shoebox in the attic. Most likely they'll be faded, they've not seen the light of day in years. But they are there, somewhere, the four of us picnicking together in the sunshine. Happy days.'

'I'll look them out, Mum. You're tired. Don't try and talk any more.'

Her mother had nodded gratefully and squeezed Rissa's hand. The next day she was gone.

Rissa had found the snapshots – smudged black and white prints, much fingered and crumpled. There was no mistaking the happiness that radiated from the young couple who sat arms entwined, smiling out into a world that would never be theirs. The two other sailors were around the same age. Three jaunty young Taffys, and all from Capel Mair. How to go about finding the right one?

'Been riding yet, Rissa?' Will's voice cut into her thoughts and Rissa started.

'What? Sorry, I was day-dreaming. No, I haven't. I'd like to, though. Be great to explore the countryside properly from the saddle.'

'True indeed. There's Bron Jenkins, Catrin's mother. She's got ponies at Brynteg.'

'I know. Catrin's given me their phone number. Might give them a ring in the morning, see if they can fit me in – oh, talk of the devil, here's Catrin now. And Ewan. Hi, you two. Over here.'

At once Will's face darkened. Before anyone could speak he rose and pushed through the tables to the two who had just entered. Catrin wore a long Indian cotton skirt and an embroidered gypsy blouse. Her hair was drawn back in a thick plait, which hung almost to her waist. She looked strained but raised a smile for Will, which swiftly vanished when she saw his expression.

'So this is why you stood me up,' Will said to her. 'Had a better offer, eh?'

'Come on!' Ewan said reasonably. He shrugged and threw Will an easy smile. 'Catrin wasn't feeling so good. I thought a drink might help. It's been a hectic week.'

Will ignored him. 'Cattie?'

Mortified colour flooded Catrin's cheeks. 'Honestly Will,

people are listening. Do you have to show me up in front of half the village?'

The bar had gone quiet, but now the hum of conversation and chink of glasses was starting up again. Will glowered on. 'Never mind that I booked us a table at that Italian joint you think so much of, planned a movie afterwards. You prefer to come drinking with someone else!'

'Get a grip, Will,' Ewan said, more forcefully. 'It's not a case of making a choice. Like I said, we've all of us been working full pelt. I suggested a drink before Catrin went off home. That's all there is to it.'

'It's the mill wheel,' Catrin burst out. 'So noisy. It gives me a headache. I've had it all day.'

Concern flashed in Will's dark eyes. 'How is it now?'

'Hammering! Is it any wonder?'

'You could be in for a migraine,' Will said. 'You need rest and quiet. I should know. Mam gets her share of migraines.'

'I know,' Catrin said. 'It's awful for Kate. This is just a bad head. I told you on the phone, I haven't been sleeping too well.'

'And that's all there is to it,' Ewan put in with rough good humour. 'So back off Will, and let's all sit down and have a drink.'

Will drew a deep breath as if to say more, clearly thought the better of it and turned on his heel and went out.

'Oh dear,' Catrin said in a low voice. 'Sorry.'

Ewan mocked a grimace and his craggy face looked suddenly boyish. 'Go on. It's I who should apologize,' he said, holding her gaze steadily. 'If you look at things from Will's point of view, our turning up here probably would appear a tad suspicious.'

'Yes. Look, if you don't mind, Ewan, I'll have that drink another time and get off home.'

'Of course I don't mind. Bit of a break, and you'll be a new girl come Monday. Good night, Catrin.'

''Night then.' She smiled at him wanly, sent the party who were now deep in conversation an apologetic farewell wave and left the premises with as much dignity as she could muster. Ewan went to join the others.

'Hello folks. What's everyone drinking? Let's make it a malt all round.'

'Not for me!' Rissa squeaked. 'It's loaded with calories.'

Fred snorted. 'Oh, to blazes with the diet, Rissa lass! You're on holiday!'

They all cheered and Ewan went to order the round.

Arriving home, Catrin parked her Fiesta in the barn, gathered up her shoulder bag and a file of notes and wearily climbed out of the car. Bron was in the main yard, checking a pony's hooves.

'Hello Catrin. You're late,' she called cheerily.

'Oh, I called in at the Drovers with Ewan and bumped into Will of all people. I'd rung him earlier to put him off. Just didn't feel like a night out.'

'Oops!' Bron made a quirky face. 'Was it difficult?'

'Quite. I coped. What's wrong with the pony?'

'Not a thing. I thought she was trotting lame but it was just a stone in her shoe. They can be a pain, these flinty tracks. You look done in.'

'I am. Don't fancy any supper, Mam. Got a bad head. Think I'll heat up some milk and go straight to bed.'

'Best thing. Take a couple of aspirin. Good night's sleep is what you need. Dad's run a couple of trekkers back to their digs.' Bron didn't provide accommodation at the farm. Her clients were boarded out at various houses in the village, and very comfortably too. 'Their car had broken down. I've rung Dewi to see to it. Dad's not back yet.'

'Oh, he'll stop talking half the night, knowing Dad! 'Night Mam.'

Evening shadows lay dark across the mossy cobblestones and overhead a flight of swallows swooped and soared about the eaves of the old pink-washed stone farmhouse. There was a smell of green growing things, of woodsmoke and the wholesome tang of horses and cattle. In the distance, the river chattered over its brown bed. Catrin heard her mother click her tongue to the pony and listened to the familiar clip-clop of hooves crossing the yard to the paddocks. The other ponies started up a frantic whinnying and came charging to the gate to greet their companion. Catrin turned and went into the house.

In bed at last, Catrin swallowed down the aspirin tablets and slowly sipped her hot milk, gazing out of the window at the sickle moon sailing over the humpy peaks of the enfolding hills. She never did draw her curtains and tonight was perfection; calm, balmy, moon-washed. All those years ago, she thought, when the mill was a proper working entity, that girl – Elin, was she called? – would have watched the same moon gleaming amongst a twinkling of stars over the same hills and—

Abruptly Catrin put down her empty mug on the bedside table and slithered down in the bed. Now was not the time to dwell on Elin or John Caradoc. Deliberately she switched her thoughts to her weaving. She pictured the loom clattering to and fro and the complex pattern emerging from the bobbins of coloured wool. It seemed to strike a rhythm. Caradoc, Caradoc, Caradoc. The painkillers began to take effect; the hot stabbing in her temple receded. Her eyes closed and she slept.

*

'John? Oh, *cariad*, how are you feeling?'

Stealthily Elin entered the shepherd's hut and went straight to the makeshift couch in the corner where John lay on a bundle of straw, covered over with blankets. He struggled up to a sitting position, wincing and putting his hand to his bound head.

'*Daro*! What a thing to happen!'

'Could be worse. The soldiers could have taken you. Killed even.' Elin's lips trembled at the very thought. She drew from under her shawl a platter of food and placed it on an upturned wooden box at John's elbow. A small flagon of wine followed. 'It's some Dada had stashed away. It should help dull the pain. Eat, now. There's cheese, a slice of meat pie and some fresh bread. Afterwards, I shall dress your wounds again.'

Though still pale and shaken after the attack three nights earlier, John tackled the fare with a healthy vigour. Elin took up a pitcher and went out to get water from the brook. When she returned John was sopping up the last of the wine with the bread.

'Ah, that was good!'

'Just hope Mam doesn't find out. This is the third time I've raided the pantry shelf when her back was turned.' Elin gently unwound the soiled bandage on John's forehead. 'Ugh, but it's deep. It'll scar.'

'Be an end to my good looks then?' He eyed her roguishly. 'Won't love me any more, will you?'

'Well … I might,' Elin parried, pouring water into a bowl. She dipped in a clean rag and dabbed gently at the wound. 'Quite appealing, a scar. Adds a bit of character—'

'Ouch!'

'Sorry. Almost done. There. It's clean. No sign of infection.

Dressing it with mouldy bread did the trick. Keep still. This will soothe. It's marigold salve.'

'Mouldy bread! Marigold salve!' John grumbled, flinching as her fingertips smoothed and smeared. 'Are you a witch with your potions and unguents?'

'I might be,' she said primly. She took up a length of clean white linen and rebound his head. 'Now your arm. What a one you are for getting into mischief!'

His wounds tended, John said, 'Elin. My father will be worried. I'll have to ask you to get a message to him.'

She bit her lip. 'It's difficult. The soldiers are everywhere. Your name is down as the ringleader of the Rebecca Riots attack. There's reward on your head. Your home is being watched. Every time your father takes a toll at the gate, a soldier questions the traveller.'

'Please?'

'Well … I'll see.'

'Tell Da I'm all right but don't let on that you're harbouring me. The less Da knows, the safer it is – for you especially. Right?'

She nodded. 'Suppose so. But I still don't see why you've got involved with all this.'

'Justice, Elin. Principle.'

'What? Dressing up in women's clothes and stealing toll-gates? Seems daft to me. Rebecca Riots indeed!'

'Rebecca's our namesake,' John explained patiently. 'Turn to Genesis in your Bible. Read about Rebecca possessing the gates of those which hate them.'

'She's in the Bible?'

'Yes indeed. That's the reason behind our disguise. We intend to remove every gate erected on every new turnpike road. A man has a right to travel freely over the land of his birth. No one should be forced to pay tithes to greedy fools who consider themselves a cut above ordinary people. That goes for the clergy too – load of hypocrites!'

'John!'

'It's true. Oh, not all I grant you. Father Hopkins is as sincere a fellow as you could hope to meet. A true Christian. Would there were more like him. Unfortunately, for every good priest there are three bad ones, and that's a fact. Elin – oh, *cariad*, I wouldn't worry you like this over nothing, now would I?'

'No, John.'

'And you'll see Da?'

'I … yes, I will.'

He kissed her tenderly. 'There's my girl. Remember, have a care.'

In the kitchen of the mill, Elin's mother surveyed her pantry shelf with a frown.

'There's funny! I'm sure I had more pie left than that. Barely enough for supper, there is. Bread gone, too.' She turned to face her husband. 'Something's not right here, Hywel. Someone's been helping themselves to the food.'

The weaver pondered. 'Could it be Elin, do you think, Marged?'

'That boy she talked to often. Caradoc's lad. Mixed up with business over the tithes, he is. I wonder – Hywel, where are you going?'

'I saw Elin slip past the mill a while back. Think I know now where she was going. Stay here, Marged. And stop looking so fashed. I won't do or say anything to harm her. Just need to get to the bottom of this.'

He took his staff from by the door and left the house. From the window Marged watched him cross the narrow wooden bridge that spanned the mill leet and take the path that led through the wooded slopes of the hills.

Gaining the shepherd's hut in its protecting copse of rowan and birch, Hywel paused a moment, then flung wide the door.

Catrin woke with a start. Light streamed in through the open door of her bedroom. Her mother stood there, her hair disordered, her nightclothes rumpled. 'Catrin? Are you all right?'

Rissa swung the wheel of her red Metro and headed off up the long track to Brynteg. It was a glorious morning, the sun bright, everywhere new-washed after a heavy dew, but for the moment the beauty of her surroundings escaped Rissa. Just now when she had called at the filling station for petrol, Dewi, who owned the premises and worked part-time at the mill, stuck his head out from under the bonnet of the car he was tinkering with. Wiping his oily hands on a bit of rag, he sent her a nod of greeting.

'Hi.' He swept her figure in white polo shirt and stretch jods tucked into gleaming black leather riding boots a smiling glance. 'Off riding then. Grand day for it.'

'Yes, it is.'

'For a moment I thought you were Catrin. Same age, both dark-haired – it's no wonder I was taken in. Would your folks come from Wales?'

'My mother was Maltese. That accounts for my dark colouring.'

'Maltese, eh? My dad went to Malta. He did a spell in the Navy when he was young. Wow, could he tell the tales!'

'Oh?' Rissa's heart had quickened. Instinctively her hand went to the locket at her throat. 'D'you think I could have a word with him sometime? I'm … interested in naval history and so on.'

Dewi looked wry. 'Not a chance. Dad's been gone these ten years. A stroke.'

'I'm sorry,' Rissa said awkwardly.

'Ah well. He was a great character. I still miss him. Left me this garage, he did. Mam's married again and gone to live in Ireland. That's life, eh?'

'Sure.' Rissa had smiled and paid him for the petrol. Disappointment had welled up inside her. It had looked like a lead at last, but it had come to nothing.

The gates to Brynteg were open. She drove in and parked out of the sun. Bron greeted her in the yard. 'Hi, Rissa. I've brought Marshal up for you. He's a cob – steady as they come. You'll love him to bits.'

'I'm sure. Is that him in the box?'

'Right.' Bron accompanied her to the stable where a chestnut head regarded them curiously over the half-door. 'Want help saddling up?'

'No, it's all right, thanks,' Rissa said, delving into her jods pocket for a polo-mint that all horses relish. 'Hi there, Marshal. There you are. Aren't you great?'

Ten minutes later she was trotting out of the stableyard, bound for a crop of forestry land that was open to riders. As she went clopping along the lane, her thoughts ranged back to the incident at the garage. Somehow, she had to find what she had come looking for.

Passing the water mill, she urged the cob on to the river path and nudged him into a canter. She had no idea what spooked him. They were cantering along, the breeze whispering past her cheeks, the river gushing by, when suddenly Marshal plunged sideways, went up in a half-rear – and took off.

'Whoa!' she cried, using her reins hard. 'Whoa there! Stop!'

It was no good. Marshal's jaw was set. He galloped on, faster, faster, hooves thundering along the flinty path with Rissa hanging on grimly, powerless to stop him.

Chapter Three

'Have a bit of sense, Marged!' Hywel said forcefully. 'If the authorities find out we're harbouring a wanted man, they'll send the soldiers in. Then we'll all be for it!'

'Authorities – tarradiddle!' Marged sniffed. 'Who's going to tell them, for goodness sake? Not me or you, and certainly not Elin! The lad's safe enough where he is for now. No one goes up the mountain this time of year, and by the time lambing comes round again and the shepherd needs the hut, all this trouble will have blown over.'

'Think so?'

'Yes, I do.' Marged smiled encouragingly at her husband, her robust face hopeful. 'Come on, Hywel. Don't you remember what it was like to be young and in love? Elin's crazy about this boy. That much is obvious. She wouldn't have got involved in such danger otherwise.'

'Well, maybe not. What about John? Think he loves her?'

'I'm sure of it. John Caradoc's a hard-working, good-living fellow and he's no fool. Elin told me he wanted to become a weaver. Think on it, Hywel. Someone to carry on the mill after us! Oh, I know he's gone against his father over this business with the Rebecca gang, but that only shows he's a man of principle. Besides, I'm not totally without sympathy with the movement myself. Not the rioting and such of course – there's some who'd join anything for a bit of fist play! Though thinking about it, I don't really see what other route there is open to them but to take the law into their own hands. It's time the common person stood up for his rights, and that's a fact.'

'All the same, woman, we're best not getting involved.'

'Tch! So what do we do? Turn John over to the soldiers and see our daughter's heart broken? I couldn't do it, Hywel!'

He sighed heavily. 'No, you're right. You truly think we're doing the right thing by hiding John? It's a risk, mind. We stand to lose everything if we're found out. The mill, our good name … maybe even each other. It'll be jail for us and the gallows for young Caradoc.'

'It won't come to that. For shame, Hywel! Letting a load of scaremongering get the better of you! John's here now and Elin's sticking by him no matter what, so it seems to me we have no choice in the matter. Now, are you coming back up to the hut with me to tell them they have our support?'

'Well … oh, have it your own way, girl!'

Marged, already up on her feet and filling a basket with food and linen bandages, threw her husband a look of relieved satisfaction. 'There's my Hywel! Come on then. Make haste, or we'll never get the cloth off the looms today! When has that big order to be delivered by?'

'Monday week at the latest. I'll do it, never fear. Even if I have to stop up all night in the attempt. You know, an apprentice might be no bad thing, Marged. We're neither of us getting any younger and a bit of help on the looms would be welcome.'

'There then, what did I tell you? God works in mysterious ways. Are you sitting there all day, or what?'

Rain had swept in while they had been talking, a drizzly

mountain mist that clung to the hair and lashes and made the steep path that wound upwards through thickets of birch and rowan treacherous to the unwary. Marged and Hywel, however, born to the area, kept to the flattish stones set into the hillside in a series of rough steps and made the ascent with little trouble.

At the door of the hut, a worried Elin greeted them. 'Mam, Dada. John's not so good. He's hot and rambling on about things. I can't understand what he's trying to say.'

'Ah. Sounds like fever to me.' Marged pushed past and went to the corner, where the injured man tossed restlessly on a pile of bracken. Elin cast a frantic look from John to her father, who still stood in the doorway.

'It's all right, girl,' Hywel said to her. 'Your mam and I have come to a decision. We're with you all the way.'

'Oh – Dada!' Tearfully Elin flung her arms around him and hugged him. 'We won't let you down, I promise. Any trouble, and John will take himself off out of your way.'

A wild muttering from the corner made a mockery of her words. Hywel shook his head in doubt. 'Seems to me that one won't be going anywhere for a while. Ah, don't worry, Elin.' He squeezed her hand, his shrewd face softening. 'You know your mam's got a way with herbs and healing, like her mam before her. Like you will have too, given time. If anyone can get him right, it's her.'

Marged, bent over the sick man, was removing the soiled bandages on his head. Seeing the wound, she clicked her tongue impatiently. 'That's a deep one. It needs borage to heal it over. I should have some on my shelf. The fever's nothing, just reaction, I'd say. A cooling potion will soon sort it out. Come back down to the house with me, Elin. You can help prepare the cure.'

'All right, Mam.' Elin pushed back her long black hair, tousled from trailing up and down the mountain through the long night. Her cheeks were pale, her eyes shadowed. 'He will … John will recover?'

''Course he will! It'll take more than a scratch to defeat that one! Your father can stay here with him while we're gone. Won't be more than half an hour,' she said to her husband.

Elin, throwing a last desperate look at the angry wound on John's head, seized her shawl and followed her mother out into the rain.

Back in the mill house, Marged set Elin to pounding the dried herbs with the marble pestle and mortar that had been her grandmother's, while she made a posset with roots and lemon juice. On the table was a freshly laundered length of linen ready to be cut into yet more bandages. Soon the living kitchen was full of the smell of infusing herbs. Pouring the potion into a bottle, Marged stoppered it with a cork from the table drawer and went to see how Elin fared.

'That will be fine. Now the honey. You make a paste, see. Be sure and use the bone spatulas to smooth it on the sore place. Never touch a raw wound with your fingers, mind, or you'll spread the infection and risk trouble yourself. Did you use mouldy bread to draw the puss?'

'Yes Mam. And cobwebs. That worked better.'

'It would, with the wound being so deep. There we are then. Put this in the basket and let me cut up that linen quickly into strips – daro! What's that?'

Outside there was shouting and the clatter and jangle of hooves and armoury. Next instant there came a loud rapping sounded on the door.

'Ho there, mistress! Anybody home?'

Hands stilling over their preparations, Elin and Marged

exchanged a look of horror. 'The soldiers!' Elin gasped. 'Mam, what are we going to do?'

Rissa came round to throbbing pain and her mind reeling. The smell of infusing herbs was strong in her nostrils. Instinctively she made to curl her fingers round the well-worn handle of the basket, and yet when she looked there was no basket there. With a groan she pulled herself to a sitting position, glancing around nervously, half-expecting to see the soldiers come tramping up the track. All that met her gaze was empty wood-land and, just ahead, some sort of glade. Everything came rushing back. Of course there were no soldiers. The horse had spooked and she had taken a toss. Rissa swallowed, passing a trembling hand across her forehead.

Shakily she unlatched the chin-strap of her tight-fitting crash hat and pulled it off, freeing her smooth dark bell of hair. There was a strange, waiting silence, as if time stood still. Gradually, into the quiet, came the sound of trickling water. Still rather confused, Rissa glanced around frowningly. Just ahead was a ring of stunted oaks, in the centre of which reared a tall boulder or monolith, its pitted, blue-black surface gleaming dully in the sunlight. It looked so old. Inexplicably, impossibly old. At its foot bubbled a bright clear spring of water. Of course, Rissa thought. This was the druid's grove with the famous touch-stone and spring that never ran dry. A little shiver touched her. No wonder she had dreamed.

And what a dream! It had been so graphic. And the girl, Elin. There'd been something familiar about her....

Marshal was nowhere to be seen and feeling slightly better, Rissa pulled slowly to her feet. The horse would have galloped for home, she decided. Taking a few reviving breaths, she set off after him down the flinty track.

Catrin was enjoying a quiet Sunday walk. Everywhere was fresh after an early shower and the sun now shone bravely. Finches twittered from the thicket of woodland ahead. Distantly came the rushing clamour of the river in full spate.

All at once the peace was shattered by the thud of plunging hooves and along the track towards her came a horse, riderless, reins and stirrup leathers flying. It was Marshal.

'Marshal! Whoa boy!'

Trying to stop his wild flight, Catrin spread her arms wide. But Marshal was not having any and skewing round her, lather flying from his dripping neck and flanks, he went charging on past, all set for home and the comfort of his stable. Catrin stared after him, her thoughts spinning. Into her mind's eye came a picture of Rissa lying on the ground.

The grove! I should have warned her, she thought, as she began to run, following the trail of churned hoofprints.

Anxiety turned to relief when she rounded the next bend and saw, coming unsteadily towards her, a figure in riding gear. Rissa held her crash hat in her hand. She looked shaken but seemed mercifully unharmed.

'Thank goodness,' Catrin said. 'Marshal's just gone past like a bat out of hell. You're OK?'

'Yes.' Rissa looked at her strangely.

'So what's the matter?'

'Nothing. You've just reminded me of someone, that's all,' Rissa said shakily. 'Marshal just took off. I've never had anything like that happen before. I simply couldn't stop him. Then he chucked me.'

About to say something, Catrin bit the words back. Perhaps this was not the moment to talk about the grove. She said instead, 'Look, you seem a bit wobbly to me. Might be wise to get you checked out at the hospital.'

'I'm fine. Just a bit stiff,' Rissa protested.

'All the same, I know Mum will feel better if we get you cleared by a doctor. I feel a bit responsible myself. You're my student after all.'

Rissa grinned wanly. 'Put that way, how can I refuse?'

They made their slow way back to the farm, taking it steadily. At Brynteg, they found Bron rubbing down the sweated, runaway horse. Marshal stood with his head over the stable door, regarding them with mild curiosity like the quiet animal he generally was. 'He's never done anything like that before,' Bron said worriedly. Her relief that Rissa had not come to any obvious harm was immense, though she readily endorsed Catrin's suggestion of a hospital check-up. 'Best to be on the safe side with a tumble. When you're through at the hospital, come straight back here. I'll have the kettle on.'

Presently Catrin was ferrying them along the road to town, Rissa a still and rather silent figure in the passenger seat beside her. Something's happened, Catrin thought. Rissa's an experienced rider, not one to be unduly upset by a spill from the saddle. Long-held tales surrounding the grove churned in her mind. Ancient folklore, spell-stones, sacred rites. She had once seen something herself.

Soon the hospital entrance reared into view. Signalling, Catrin turned in and found a parking slot.

In the A & E department, they gave the necessary details and settled down in the stuffy, overheated waiting area for the usual long wait. Opposite them, a mother with two small children sat reading them a story from the pile of rather tattered books. A youth in jeans nursing a roughly bandaged hand sent them a rueful smile. Others sifted through magazines, a restless eye on the clock. 'Fancy some coffee or tea?' Catrin said. 'It's only from the machine but it's not bad.'

'Tea would be great,' Rissa replied.

Catrin went to get it, lacing Rissa's liberally with sugar.

'Lovely,' said Rissa, sipping. Some of her colour had returned now. Catrin took a deep breath. 'Rissa. Back by the grove, when you said I reminded you of someone, what did you mean?'

Rissa's hand began to shake uncontrollably and hurriedly she put the plastic beaker of hot tea down on the low table in front of them.

'You're not going to believe this, but something happened out there. Something really weird. I can't get it out of my mind. Can't get my head round it either,' Rissa added with a small self-conscious lift of her shoulders.

'It's the grove, isn't it?' Catrin swallowed and took the plunge. 'You've had a seeing. What my gran would call a waking dream.'

Rissa shuddered. 'Tell me about it! That place! So creepy!'

'So what happened?'

'Well, one moment Marshal had ditched me,' Rissa said. 'The next I seemed to be transported back to another century. Catrin, it was so real! There was this girl, Elin. She was the image of you. No, that's not quite right. I think there was a resemblance to both of us. Anyway, she was harbouring this guy she was sweet on. Um ... Caradoc, that was it. John Caradoc. He'd been heading some riots or other and got himself hurt in a skirmish.'

Catrin's heart began to thump. 'It was the Rebecca Riots. Elin's parents were called Hywel and Marged Rees. They lived and worked in the mill in the nineteenth century.'

Rissa stared at her. 'You know? But ... but how come?'

'I've dreamed about them too. I had another one only last night. John was hurt during one of the raids and Elin hid him and nursed him.'

'In a shepherd's hut. But ... this is ridiculous. There's got to be some sort of evidence that the place actually exists. The hut. Is it still there?'

'The ruins of it are,' Catrin said. 'You'll find it about halfway up the hill, right in the wood. In the winter when the trees are bare you can see the grove from up there. It's spooky, the grove.' Her mind cast back. The voices, whispering. The crawling silence. 'I once saw something there when I was small. It really freaked me out,' she finished in a low voice.

'What was it?' Rissa asked nervously.

'Well, there was chanting and I saw figures. It was very vague and shadowy like looking through mist. More an impression than an actual seeing. I was up there playing with my doll. I dropped it in fright and ran. I kept away after that.' Catrin heaved a sigh. 'Odd thing, remember when you turned up on the path that day and found me asleep? That was when I experienced my very first dream about the mill. I've had them on and off ever since.'

Rissa picked up her tea, gulping it down. 'Think I need something stronger,' she murmured in a voice that shook.

Catrin, seeing the girl's white face, said, 'Look, I should try not to get too wound up about it. There's sure to be a perfectly rational explanation.'

'Think so? I think it's weird. What's going on? Why us?'

'It's got to be the grove,' Catrin said rationally. 'Like I said, it's got a reputation. Ask anyone. Ask Ewan even. He's not a local man but you don't see him walking often in that direction.'

'OK. Fine.' Rissa sounded anything but fine but Catrin

allowed her to continue. 'Let's try and look at it logically. We both hone in on this incident from the past. Rebecca Riots, the miller and his folks. They're in the thick of it because of this John Caradoc guy.'

'Right. It sounds as if your dream was a continuation of mine. I'd got up to where I was hiding John and treating his head wound. It was a terrible gash.'

'You?' If anything, Rissa went a shade paler. 'You mean you actually felt you were Elin?'

'Well, yes. Yet I can see myself too. Wasn't it the same for you?'

'I suppose ... yes, it was.'

The nurse bustled in for the next patient. There was a flurry of movement as the young mother gathered up her offspring and hustled them through to the doctor. Rissa glanced with agitation at her watch. 'We're going to be here all day at this rate. I'm beginning to wish we'd never come.'

'Never mind,' Catrin said placatingly. 'Want some more tea?'

'No thanks. I just want to get to the bottom of this Caradoc business. Why don't we do some research? There's got to be a record of previous mill owners somewhere.'

'There is. It'll be in the deeds. Heritage are in charge of those so we can count that out. There are the church records, of course. I might have a book somewhere on the Rebecca Riots. I'll look it out for you.'

'Great. Thanks. Gosh, isn't it hot in here? Wouldn't mind a cold drink if there's one going.'

'They sell cans at the hospital café. I'll see what I can rustle up.' Catrin rose, mustering a smile. 'Don't go away!'

As she sped along the corridor, shoes squeaking on the rubber floor, Catrin's mind was in turmoil. At least now she wasn't alone. She'd been beginning to think she was losing it!

Thing was, why was it happening? And why was Rissa involved, of all people? It didn't make sense.

At the café she purchased some cans of orange and hurried back. The queue in the waiting area had diminished again. 'They've brought another doctor in,' Rissa said. 'Things should speed up now. Oh, orange. Lovely.'

In due course Rissa was seen and subsequently given the all clear, but warned to see a doctor should she have any further trouble. Not long afterwards they were sitting in the comfortable farmhouse kitchen at Brynteg, enjoying copious cups of tea and generous slices of Bron's raspberry sponge cake.

'I'll worry about my diet tomorrow,' Rissa said, accepting a second piece. 'Mmm, wonderful.'

Over her teacup, Catrin eyed her friend. Rissa looked more herself now, she was glad to see. Together they would sort out the dream business. As Ewan was wont to say, no matter what happens, it can be sorted. Conjuring up an image of Ewan's rugged face and shrewdly appraising grey eyes, Catrin smiled to herself. It was good to think he'd be around for the next few months, until the mill and its workings were fully tried out. Only the other day Glenys was saying how Capel Mair Mill would not be the same without him. Catrin could not help but agree.

Later she hunted out the slim volume of local history and the next morning, as her group gathered together in the weaving room, she handed it to Rissa.

'There isn't much on the riots,' she said, her eye on the chattering party. 'John Caradoc's name is mentioned. He was the leader for this district. Anyway, see what you make of it and we'll have a chat sometime. How d'you feel this morning?'

'OK. Bit sore, but nothing I can't cope with,' Rissa said, glancing up as the door swung open and Fliss appeared, smiling apologetically.

''Morning everyone,' Fliss sing-songed. 'Sorry to be late. Is it weaving today? I'm itching to try the big loom.'

'Right then, let's make a start.' Catrin fixed her mind back to work. 'Have you all got your pattern book? Turn to the wedding ring design on page ten. Now, we've covered the acid and natural dye processes. Today we're concentrating on the actual weaving. Just gather round the loom, please. I'll demonstrate the tension and show you how the shuttle works, then you can each have a turn.'

They had completed the first section of pattern and were about to start on the next when the loom suddenly juddered and stopped. Outside the window, the mill wheel swung to a halt.

'Drat,' Catrin muttered. 'It must have jammed or something.'

'Want me to fetch Ewan?' Glenys said.

Catrin shook her head. 'It's OK, I'll go. It must be about coffee break time. You all go ahead. I'll meet you in the café later.'

Ewan had already noticed the silent wheel and was coming out of the room he used as a studio as Catrin appeared on the exhibition gallery. He looked exasperated. 'I know, I know. You don't have to tell me. The confounded thing's playing up again. Where's Dewi?'

'Think he's gone into Cardigan to the suppliers. He should be back shortly. Can I help?'

'Possibly. Just mind you don't fall in the mill leet, that's all. One disaster's enough for one day. Blasted thing. Whatever's wrong with it?'

Grumbling to himself, yet still maintaining his look of dry humour that Catrin had to admit she found so arresting, Ewan picked up his toolbox and led the way outside and over the narrow bridge to where the wheel hung still and silent above the frothing water. A swift foray into the workings and the architect had his answer.

'Cogs have jammed. Apparently it was a weakness in this type of mechanism. If you could pop back inside and put on the brake, Catrin, I'll soon have it fixed.'

With a few adjustments to the workings, Ewan had the wheel turning again. 'All the same, it shouldn't have jammed,' he said as they came away. 'I made a few modifications to the original design which should have solved the matter.'

'Was that the wrangle you had with the Heritage people?' Catrin asked, recalling the correspondence that flew back and forth with Ewan getting more and more irate with every letter.

'Yes.' He laughed shortly. 'You know Cadw. Everything to be restored exactly as it was right down to the very last nail or else! They wouldn't let me go ahead with the new concept I'd worked out, so I had to bring it more in line with the original. Blasted nuisance! If they were less keen on having things just so, there'd be no problem now. As it is....'

He shrugged and off they went to the café, where frothy cappuccinos and homemade biscuits awaited. 'All sorted,' Catrin cried, flopping down into a chair next to Rissa. One of the new intake had joined the group, a young girl called Roz with curly red hair tied back from an animated face.

'I love the way they've incorporated the exhibition gallery and the workshop,' she was saying eagerly. 'Then there's this café as well. It's all really lush. Reminds me of a place we used to visit up north. It was a mill that had been converted into a restaurant. My dad's a naval officer so we get around quite a bit.'

'My father was in the navy once,' Catrin said, sipping coffee. 'It was before he and Mam were married. You'd have thought it would have been hard for him, being tied down to a farm after years at sea. But Dad didn't seem to mind. Great, to see something of the world before you settle down. Were you thinking of the same sort of future, Roz?'

'Possibly. Music's my thing. Wouldn't mind joining the Band of the Royal Marines – if they'll have me!'

Catrin had failed to notice Rissa's sudden stillness. Rissa said, 'Didn't know you had a nautical background, Catrin.'

'Wouldn't say that,' Catrin said with a laugh. 'Dad and two schoolmates of his had a thing about the sea. When they were old enough they all joined up together.'

'Oh?' Rissa sounded suddenly breathless and Catrin knew a stab of alarm. Perhaps the girl should have rested up today. 'You OK?'

'What? Oh, sure, thanks.' The others had started up conversations of their own. Rissa said, apparently casual, 'It's great when friends keep in touch. I expect your father enjoys a good memory-lane natter with the others.'

'Well, one of them died a few years ago. He was Dewi's father, who owns the garage, you know. The other's James Emmet. He's a chartered accountant now with his own business in Cardigan. Dad has him for the farm accounts so yes, they're still in touch.'

Catrin glanced up to find Ewan's eyes on her across the table. He smiled. For a long moment their gaze locked and Catrin's pulse began to race alarmingly. Confused, she tore her gaze away and pushed aside her empty coffee mug. 'Oh well, back to it. You ready, everyone?'

'Slave driver!' someone groaned, and amid a lot of laughter they all got up and made for the exit. Rissa was the last to leave. Beth Marriott, clearing the tables, thought the girl was unusually quiet and put it down to the fall off the horse.

*

Will pushed through the doorway of the newsagent's in Cardigan and practically cannoned into Rissa.

'Rissa! Hi there! How are the bumps and bruises?'

'Hi, Will. I'm fine, thanks. How come everyone knows what happened? It's embarrassing. As if falling off a horse wasn't ego-busting enough!'

'Shouldn't worry about it. You can't keep anything secret in Capel Mair, and a bruised ego soon mends. Fancy a cup of tea? I was just going for one.'

'Lovely, thanks.'

Having purchased his farming magazine, Will ushered Rissa into the teashop on the corner and said he'd get the order. 'No milk or sugar for me,' Rissa said, adding a word about her diet.

Will laughed. 'You should take up farming. You could nosh as much as you wanted then. There's nothing like hiking up and down mountains after sheep for keeping you good and trim.'

'I'll take your word for it.'

He was soon back with the steaming cups of tea. Rissa eyed him narrowly across the table. 'Thanks. You're looking very smart. Don't think I've ever seen you out of working togs.'

'Thought I'd best spruce myself up. I'm here to see the accountant.'

'Oh? Would that be James Emmet?'

'Right. He's a local lad. All the Capel Mair folk deal with him. Know James, do you?'

'Not at all. Catrin mentioned he'd been in the navy with her father. I was curious. My mother once knew someone from here who'd been stationed in Malta where she came from. It was years and years ago.'

'That right? Why don't you ask Llew if you want to know more? There's nothing he likes better than a good jaw. What you doing out of school, anyway? Has Catrin given you a free afternoon or are you skiving off?'

'Now would I do that? Catrin's doing workshops today with the new intake. Can't be easy, keeping up with the flow. I know she's got Glenys as a spare pair of hands, but Catrin's the brains behind it all. I really admire her for it.'

'Catrin's a glutton for hard work,' Will said tetchily. 'Just wish she'd put her thoughts into Ty Coch. Farming's taking a beating lately and our place is no exception. Few new ideas might help to get it back on its feet again.'

'I'm sorry.' Rissa's voice was quiet. 'I know a lot of farmers are having to sell up. It seems such a shame. Though I really don't see what Catrin could do about things.'

'No.' Will swallowed. He shouldn't have said what he did. 'Forget it. Bit worried, that's all. Farm on the brink – there's no money in sheep any more and you can't do crops or dairying on hill pasture like mine, the land simply isn't suitable. Then there's Mam, not in the best of health.'

'Not easy for you.' She sipped tea reflectively. 'Have you thought of going in for specialist breeds for the fleeces? Catrin was saying how hard it was to get merino. Don't know how viable it would be commercially, but with the sudden swell of interest in traditional crafts I should think there would be a demand. Goats too. And alpacas – alpaca fleece is much sought after. Are they easy to keep?'

'You need to be able to run fast!' Will said with a quirky grin that completely altered his face. 'Seriously though, it's a thought. There are other tourist mills in the area beside Capel Mair. They just might be interested as well. Thanks, Rissa. Any more ideas gratefully considered. Have you any?'

'Only what probably half the farmers in the country are plugging and that's giving guided tours of their farms to groups of schoolchildren and showing them how it's done. Isn't there a government scheme for that?'

'Possibly. Wouldn't be any use for me. I'm hopeless at explaining things. I've got no patience at all. And Mam's not fit enough.'

'I'd do it given the chance! I'd quite enjoy working with kids. Almost went in for teaching but I didn't fancy the palaver that goes with it nowadays, the national curriculum and so on. I'd want to be in the classroom. Hands-on every time for me.'

'Me too. The red tape with present-day farming has to be seen to be believed. Want another cup?'

'Not for me, thanks.' Rissa began to get her things together. 'I'm going to take shots of the bay while the sun's out. It makes the sea such an incredible blue. You're so lucky living here – though I don't suppose you appreciate it when you see it all the time.'

'Oh, I think I do,' Will said, standing up with a smile. 'Wouldn't like to live anywhere else, no way.'

Outside the café, they said goodbye and Will watched Rissa go walking off with her eager stride. She might be on to something with that rare breeds idea, he thought. Big, commercial mills had no interest at all in the specialist fleeces, so the prospect of producing them had never entered his head before. Now, he might just go for a change of farming policy. Nothing ventured nothing gained, as his dad used to say. The local sheep and cattle marts sometimes turned out a few random breeds. Failing that, didn't James deal with the smallholders and rare breed enthusiasts? He might know of a likely source.

Feeling more cheerful than he had in weeks, Will waited for a break in the traffic and darted across the road, gaining the accountant's premises in perfect time exactly as the previous client was leaving.

'You've bought in thirty breeding ewes?' Catrin said. 'But that's wonderful! Merino fleece is like gold! I can never get enough of it!'

Will laughed gently down into her glowing face. They were sitting outside in a pub garden enjoying a quick snack before going on to Cardiff to the theatre. To judge by the admiring gleam in Will's eyes, Catrin was glad she had made an effort and put on her new dress and strappy shoes. It had been weeks since they had enjoyed a relaxing time out together. She had been disconcerted to find that she had not missed him as much as she should. There were times when she wondered if their relationship was dwindling to a natural end. Now it felt good to be at Will's side again, the two of them looking forward to the evening ahead.

He said, 'James gave me the name of a Southdown breeder, too. Are they any good for your purpose?'

'Yes, very much so. And if you can get some Jacobs—'

'Hang on! This is just experimental. Let's see how we go with these first. If it sparks an interest we can go on from there.'

'Right.' Catrin swallowed. The inference that they were in this together had rekindled that old feeling of being trapped. 'Where does James Emmet come into this?' she asked, twisting the subject slightly.

'Bumped into Rissa in town.'

'Oh? Was she all right? I won't forget having to hawk her off to hospital in a hurry. Nor will Mum. She was really done at having of one her horses misbehave.'

'Ah well, that's animals for you. Rissa was fine. The sheep were her idea, actually. I was on my way to the accountant so I picked his brains about likely breeders. James gave me a whole list of people. Amazing how popular these rare breeds are becoming. Very soon they'll not be rare any longer!'

'True,' laughed Catrin. 'Poor Rissa! You can laugh, but I think she's still feeling the effect of that fall. She didn't turn up at class again this morning and that's not like her.'

'Shouldn't worry. I'd say Rissa's tougher than she looks. She was quizzing me about your dad's experiences in the navy. Something to do with her mother being Maltese, can't really remember. I suggested she asked him herself.'

'He won't say much. Dad's surprisingly reticent about his time at sea.'

'That right? Have you had enough to eat? Let's make tracks then or we'll not find a parking space.'

The play was everything Catrin had expected and the memory of the enjoyable evening stayed with her all weekend. No more dreams, happily. On Monday she arrived at the mill refreshed and ready to start another busy week – the final week in the course for her first batch of students, as it turned out.

'I was wondering about an end-of-course party,' Catrin said to Beth, having called at the Mill House on her way home. Greg was still at the mill, going over the workings of the wheel with Ewan, since it was still giving cause for concern.

'Lovely,' Beth said, pouring tea. 'Just milk, isn't it? Biscuit?'

Catrin helped herself to an almond cookie from the tin. 'I don't mean anything lavish. Just a few eats and some wine and maybe some background music if anyone wants to dance. We could clear the foyer and hold it there. Be a bit cramped up in the gallery.'

'Good idea. How about quiche and a variety of salads for the buffet? Maybe cold meats as well. Early strawberries are in. We could have strawberries and cream and maybe a pavlova—'

'Shut up!' Catrin laughed. 'My mouth's watering at the very thought! Oh – there's your phone ringing.'

Beth went out into the hallway to answer it and Catrin, feeling very much at home in Beth's cosy parlour, helped herself to another biscuit and nibbled it reflectively. As part of the early refurbishing, the Mill House had been totally gutted and rebuilt. The pretty room with its stripped beams and smooth walls bore no resemblance at all to the dark, low-ceilinged little dwelling in Catrin's dream, and she wondered not for the first time if she had allowed her imagination to get the better of her. Of course, there was Rissa's experience as well. Maybe that too could be explained. Could they both have watched the same film recently? Memory was a strange tool that could play tricks on you. Easy to believe that a scene from a film or even a passage read in a book actually happened. She had not had time to do any research into the mill's past herself and Rissa had not been very forthcoming, so Catrin assumed the girl had met with a deadlock.

'That was Greg saying he'll be late for supper – yet again!' Beth said, coming into the room. 'It's the boys' after-school swimming club too. I'll have to go and pick them up myself.'

'Then I'll make myself scarce,' Catrin said, getting up. 'Thanks for the tea, Beth. We'll talk again about the party.'

'Of course. See you then, Catrin.'

Bidding her friend goodbye, Catrin let herself out of the back door. From here there was a view of the village straggling up the hillside and the square-towered Norman church at the top. On impulse Catrin decided to take that route home.

Glenys had already left and Catrin's was the only car left on the hard standing reserved for staff. Piling her pattern books and files on the back seat, since she had tomorrow's notes to glance over, Catrin jumped into the car and drove off. As she approached the church she saw, parked outside the gates, Rissa's Fiat. At once Catrin pulled in behind it. Getting out of the car, she entered the churchyard and went walking up the path between ranks of mossy old headstones in search of her friend.

Towards the side of the church, the current graveyard lay neatly mown and cared for, but here where the graves dated back a couple of centuries and more the grass was long and starred with daisies and tiny blue flowers of periwinkle.

The sun sent brilliant shafts of light across the valley and as Catrin gained the end of the row she was suddenly blinded. Squinting through the dazzle, she saw that a figure stood before a grave over by the church wall. It was Rissa. She seemed absorbed.

'Rissa!' Catrin called, stepping over the long grass to join her. As she approached the grave Catrin became aware of a creeping sadness. The closer she got, the stronger it grew. It was so powerful she wanted to turn and run away. But before she could succumb to temptation Rissa had glanced up, a glazed expression on her face. She gave a small salute of recognition.

'Hi, Catrin. Look what I've found here.'

In silence Catrin came to stand beside the other girl, forcing her gaze on the black granite headstone. The name inscribed on it was that of Elin Caradoc.

Chapter Four

Twelve years I was a maid
One year I was a wife
One day I was a mother
And then I lost my life

Catrin and Rissa gazed in shock at the pitiful epitaph. Above the verse, Elin Caradoc's name was carved deeply into the black granite stone, and her dates.

'Born March 8th 1820, departed this life November 22nd 1842,' Rissa murmured, battling with such a perilous feeling of sorrow that it threatened to overwhelm her. 'Only twenty-two when she died. Heck.'

Catrin, her face plainly showing like emotions, gave a sad little sigh. 'How awful for her parents, to have lost a daughter like that.'

'Awful for John too. One short year together. They didn't have long, did they?'

'No, not long.'

'I wonder where they lived after they were married. If John Caradoc was still a wanted man, and I guess he must have been, they could hardly have stopped in the district.'

'True. Perhaps they fled the country.' Catrin gestured towards the headstone. 'There's no mention of the baby being interred here with her. It must have survived. Wonder what happened to it?'

'Wonder what it was? Boy or girl?' Rissa spread her hands helplessly. 'It just adds to the mystery, doesn't it? There are so many loose ends. Perhaps Elin and John's marriage was kept secret. In that case they could have lived here quietly, with John helping the miller with his work. On the other hand, they'd have felt safer away from here. I know I would have.'

'But Elin's buried here. Maybe she came back home to have her baby.'

'And when she died the Reeses brought up their grandchild as their own. I'd love to know what happened to them in the end. The mill was burnt down, wasn't it? Maybe they perished in the blaze. Or did the fire happen later, after the workings had closed down? Oh, it's no good, Catrin. I've just got to get to the bottom of all this.'

'I feel the same. Let's go round all the graves and see if the others are here.'

'I have done,' Rissa said flatly. 'I've scoured this churchyard until I feel I know every inscription on every grave. They're not here. Neither is John. Odd that. You'd think he and Elin would have been together.'

'Maybe he didn't hang about after she died. Maybe he took his child and went to England. London probably, that's where most people fled to when they wanted to escape something. Easier to lose yourself in a crowd.'

'True. Hywel and Marged wouldn't have gone with him though. They'd have stopped here and worked the mill. I can't understand why they're not here.' Catrin flung a hopeless glance around at the towering black stones of the graveyard. 'What about consulting the church records?'

'We could always try. Is the church open?'

'Usually. The chest where the books are stored won't be, though. We'd have to get permission anyway. The rectory's on my way home. I'll call in and ask if you like.'

Rissa nodded. 'Right. Ring me, let me know the score. If you get the go-ahead I'll come with you to look. You've got my mobile number? Good. To be honest, right now I'll be glad to get back and put my feet up. This discovery has knocked me sideways.'

'Me too.'

Their gaze met and slid away. The same thought had slid through both girls' minds. In all probability more dreams lay ahead. A sad chapter of events was likely to unfold. How could they bear it? And why them? As always, the answer evaded.

The sun was going down in a blaze of crimson and gold, but over to the east darkness was gathering. Rissa shivered. 'Come on, let's go.'

At the church gates they parted company. Catrin climbed into her car and swept off along the quiet mountain road. Rissa waited until she could no longer hear the hum of the engine and then walked back to her holiday flat. She made herself a mug of coffee, resisted adding sugar and took it through to the living-room, turning on the television. With a sigh of pure relief she subsided on to the sofa.

A popular sitcom she generally enjoyed was just starting. Rissa put her coffee on the table at her elbow and curled up to watch the show. Presently her eyes grew heavy. From the television set the strident laughter and slick talking television voices grew distant and faded. Seconds later she was fast asleep.

The dream was waiting for her. Stark, violent.

'I demand to speak with the miller. Where is he?' The captain was tall, arrogant in his red and black uniform, badges glinting across his chest. Behind him outside the door, the small platoon of soldiers were ogling at Elin, trim and pretty in her blue gown and patterned shawl. One of them nudged his mate and sniggered.

Boldly Elin clutched the telltale basket of linen bandaging and healing herbs to her. Deep down, she was quaking with fright. 'My father is occupied with his work,' she said stoutly. 'Anything you wish to say can be spoken to us.'

Her mother, after the first fright, suddenly collected herself. She drew her dumpy body very upright and raised her chin, throwing the soldier a steely glower. 'What is it with you? How dare you come tramping in here like this? Look at my floor. Look at it! You've brought half the mountain in on your boots. Did your mother never teach you any better?'

Snorts of smothered laughter resounded from beyond the door. The captain looked down at his boots uncomfortably. Elin resisted an hysterical urge to laugh. Her mother was fiercely houseproud and could be formidable when it came to defending her home.

Elin darted a frantic glance through the unshuttered window, just catching the sight of her father's wiry figure disappearing into the mill. Her knees went weak with relief. Da must have seen the soldiers from the hut and put two and two together. He'd have slipped down the back way and approached the mill over the bridge. In the next instant she heard the thud and clank of the loom starting up.

The captain was also alerted to the sound. 'Confound you, woman. I demand to speak with your man.'

He shouldered his way out of the house and strode to the mill, the soldiers behind him, armoury and spurs chinking as they went. 'Ho there, miller. Open up I say.'

The heavy old door of the mill opened and Hywel stood

there. He put on an affronted face. 'What's all this about? *Daro*, there must be half the army by here. Can't a man go about his work without being interrupted? I've had to stop the loom, and I was in the middle of a pattern.'

His protests were brushed aside. The captain reached into his saddlebag and drew out a roll of paper, opening it. On it, beneath a wanted notice, was printed John's name in bold black letters 'Have you seen this man? I want the truth now?'

Hywel's face tightened. 'What else would an honest church-goer give you but the truth? If it's the Rebecca rabble you're after, I'm only too pleased to help.'

Elin caught her bottom lip. She couldn't breathe. Surely Da wouldn't give John away?

Hywel stepped out a little way along the path and gestured across the valley to the wide sweep of pine-clad hills beyond. 'This morning I was up early, see. Had to get the loom set up. It would have been just after sunrise and I could have sworn I saw movement over there. It was in the forest, high up amongst the trees.'

'What, over there?' The man looked aghast. 'We'll have to cross the river then.'

'That's right. You'll need to take the bridge, mind. The current's strong. You won't be able to swim the horses across. They'd be swept away.'

The captain cursed roundly. 'Dammit. It's an hour's ride at the very least, and then we'll have to man a proper search. I'd lay bets that forest goes on for miles.'

'It does indeed,' said Hywel succinctly. 'Great place for hiding, the forest. There's caves too, up in the mountains. You never know, your man could be holing himself up there.'

'Aye. Ah well, we'll be off then. But I'm warning you, miller. Any sniff of trouble from this quarter, and I'm pulling you in for questioning. And that goes for your wife and daughter too. Right men. Mount up.'

There was a flurry of movement and with a clash of steel and thudding hooves the soldiers had leaped astride their horses and had gone. Elin let out a gulping sob and flew across the forecourt into her father's arms.

'Oh, Dada. You've got rid of them. How can I ever thank you? For a moment I thought ... I thought—'

'Ah, for shame, girl! You surely didn't think I'd stoop to kowtowing to the likes of them, did you?' His voice was full of rough affection. 'Anyway, they've gone, praise be. Away up to the hut with you, now. That young whippersnapper needs attention.'

Giving him a final hug of gratitude, Elin picked up her basket, bid farewell to her mother who was busy wielding a broom in her kitchen, and sped off up the hill.

Reaching the grove, Elin paused, and then entered the circle of stunted oaks. She walked up to the touchstone, placed her hands palms downwards on its roughened surface and whispered a few words of thanks. For all she went to chapel regularly of a Sunday, it was just as well to acknowledge the older beings too. At her feet, the water of the spring rippled and danced. Elin drew a stoppered jar from her basket and filled it. The water was reputed to have healing qualities. If anything could make John better – in addition to Mam's herbs, of course – it was this.

Making a small bow of obeisance, Elin took up her basket and hurried on to the hut.

Rissa woke with a start. Her head was slamming and her throat felt thick. Over in the corner of the room the television set blared, one of those hideous chat shows she loathed. Rissa groped for the remote control and flicked it off. Before her on the table, her coffee was cold, the milk congealing in a murky skin on the surface.

The dream. Earlier in the churchyard she had wondered how long it would be before the past revealed itself again. She had not imagined it would happen so soon. It struck her that the dreams – timeslips, seeings, whatever – were occurring with more frequency now and with frightening clarity. It was almost as if the past was trying to take her over.

Abruptly Rissa stood up and moved to the window. Down in the courtyard, the new holiday visitor with the glorious red hair was chatting to Greg and Beth Marriott. Beyond, the mill-wheel turned busily, churning up the waters of the millrace. Only five more days left now of the course, and then Rissa would be going home. She knew with absolute certainty she could not do it. Somehow, she would have to think of a way of staying on.

The following day, Catrin looked out of the gallery window and saw Ewan and Rissa deep in conversation. The drifting rain of the morning had stopped and Catrin, feeling in need of some fresh air, decided to join them.

First checking that the loom was prepared for the afternoon session, she left the gallery and ran lightly down the wooden stair and out.

'Hi, you two. You're both looking very serious. Is everything all right?'

'I think so,' Ewan said. 'Seems Rissa's decided to stop on and she wants somewhere to park herself.'

Rissa nodded. 'I had this brilliant idea last night. I thought why not stay on as a sort of working student, you know.'

She met Catrin's gaze hopefully. In fact Rissa had already mentioned she was thinking of staying on when they had met up to consult the church records. Catrin smiled. 'Sounds great to me. Have you spoken with Greg about it.'

'Yes. He's agreed to my working here, it's just the accommodation. The holiday flats are booked up for the season.'

'I see. Mam might have a room vacant until the trekking season hots up. Want me to ask her?'

'Actually,' Ewan put in, 'I thought that empty cottage of yours might be suitable. The one by your farmyard?'

'Oh, you mean Ty Coch Bach. It doesn't belong to us. It's on Will's side of the boundary. You could always ask him. It was the cowman's cottage. It's stood empty since old John and May Evans retired and went to live with their daughter. May was a stickler for having things just so. It'll be in good nick.'

Rissa's face was growing more hopeful by the second. 'Oh, I hope it's available. Be just my luck for a new tenant to be moving in this very week.'

'Doubt it,' Catrin said. 'Will hasn't any cows any more and I don't think he's taking on staff anyway. I should slip up there and see. Will's usually home for lunch and Kate's sure to be there. Have you met Kate?'

Rissa shook her head. 'No.'

'She's really nice. Not enjoying very good health at the moment I'm afraid, but she loves having someone to talk to. I'm sure she'll make you very welcome. There's a short cut if you feel like a walk. Follow the track behind the mill and you'll come to Ty Coch. Quicker than the car. The road takes you miles off route.'

Rissa grinned. 'I'm on my way. See you.'

She went dashing off. Ewan turned to Catrin with a smile. 'I was coming to find you. I'm going to visit a mill with a similar wheel set-up to this one this evening. I wondered if you'd like to come. It's over the border.'

'In England?'

He laughed. 'Don't say it like that. It's not the far side of the moon. Couple of hours should do it easily. From what I can gather it's a slightly broader set-up than ours. They do spinning sessions and have a special room for dyeing and so on. Might be something to consider for the future.'

Catrin's eyes shone. 'Indeed yes. Thanks, I'd love to come.'

'Fine. This evening then? I'll pick you up about five-thirty. You won't be too pushed?'

'Not at all. I'll look forward to it,' Catrin said.

She was outside waiting for him when he pulled into the farmyard.

'Hi.' Ewan leaned across and opened the door and Catrin jumped in. 'Hi there. Mam wanted to do a flask and eats but I said no. Hope I did right.'

'Absolutely. They're bound to give us coffee and we can always grab a meal on the way back. There's a nice little pub I know, The Golden Thatch. They do a fish supper you'd die for.'

'Lovely.' Catrin fastened her seat belt and sat back as Ewan sent the car bumping off down the rough-made drive, heading through the hills. Soon they were speeding along the coast road, the late afternoon sun glinting on the sea and sending shifting shadows across the mountain road. Ewan had a tape playing, Mozart, a gentle violin quartet.

Catrin swallowed a yawn. Last night she had slept only fitfully, wound about with dreams. Nothing ... specific. In her dreams, troubled, disjointed, she had been aware of the pounding of the wheel in the millrace, of shouting and the urgent scupper of iron-shod hooves on a flinty track. At one time she seemed to be in the grove, feeling its sleeping power. Then she was with John, accepting the piercing sweetness of his kiss, responding. Only it wasn't John but Will's embrace she was experiencing, comfortably familiar but lacking the blazing joy of the other.

Time and again she had jerked awake and lain staring into the darkness, her heart beating a wild tattoo in her ribcage. Towards dawn she had slept, deeply, to be awakened it seemed only minutes later by her radio alarm.

After that the day had sped by, scarcely allowing her time to think. Ewan's offer of a trip out – even if it was work-related – had come as a respite.

Aware of him now at her side in the warm, safe cocoon of the car, Catrin felt a strange contentment stealing over her. She closed her eyes and allowed herself to relax.

Ewan, glancing at her sleeping face, decided to pull in for a while. They had made good time. Catrin would feel all the better for a good rest.

When she awoke the car had stopped and the light had thickened to evening. She blinked, confused, wondering for a moment where she was. Seeing Ewan beside her studying the road map, realization washed over her. 'Oh, what must you think of me? To zonk out like that. Honestly.'

Ewan just laughed. 'You looked exhausted. Not surprised really. You never stop. Mill all week, helping on the farm at weekends. It's all go. We're not far from our destination now. I thought it best to stop and give you time to get your act together.' He paused, his eyes narrowing. 'Catrin, what is it?'

'I—' She swallowed. She must have been asleep for all of two hours and she had not dreamed once. Suddenly it was too much and she found herself blurting out all that had happened into Ewan's startled ears.

He listened, not interrupting, frowning a little, until she stammered to an embarrassed stop.

'You must think me mad,' she said in a low voice. 'Am I going crazy? I'm beginning to think I might be.'

'Not at all.' Ewan's voice was bluntly reassuring. 'You – and Rissa too by all account – have plainly picked up on some vibes.'

'Yes but … the grove and so on. I really fear the place, always have. It's so stupid. I tell myself this is the twenty-first century. We're supposed to be civilized. Spooks and superstition belong in the past. But it doesn't seem to make any difference. Elin felt the same about the grove and you know how fiercely they followed the Church and its teaching in her day.'

'Yes. Thing is, that particular part of Wales is steeped in legend and old mysteries. What you have to remind yourself is that Christianity as we know it is only a very thin veneer spread over the hundreds of earlier centuries when people worshipped the old gods and superstition ruled.'

'What you're saying is the old ways stick.'

'Very probably. Especially in druid groves and stone circles and other such places where the energy is very concentrated.' He drew a breath. 'Generally the best way to exorcise, if you'll forgive the pun, any type of worry or trauma is to face it. Have you done any research on the miller and company?'

'Well, last night I went with Rissa to look at the church records. Elin's birth and death are recorded and her marriage to John. Hywel's birth is there too. All his side of the family, the Reeses, were Capel Mair born so they're all registered in the parish. Marged must have come from away. She's not mentioned.'

'No record of burial?'

'No. Odd, that.'

'What about the baby?'

'It was a little girl. She was baptised Marged Sian. They must have named her after the grandmother. That's as far as it went.'

'I see. Tell you what, I'll see what I can find out about the background of the mill. The dates tie in. We know, of course, that much of it was destroyed in the fire of the mid 1800s, though there's no history of anyone perishing in the blaze. And seemingly no attempt was made to rebuild. There'd be many other mills in the area at the time, so I daresay people simply took their custom elsewhere. Maybe your couple – the Reeses? – retired to some other village. That'd account for them not ending up in the local churchyard.'

'I guess so.' Catrin smiled wanly at him. 'Thanks, Ewan. Talking it over has made me feel heaps better.'

'Good. Feel up to carrying on?' He fired the engine. 'Fifteen minutes and we should be there.'

As Ewan had said the English mill was a bigger venture than Capel Mair. Running now for several years, the existing outbuildings had been utilized into workshop areas for spinning and other crafts. Whilst Ewan discussed the mill-wheel and its workings with the resident architect, Catrin was given a thorough tour of the premises. Excursion over, Catrin wandered into the mill proper to wait for Ewan.

It came over her with perilous suddenness; a tortuous feeling of being pressed in all sides. Panic grabbed her. She was finding it hard to breathe and the clank and judder of the machinery was more than she could tolerate. She had to get out.

She stumbled out into the reviving evening air and went to stand on the stone bridge, under which the water flowed deep and slow. There was none of the dance and chuckle of the Capel Mair river that hurtled over brown stones through deep mountain gullies on its course to the sea. This was a land of quiet water meadows and wide skies, flatter, greener, lush. However, the sound of the wheel was just the same. Try as she might,

Catrin could not escape it. She stood clutching the parapet of the bridge until her knuckles whitened, staring into space, the past taking her inexorably over.

Bullets whistled through the air. John glanced up, his eyes widening in shocked surprise as they took in the small band of soldiers at the foot of the hill. He turned and began to run, stumbling up the steep mountain path, his boots slithering on the gritty shale. The men shouted and gave chase. Trained to the terrain and in prime physical condition, they quickly gained on him. Rough hands seized him, holding him kicking and struggling in fierce desperation—

'Catrin! Catrin, wake up. It's me. For God's sake what is it?'

Ewan's voice dragged her roughly back to the present. She stared blankly in his direction, not seeing him. Everything was spinning. She felt her knees buckle and heard the flow of the deep water perilously close. 'John. They've got John,' she gasped.

Ewan's arms came round her, supporting her. He led her away from the river bridge and sat down with her on a low stone wall, rocking her like a child until the trembling and gulping sobs ceased. Drained, still sensing the shrill echoes of what she had just experienced, Catrin buried her face in the warm comfort of Ewan's jacket and tried to remember what she had seen. Had John escaped capture? She didn't think so.

'You broke the dream. You broke it! Now I'll never know what happened,' she choked.

Ewan held her from him. 'Dammit Catrin, I had to do something. You were standing there staring at nothing. I saw you leave and followed. You very nearly fell in the river. It's deep with hidden currents. You'd have been sucked under for sure.' His tone softened. 'You look all in. Let's go and find that pub, eh? Stiff drink and some food inside you, and you'll be a new woman.'

'Listen Dad, I'm staying on here at Capel Mair,' Rissa said into the phone. 'It's really terrific here. Greg's agreed to take me on as a working pupil.'

'Meaning they'll work you to the bone and expect you to be on call twenty-four hours a day.' Her father sighed over the miles. 'Still, if you're sure it's what you want.'

'I am sure. I've even got somewhere to live – at least, I think so. I'm going up there after this call to finalize things.'

'Somewhere to live?' She heard his tone change. 'How long are you thinking of stopping then? A month? Six months? Does Mike know about this?'

'Yes. I rang him earlier.' Rissa bit her lip. Mike hadn't sounded too pleased either. He had suggested hiring a car and coming down for a week. She had tried to put him off. He'd only want to drag her out sightseeing and she had more important issues pending. 'Mike was a bit miffed, to be honest.'

'I'm not a whit surprised.' Her father's tone was wry. 'He's up for promotion at the museum, did he mention it?'

'No. That's wonderful news. I'm really glad for him.'

'Odd he didn't say.'

'Oh, he was probably waiting until it's all signed and sealed. You know Mike. And I had the feeling he wasn't missing me all that much. It's you I'm concerned about.' Rissa paused. Her father was not in the best of health. Maybe she should have checked before going ahead with her arrangement. 'Dad, you are feeling all right? You don't really mind my not coming home just yet, do you?'

'Of course not, Rissa. Whatever makes you happy, you know that. How's the cash flow situation?'

'Fine. Greg's offered me some hours in the café. It'll relieve Beth a little and give me some extra pennies as well.'

'I'll put a cheque in the post, just to be on the safe side. No, don't argue. You never know when you might need it. You'll have to pay a bond on that cottage, for a start.'

'OK, I give in. Thanks, Dad. Got to scoot now. Love you.'

She put down the phone with a smile. Her father seemed to be coping reasonably well without her. She knew that Mrs Brooks went in every day to cook and clean and if Dad wanted company, there was his club. As for Mike, well, if this promotion came off, he was not likely to be free to take holiday leave just yet. The museum would expect him to be around for the usual invasion of tourists and trippers, if she knew them. Which left her satisfyingly free for the summer.

On that positive note Rissa picked up her embroidered black sack-bag and left the flat. A warm breeze ruffled her hair as she toiled up the track behind the mill. She breathed in the freshness of early summer greenery and listened to the now familiar chuckling of the river as it thrashed its way over slippery rocks and boulders. Stark seeming at first, with its greystone cottages and damp skies, the countryside was now beginning to inch its way into her heart. London and Mike seemed light years away. She was glad to be stopping on.

At Ty Coch, long, low, white-painted, Kate Meredith was washing up the lunch dishes. Will sat at the table, his face hidden behind a weekly farming paper. He flung it aside when Rissa appeared, smiling a welcome. 'Well, look who it is. Mam, this is Rissa. Told you about her, remember?'

'I do.' Kate dried her hands and offered one to Rissa. 'Hello, Rissa. Nice to meet you.'

'Hi there. Gosh, I can see where Will gets his dark hair and eyes. You're really alike.'

'Only Mam's much prettier,' Will said, jokingly. 'Sit down, Rissa. Have a cup of tea. Come on horseback, have you? Had any good falls lately?'

'No I have not.' Rissa sent him a grin. 'Some folk have long memories. I'm on foot, if you must know. I want to ask you about the cottage on your boundary. I wondered if I could rent it for a few weeks.'

'John and May's place, you mean?' Kate said, pausing from filling the kettle for tea. 'It's been empty all winter. It might be damp.'

'A fire would soon sort that out. I keep meaning to light the Rayburn, only I never seem to get round to it.' Will was regarding Rissa speculatively. 'What's this all about then?'

Rissa explained. 'I'm stopping on, for the whole of the summer if possible. Depends on the cottage.'

'Don't you want to see it first? It's nothing fancy. Not the sort that's usually rented out as a holiday cottage. It's too close to Brynteg's calf-sheds and stables. You get a whiff of farmyard when the wind's in the wrong quarter.'

'I don't need anything fancy, and I like a farm smell. It's healthy.'

Kate put a mug of strong hot tea down in front of her, offered shortbread from a tin, and refilled Will's tea-mug. 'It would be nice having a neighbour again, Will. It's been quiet since May left.' She held her son's gaze. The rest of her thoughts passed unspoken between them. The rental for the cottage would come in handy too. She said to Rissa, sensibly, 'First go with Will and take a look at the place. If you think it will suit, I'll go down there and give it a good airing. Don't worry about bed linen and crockery and so on. I've plenty here you can use. And Will can stock up the woodpile, save you buying coal.'

She smiled, brightening by the minute, plainly delighted at the prospect that had come right out of the blue.

'Seems Mam's got it all worked out.' Will laughed.

'Yes, she has.' Rissa smiled at the woman. 'Thank you. I'm sure it will be fine.'

Rissa sipped tea. She had taken immediately to Kate, who was obviously not strong and could do with a bit of cheering up. Bron Jenkins was equally as pleasant and would be good to have as a neighbour. As well as pursuing the history of the mill, Rissa had her other research to follow. The cottage, bang on their perimeter, couldn't have been better placed for observing the elusive Llew as he went about his chores. Somehow she had to get into his confidence. Rissa was sure it was not beyond her capabilities. Trouble was, what effect would this deliberate raking up of the past have on his wife? She liked Bron, didn't want to hurt her. If Llew turned out to be the third Taffy, then that made herself and Catrin half-sisters. How would the Jenkins family cope with a momentous revelation such as that?

Chapter Five

With a sigh, Catrin pushed aside the copies of the deeds of the mill that Ewan had passed on to her that morning.

'Do they throw a light on anything?' Ewan asked from the window seat of the gallery. They had taken to sharing their lunch break up here, away from the crush of the mill café which tended to get overpowering now that the tourist season was warming up. Ewan bit into the ham and salad roll that Beth had sent up and raised a quizzing brow at Catrin.

'Not really,' she replied. 'There's nothing here I didn't already know. The Reeses ran the mill until the fire in 1843. That's the final date given. They must have moved away afterwards, baby granddaughter as well. Don't know about John Caradoc, though. Poor fellow. He'd already suffered the loss of his wife. He wouldn't have wanted to lose touch with his little daughter as well. I suppose he must still have been around.'

'Depends what sort of price the militia had put on his head. He was guilty of wounding one of their ranks, remember. If the chap died of his injuries....' Ewan shrugged and offered the plate of rolls. 'Eat up. You need the energy. You never seem to stop working.'

Catrin took one with a smile. 'Thanks. It's actually my Saturday off tomorrow. A whole weekend to myself. Bliss.'

'A well-earned break, I'd say. Have you got anything planned?'

'It's Festival Week at Lampeter. Will wants to go and have a look. You'll never believe it, but the History Society is staging an incident from the Rebecca Riots.'

Ewan laughed shortly. 'No getting away from it, is there?'

'Seems that way. They're doing the bit where Rebeccaites from all over Cardiganshire banded together and marched upon Lampeter to destroy the four tollgates. The Rebeccaites had the sympathy of the people by this time, and there wasn't much the militia could do about it. Apparently a band of musicians preceded the march and all the townspeople cheered. It's just the thing for Festival Week. Everyone will be in costume and the town is always dressed up Victoriana anyway.'

'Great tourist attraction.' Ewan sent a look of concern. 'Realistic, too. You should have a care.'

'What d'you mean?'

'These trances you have. This is the very sort of situation that could trigger one off. Does Will know about them?'

'Well, no.'

'Then you should tell him. If it were me, under the circumstances I'd steer clear of taking you to this sort of entertainment. I'm serious, Catrin. I think it could be asking for trouble. It's up to you, of course.'

'It'll be all right,' Catrin said, a faint quiver of uncertainty in her voice. 'I can't very well put Will off. He doesn't often get the chance to get away from the farm. He's looking forward to it. Anyway, it'll be all noise and bustle. I'd defy anyone to go lapsing into dreams with that sort of racket going on.'

All the same, it happened.

*

Will had picked her up early to get a parking slot. Lampeter heaved with people, locals and tourists alike making the most of the good spell of weather and coming to see the show. The little university town was decked for the occasion. Bunting, criss-crossing the main street, fluttered gaily overhead. Pavements and shop fronts were bright with flowers. Onlookers waved and cheered as the procession advanced, the band playing rowdily, the actors in their sturdy country garb brandishing poles and firearms and hollering at the tops of their voices.

Hemmed in with Will amongst the crowds on the narrow pavement, Catrin suddenly experienced the strange spinning sensation in her head that marked the onset of a slip in time. Desperately she tried to fight it, clutching Will's arm for all she was worth. But the air had grown colder, was tainted with smoke from the chimneys, and the reek of horse dung that littered the street was sour in her nostrils. The shouts of the throng and the marchers had a deeper significance. Beneath Catrin's feet the ground was muddy shale and the sweaty press of people around her, most of them clad in rough homespun, were shouting in their own tongue.

'*Dynion da! Dynion da!*' Good men! Good men!

John Caradoc marched past heading his band of men. His face was worn and sad, though the fire of battle still lit his eyes and he held his head proudly as they headed for the fourth and final tollgate on the far side of the town.

Standing inside a doorway of a row of terraced houses that opened directly on to the street was a soldier. His eyes were on Caradoc. Vanishing into the house, he appeared again presently, his red and black uniform abandoned for dark breeches and jacket. Without looking to right or left he melted into the procession.

The scene fractured and changed, taking shape again.

John Caradoc was striding up the last lap of the flinty track to the mill. In the yard, the weaver's cart stood loaded with bales of cloth, pony waiting patiently in the shafts. John threw a searching glance over his shoulder, and then entered the building. Hywel was at the loom, overseeing a growing length of cloth in blue and white woollen.

The pattern brought John up short. Fashioned in a complex arrangement of whorls and knots, it was the design Elin had been working on when fate had struck its cruel blow. He pictured her, the quiet darkness of her, the laughing brown eyes … and his heart contracted fiercely. They had called it the Wedding Ring design and planned to make it their own. It was to be their bid for the future. Only for Elin there had been no future. To have gone like that, without even knowing the joy of holding her child in her arms. John swallowed, fighting back the impulse to rage at life and the way it gave, and snatched back when you least expected it.

Hywel glanced up and saw John standing there. 'John, man. How went it?' he shouted above the hectic clatter and thud of machinery.

'Well enough. We did for all four tollgates. The militia kept their distance.' John pressed his hand to his head, where the merciless throb of the old wound echoed that of the more recent one deep within him. 'It's been a long day.'

'Man, you look fit to drop. Sit down and rest yourself.'

'I'm all right. It's nothing one of Marged's potions won't sort out. How's the little one? I thought I heard her crying in the night.'

'Ah. Teething, Marged said she was. She's perky enough

now, bless her. In the crib by the hearth she is, keeping her grandmother company.'

'That's all right then. Want me to take over for a while, Hywel? You've been at it all day as well by the look of things. Is that stuff outside waiting to be delivered?'

'Well, yes. Best if I go, isn't it? You never know if they might send the troops routing again. If you could keep the loom rolling while I see to it? Marged wanted some shopping. I can drop her and the baby off at the village on the way.'

John took his place at the loom and Hywel left.

As the weaver crossed the yard, a figure melted into the shadow of the trees. The man in sombre brown stood watchful, catching his breath after the lengthy tramp through the hills in the wake of his quarry. Seeing the weaver and his wife, baby in her arms, go rumbling off in the cart, he turned his gaze to the mill where Caradoc could be seen bent over the loom. Ambition glinted in his eye and his mouth twisted into a satisfied smile.

'Cattie? Cattie, what is it? What's wrong?'

Catrin came round to Will's voice ringing in her ears and a clammy feeling of faintness. Figures swam mistily across her inner vision. Her heart hammered to the fading clank of machinery. A half-woven length of dark-blue woollen with a distinctive white pattern flashed briefly in her mind and was gone.

In the street the jaunty procession had now moved out of sight and the crowds were beginning to disperse. Catrin took a long breath. 'I'm fine. At least, I will be in a minute.'

'You don't look it,' said Will, guiding her away from the mildly curious eyes around them. They stopped at the entrance to a side road. Will gazed into her face. 'You're white as a sheet. Did you feel faint?'

'No, it wasn't that. I … just lately I've been getting these peculiar dreams. I dream I'm back in the days when Capel Mair was run as a proper mill and … well, I suppose the procession reminded me.'

'Dreams? About the mill? Come on! It's not surprising, mind. You put far too many hours in over there. Look, the Black Lion's just across the road. Maybe a brandy—'

'No. No really.' Catrin wished he wouldn't fuss, and then felt guilty. He was only showing his concern. 'Cup of coffee would be nice, though.'

'Right. Are you fit to walk?'

'Of course.' She smiled at him shakily. The buzzing in her head was easing and she felt more in command of her limbs. 'It was the crush and the shouting. You know I'm not good in crowds.'

Much of the tension left Will's face. He looked suddenly amused, the way he used to when they were youngsters and she had done something he considered particularly absurd. 'Come on then, Cattie. Let's see if the pub can rustle up something to eat. Don't know about you but I'm famished.'

He fetched Catrin a playful slap on the back, more like a brother than a future spouse, she thought, in a sudden illuminating moment. Ewan wouldn't have responded like that. Ewan would not have brought her here in the first place. But then Will wasn't to know, was he? And if he had? If she had confided in him from the start, would he have taken her dream sequences seriously, the way Ewan had? Frankly, Catrin doubted it. Soberly, she fell into step and let herself be guided across the road to where the double doors of The Black Lion stood open and welcoming.

*

Rissa was rearranging the furniture in the small living-room of the cottage when there was a light tap on the front door, which opened directly off it. 'Anybody home?' called Catrin's voice.

Giving the dresser a final shove, Rissa went to let her friend in. 'Hi there. I'm having a change round. What do you think?'

'I like it,' Catrin said with a cursory glance around. 'It gives you more space this way. How was the move?'

'Just fine. I'm going to love it here.' Rissa paused, taking in the other girl's rather pensive expression. 'What is it? It's happened again, hasn't it? The dreams. Oh, Catrin.'

'It was in broad daylight this time, plump in the middle of town. It's Lampeter Festival Week.'

'I know. I thought I might go along with my camera but there was too much to do here. Was it a good show?'

'Too good, as it happened! I was with Will, cheering on the carnival procession and … and—'

Rissa took Catrin's arm. 'Steady on. Let's sit down, then you can tell me about it.'

They subsided on to the shabby sofa and Catrin told Rissa what had happened yesterday at Lampeter. 'Ewan warned me to watch out and he was right.'

'You've told him about it?'

'Some of it. I was afraid he'd think I was being neurotic, but he didn't at all. In fact he was very understanding and sympathetic – which is more than you could say for Will yesterday.'

'Oh, Will's a farmer. His sort don't go in for visions and flights of fancy.'

'Is that what you seriously believe it is? A flight of fancy?'

'You know I don't.' Rissa touched her friend's hand reassuringly. 'What's happening to us is frightening. It scares me witless half the time, so I know how you must have felt yesterday. At least we're in it together. It would be far worse to be going through it on one's own.'

'True.' Catrin gave a wobbly smile. 'Rissa, this business over the fire. A mill wouldn't go up in flames without due cause, would it? I think the militia guy had something to do with it.'

'You think he fired it deliberately to flush John out, while the Reeses were away from home? Cool!'

Catrin shuddered. 'It's sick. What a vile thing to do. To deliberately destroy someone's livelihood.'

'Mm. Supposing the plan worked and John was captured. Other than the death penalty, what's the most likely punishment for his sort of crime?'

'Deportation, I should imagine.' Catrin broke off, her gaze narrowing on one of her own woven throws that was draped across an easy chair. It was in her Wedding Ring weave. 'That's the pattern I cooked up for my finals at college. It's very like the one I saw on the loom in my dream.'

'It is? Celtic-type motifs all look similar to me.'

'They're not when you study them. The knots and scrolls are quite different. The one I saw was Elin's design, one she was creating just before she died. Each mill had its own set of patterns, see. The young Caradocs would be aiming to bring this one out when they took over Capel Mair from Elin's father. Maybe Hywel used it instead in Elin's memory. Who knows?'

Rissa stared at her in astonishment. 'And you thought up the very same design without consciously knowing it? Wow! That's freaky.'

'No, it wasn't the same. I had something like it in mind but it didn't turn out right. The one on the loom was far more intricate than mine. It was really lovely. Where's my bag? Ah, here it is. There should be a sketchbook inside. Yes. Look, this is how it was.' She sketched a quick design on the paper. Two loops interwoven with a central heraldic knot, and other rings branching out in a complicated series of whorls and leaves, reminiscent of entwining ivy tendrils. 'I'm going to work this out on a grid. It won't be easy but I must try.'

'Rather you than me,' Rissa said ruefully. 'It looks impossible!'

'It'll be more straightforward on graph paper. Tomorrow I'll go into work early and map it out. Oh, that reminds me.' Catrin looked up. 'Greg said to fill you in on the leavers' party details. He thought Friday evening might be the best day to hold it.'

'Fine. What time about?'

'Seven till tennish? It doesn't have to drag on till late. Some people will be planning an early start for home on Saturday.'

'True. Just think, if Greg hadn't taken me on the workforce I'd be joining them. Ugh, what a thought! So what's my job to be?'

'Helping Beth with the eats. She's doing a buffet supper, but you know Beth. It'll be an absolute feast! Greg's put himself in charge of the drinks and the music. Oh, and if you and Dai wouldn't mind first clearing a space in the gallery for the dancing, that would be a big help. Shove the trestles down one end for the food. It might be best if we stopped on after work. There's a lot to be done.'

Rissa mocked a groan. 'Tell me about it! At least I won't have to worry about dieting any more. A few weeks of this and I'll be positively sylphlike! I'll get pen and paper shall I? Then we can make a list of what's to be done.'

They had just finished when Will turned up at the cottage, two mud-splattered sheepdogs panting at his heels.

"Morning,' he greeted from the doorway. 'I've got the dogs

so I won't come in. Hi, Catrin. How's things this morning? Have you told Rissa how you almost passed out on me?'

'I mentioned it, yes.'

'You've been overdoing things at the mill, that's your problem,' Will said bluntly. He nodded towards Rissa. 'Mam says you were asking about the farm and she told you I'd show you round. I've got an hour to spare, if it's convenient?'

Rissa jumped up. 'Yes. Great. I'll get my wellies. What about you, Catrin? Are you coming as well?'

'Oh, I'd better get off home, thanks. I promised Mam I'd take a party of trekkers out. I'll see you in the morning, Rissa.' Briefly, Catrin's gaze flickered over the other girl struggling into her new rubber boots acquired with country living in mind, and moved to Will watching them from the doorway. Did he have to be so dismissive over her experience? Ewan had been far kinder to her when a similar thing had happened at the English mill. It didn't say much for their engagement. A sadness crept over Catrin, a sadness born of genuine tiredness and a sense of losing the threads that had made up the familiar pattern of her life for so long. She gathered up her belongings quietly and left the cottage.

Ready at last, Rissa pulled the door to behind her. 'Right, Will. Lead the way.'

'Do you want to do the land first, or the yard and buildings?'

'Oh, wherever the animals are.'

'Yard then. The new sheep have arrived. They're in the barn for now, till they've had their jabs.'

'Jabs?'

'Inoculations. Vaccination doesn't come cheap, but sheep are forever finding something to die from so it's a false economy not to get all incoming stock done. No need to lock the door. 'Tisn't exactly the M6 up here, is it?'

They went out into the gentle warmth of a perfect late-spring afternoon. The cottage on the boundary of the two farms over-looked Brynteg with its row of stables, its barns stuffed with hay and straw and its stackyard with milking parlour and pig units. Will turned his back on the bigger farm and led the way upwards, clambering over stiles set into drystone walls and crossing fields where the grass became sparser the further they climbed. Curlews called overhead and all around, gorse blazed gold under the sun. Here and there, pushing up amongst unfurling fronds of bracken, bluebells and wild campion gave off their drenching scent.

Rissa, striding out to keep up with Will's long-legged lope, inhaled deeply and sighed. 'If ever there's heaven on earth, it's got to be here.'

'Come back in the winter and see if you think the same way,' Will said.

'Is that an invitation?'

'What do you think?'

Will sent her the swift, sweet smile that totally changed his rather dour everyday face into one of pleasing good humour, and Rissa felt her heart respond with a treacherous bump. Suddenly awkward, she tried to pass off the moment off. 'I'll be back in London then, getting on with my career, I hope. Don't ask me what. At this moment I haven't a clue.'

The going became steeper and soon Ty Coch came into view, a long low farmhouse amongst a huddle of buildings, the red-painted walls now faded to a nondescript pink.

'Why don't you paint it white?' Rissa said musingly, panting a little after the climb. 'With glossy black window frames and doors. It would look great.'

'Think so? Ty Coch's always been red as far as I know. That's what it means. Red House.'

'Then do it white and change the name to Ty Gwyn.'

'My, Welsh now, is it? You'll soon be talking like a native!'

'I wouldn't bet on it,' Rissa said, rueful. 'It's too difficult. I once spent some time in Germany and it didn't take long to pick up the language. Same with French. But Welsh defeats me. It's so fast. I swear you make it up as you go along.'

This prompted a shout of amusement from Will, which sent a small flock of ewes that had trailed after them fleeing off in alarm. The dogs immediately gave chase. 'Fly! Mossie! Come-by!' Will bellowed, whistling piercingly to back up his command.

'Oh, don't,' Rissa laughed, clamping her hands to her ears. 'You're deafening me! I'm glad I'm not a dog. I couldn't stand the strain.'

Will gazed at her, a strange mixture of emotions chasing across his dark eyes, and Rissa's laughter died on her lips. 'Ah, Rissa girl,' he said softly. 'I wouldn't want you to be anything but yourself.' And he reached out and aimed a playful but disturbingly tender cuff on her chin. 'Come on. Let's go and see those new arrivals.'

Will took Rissa on a tour of the farm, showing her the stone-built barns with the low doorways and steeply sloping roofs, which like the house dated back three centuries or more. She gazed in growing wonder at the defunct dairy, now used as a general store, yet still containing the original slate mixing slabs and wooden butter churns of yesteryear. It was wonderful. There was so much potential here that her mind whirled. It could be used in so many different areas. A film set or a background for a TV serial. A working farm museum. Yes, that was it. 'Will,' she blurted. 'I had no idea it was like this. A bit of work and you could really make something of the place!'

Will's face clouded. 'Meaning we're way behind the times. Huh, you don't have to rub it in.'

'No, I didn't mean that at all. What I was trying to say is you could get a government grant and do Ty Coch up as a commercial enterprise. I visited a working farm museum once. It wasn't a patch on Ty Coch and it was doing a bomb. You couldn't go wrong here. It's just amazing. Look at that wonderful old stone well. And the dairy and cheese room with the apple store above. And this lovely cobbled yard and those old stables. It's all so quaint. It's—'

'It's a mess!' said Will tightly. 'Farming's a mess. There's no future in it any more. Three centuries of Merediths have farmed this land, and for what? Precious little, the way things have turned out. It's nothing but hardship and worry.'

'So you move with the times and try a different tack.'

'But I'm a farmer, not a museum curator! Don't you understand that? I'd sooner see Ty Coch razed to the ground than turned into some fancy concern I could never be happy with. I'm surprised you can suggest it. Oh, I've got things to do. I'm going!'

He directed her a final blood-chilling glower and went stomping off. Rissa stared after him, thoroughly shaken, her good intentions falling miserably about her. She hadn't meant to hurt him. She had only wanted to help and now he was furious with her, and just when they were getting on so well. Tears choked her throat, sudden, unexpected. She heaved a shuddering sigh. Why was life so complicated?

At that moment the back door of the farmhouse opened and Kate stood there. 'Did I hear shouting? Oh, it's you, Rissa. There's lovely to see you. But you look upset.'

'It's Will,' Rissa said hollowly. 'Or maybe it was my own fault. I got carried away with an idea I had for the farm and he took it all wrong. Me and my big mouth!'

Kate smiled kindly. 'Oh, I shouldn't take it too hard. Will's got a lot of worry at the moment. He's bound to be a bit touchy. Come on in and have a cup of tea. You can tell me about this scheme of yours if you like. Seeing things through new eyes is not a bad thing. You never know, this might be just what we need.'

In the event, Kate's response proved very different from that of her son. 'I think you could be on to something here,' she said thoughtfully. 'A start's already been made with the mill, and there's Bron's and her pony trekking venture. A working farm museum would be an added tourist pull. I'll speak to Will myself if you like. It would only be a summer concern after all. For the rest of the year he'd be farming as always – only with some profit behind him, God willing!'

Heartened, Rissa found herself telling Kate about her home in London and Mike. 'We've been together since sixth-form – well, on and off. Mike was one of the reasons I came here. I felt I needed space to think things out.'

'And have you reached a conclusion?'

'I guess so. I don't really miss him. That says a lot doesn't it?'

Kate poured more tea. 'What about Mike? Will he be upset if you finish?'

'Oh, he'll survive. We'll still be friends I expect. It's Dad I worry about. He's not been himself since Mum died. He and Mike get on so well. I wouldn't want to upset Dad more than I need to.'

'Oh, I think you'll find your father tougher than you realize. He won't want you to make a mistake and marry the wrong one. I know I wouldn't if it was Will.'

'I'm sure you're right,' Rissa said. 'I feel guilty for not going home as planned as well, though Dad insisted he was all right. He told me to stay on for as long as I wanted. He's such a love. He's always been very understanding.'

'He sounds wonderful. The sort of father everyone wants. I'm sure that once you've made up your mind what you're going to do, the rest will fall into place.'

'Yes. Thanks for listening, Kate. You've been a great help.'

'Think nothing of it. Are you going? You don't have to rush off.'

'I must. There's still a lot to do at the cottage and it's work tomorrow. I'll be too shattered afterwards to do anything but collapse into bed!'

Rissa said goodbye and left. Reaching the cottage, she caught a glimpse of Llew in the farmyard and was surprised when he waved and called out to her. Bemused, her mind still full of Will and Ty Coch, she stood by the back door and watched him approach. This was her first meeting with Catrin's father. She gave herself a mental shake and remembered why she was really here. Come on, this is Llew, the possible third Taffy. This is why I came here in the first place!

She mustered a smile. 'Hi there. Lovely day, isn't it?'

'Yes indeed,' Llew said sociably. 'Nice to see the cottage occupied again. Are you well?'

'I'm fine, thanks. And you?'

'Oh, can't grumble.'

Sunlight stippled the yard and buildings, lending warmth to the starkness of local grey stone and slate. A pair of early swallows swooped and soared about the eves of the farmhouse, seeking their old haunt. Llew rested his elbows on the dividing wall and sent Rissa a smile, friendly, full of charm. Rissa heart lurched. It was *her* smile – Catrin's too, if the truth be known. Dear goodness, she thought, it's got to be him at last. And if this truly is my real father, that makes Catrin my half-sister.

Llew said, 'You'll find it quiet here. Bit dull, maybe?'

'No … not at all. I do more chatting to people here than I've ever done before. Back home in London everyone's tearing about as if there's no tomorrow. I was the same myself. I haven't spoken to our neighbours in months.'

She knew she was gabbling. The full implications of what she was doing hit her like a physical blow. It wasn't only her future and that of the man standing in front of her she was about to change, but Catrin's and Bron's too. She had grown fond of them both. She didn't want to hurt them. And there was Will. She liked Will more than she cared to explore right now. And Kate was terrific. Had she any right to tamper with the existence of these dear people, merely to satisfy her own need?

All at once it was painfully too much to cope with, too difficult a situation all round. Instead of quizzing Llew as she had planned to do she decided to back off. She had come a long way and waited a long time to meet her natural parent. Another few days would make no difference.

'Ah well, it's a different out here,' Llew was saying. 'In the country you never know when you might need one another and you make an effort to get on. It's no bad thing.'

'That's very true.' He was so ... well, nice. A good man. Quiet, genuine as were the rest. What right had she to blast all their lives apart? She had a good mind to leave it be. Forget it. Rissa said, 'Oh well, I must go inside and finish unpacking. Nice meeting you. 'Bye for now.'

'Goodbye ... er, Rissa, is it?' He smiled again. *That smile!* 'See you again, Rissa.'

Rissa nodded and went in, thankfully closing the door.

Ewan frowned over the blueprints of the mill wheel. The blasted thing was playing up again. At this rate it would never last the season out, never mind another half century or so as was intended.

Beyond the door in the gallery, Catrin's voice could be heard giving instructions to Rissa and the ever-willing Glenys. How that woman managed to juggle a young family, home and job and still keep smiling Ewan could not imagine.

There was a tap on the door. It was Catrin. 'Ewan? Are you ready? It's gone seven. The guests are starting to arrive.'

'Coming.' Closing the file on the papers, he gave himself a quick check in the mirror. He hoped his lightweight slacks and cashmere jersey hit the right note in casual eveningwear. It had been a long time, and all at once, despite the anxiety over the wheel, Ewan found himself looking forward to the evening ahead. Smiling faintly, he went out to help host the party.

Beth had done them proud with the refreshments. Two long trestle tables, suitably decked in white linen, groaned under the weight of the food. There was cold beef, cold ham and chicken, a whole salmon resting on a bed of crisp lettuce, salads galore and a choice of vegetarian dishes for those who preferred it.

Greg, an avid jazz enthusiast, had got the music playing quietly and over in the corner a young couple were dancing, quite oblivious to the rest of the company.

'Ewan, there you are,' Greg called. 'Shall we have the wheel going? I've just heard the press are paying us a visit. Just the local rag, but it would be good for them to see everything working.'

Ewan groaned inwardly. 'OK. I'll go and switch it on. Want to come, lads?' he said to the two small boys, well-scrubbed for the event and no doubt equally well threatened to be on their best behaviour.

'Sure are,' said Sam and Oliver together, and followed Ewan out.

They found Catrin in the weaving-room, putting some

finishing touches to a display. She threw the two boys a smile. 'Hi there. Are you helping Ewan with the machinery?'

They nodded importantly. Ewan said, 'I intended having a look at the wheel this weekend. Just hope it doesn't let us down tonight. Greg says the press are coming.'

'I know. That's why I'm messing about here instead of enjoying myself with the others. The newspaper's running a feature on local tourist attractions, so they'll want to take pictures.' She bit her lip. 'It's serious isn't it, this problem with the wheel?'

Ewan grimaced. 'It could be. There's friction in the main cogs. It was always a handicap in the old days. I expect if it went wrong then they'd have had no choice but to close down the mill and fix it themselves. It would have run again for a while, and then started to falter again.'

'Is that the reason why the mill caught fire?' Disappointment crossed Catrin's face. 'I was working on another theory.'

'No. In that instance the entire building was gutted. You'll remember what it was like before work started on it. Even the roof was gone. That particular blaze must have started inside the mill itself. This is something different. I've called Heritage's attention to it. They sent one of their minions out to look at the matter, but you know them. They always know best. They seem to think we're all right for the season. I tried to argue it out.'

'And?'

'No response. In the end I gave up and decided to hope for the best. Going to suss out that English mill was a big help. I think I've cracked how to overcome the problem. Thing is, presenting it on paper in such a way that it doesn't overstep the rules laid out by the Heritage people.'

'Is it a big job?'

'The paperwork? Fairly. I should have it all tied up by the

autumn. Just hope the dratted wheel lasts out till then. Is that the music hotting up? I'd better get the machinery in motion. Come on you guys, through to the control room. And remember. No fiddling with things behind my back or there'll be trouble. Understand?'

'Yes.'

'Right. Who's turn is it to man the switch? Oliver's? Off we go then.'

The old millwheel swung into life and the building echoed to the now familiar judder and roar of machinery and water. The party was soon in full swing. Beth spirited the little boys away to their beds. Will put in an appearance and was dragged off by Catrin to dance.

Everything was going well and Ewan began to relax. He danced with Rissa and then Catrin and even coaxed Glenys out on to the floor.

He was dancing with Catrin again, a slow moody blues number, when she happened to glance out of the double doors which were open to the warm night. The mill was floodlit, the wooden bridge and wheel brightly illuminated.

'Funny,' Catrin said, stopping. 'I could have sworn I saw someone on the bridge. We did put the barrier rope across?'

'Yes. I checked it myself earlier.' He guided her to the edge of the dance floor and looked searchingly into her face. 'Sure you feel all right?'

'If you mean, am I about to be drawn into one of those hateful trances, then no, I'm not. I feel perfectly fine and—'

'Can anybody smell burning?' said someone loudly from across the room.

The dancers came to a halt. Greg turned off the music. Without the blare of the jazz band and the chatter and laughter, it was apparent that the wheel was no longer in motion. Right on cue the main door opened and a man from the newspaper office appeared with his camera slung over his shoulder.

At the same time a plume of smoke rose above the wooden framework of the mill wheel, and from the control room the alarm began to bleep. 'Fire!' shouted another voice. 'Quick, call the fire brigade! The wheel's on fire!'

Chapter Six

Tongues of orange and crimson flame licked up from the far end of the mill, billowing smoke into the blackness of the summer night. The tranquil babble of the river was overlaid by the crackle and roar of fire, and the shouts of the firemen as they organized hoses and ladders. Shocked and shivering in their flimsy evening wear, the group of party-goers stood in the safety of the courtyard where Greg had ordered them, and watched the fire take hold.

'So quick,' gasped one.

'It's all that internal timber,' said another with all the relish of the true pessimist. 'The mill's a gonner!'

'Getaway!' his companion snorted. 'Those guys will soon have it out, you'll see!'

Some of the residents were agitating over their belongings. Those who were due to leave the next morning had their luggage stowed into the boots of cars, ready for the off. That of the new intake remained in the barn accommodation opposite, now declared worryingly out of bounds.

Under Greg's direction, members of staff strove to rescue whatever they could from the apparently doomed mill. The newspaper reporter darted hither and thither amongst them, snapping shots from every angle and generally getting underfoot. 'One moment of your time, sir,' the man said, collaring Greg with notebook posed as he strode past with an over-flowing box of papers from the office.

'Not now,' Greg snapped, and hollered to Ewan, 'D'you get the computer? Good man. I'll fetch the monitor. Dewi, see if you and the lad can dismantle the loom between you. If not shift it somewhere less vulnerable.'

'Right-oh.' Dewi charged off.

'My blueprints!' Ewan ran his eye over the hastily-crammed boxes on the ground under the trees. 'Can't see them with this stuff. Hang on, Greg. I'm coming with you.'

The two men went sprinting back into the mill. So far the fire was contained to the control room at the other end of the prem-ises, where it appeared to have started. The gallery and workshop level, with the staff quarters and storage areas underneath, were as yet reasonably secure from the blaze.

Catrin and Rissa, breathless from the frantic dash to empty the workshop from all removable stock and effects, seized a moment to get their second wind. Their clothes were crumpled and soot-smudged, their eyes red-rimmed from the smoke that was beginning to seep through the levels. Catrin's long hair had come loose from the elegant style the hairdresser had taken such pains that afternoon to create, and hung in damp, smoke-encrusted tendrils around her hot face. Rissa ran trembling hands through her shorter locks, sticky with perspiration and smuts.

'Oh-my-God!' she groaned, gazing in horror at the burning building. 'We could have been trapped in there. Imagine!'

'I don't want to,' Catrin answered shakily. 'Look at it!'

'I know. It's the end.'

''Tisn't! It can't be!' Temper flared, quick and fierce. 'It's all right for you, Rissa. It isn't your career at stake. You'll be going

back to London and your own life, whereas the rest of us—'
Catrin bit her lip, and the anger that had risen so swiftly and
unexpectedly faded away, leaving her limp and exhausted.

'I only meant,' Rissa began, but Catrin waved her explana-
tions aside. 'It's all right. I'm sorry. I shouldn't have lost my
rag.'

One of the firemen was training a hose on the wooden
bridge. 'Isn't that Will?' Rissa said. 'Over there by the bridge?
It's hard to tell in that protective gear they wear.'

'Where? Oh yes, I see. Yes, that's Will. He does voluntary
work for the local fire service. He trained up as soon as he was
eighteen, and he's been part of the team ever since.'

'Well! That's community spirit for you!'

'Mm. Lots of them do it. Here's Greg and Ewan back again.
Is that everything from inside?' Catrin asked the men,
gesturing towards the random heap of office equipment and
small items of furniture. Boxes of wool and others containing
spinning and weaving tools from the workshop made up
another pile. Balanced on the top, Catrin's spinning wheel
rotated lazily.

Greg nodded. 'Just about. Dewi and the lad have done their
best to clear the lower level. Couldn't do anything about the big
loom, unfortunately. It's devilish hot in there. If they don't get
the blaze under control soon the whole lot's going to go up.'

Both men were sweating and out of breath. Ewan had a
smear of oil across his forehead from an initial futile attempt to
staunch the flames that flickered around the wheel. Greg's
designer shirt, purchased especially for tonight's festivities,
had a rip in the sleeve. Lapsing for a moment into bewildered
stupor, Greg inspected the damage blankly. 'Beth won't be
pleased. This shirt cost the earth.'

Ewan, frowning at the nightmare before him, muttered

something about needing to see the wheel, and then ducked his head and made a sudden dash for side of the mill where the flames were fiercest.

'Ewan!' Catrin shrieked. 'Come back! You'll get hurt!'

Her cry was echoed by Greg. 'Come back you fool! You can't do anything there. Come back, will you?'

Ewan's route was effectively blocked by a stocky fireman with a hose. 'Sorry sir. You can't go that way. The bridge isn't safe. Where's the boss?'

'What?' Ewan flung a last despairing look at his goal and seemingly gave up. 'Oh, Greg Marriott, d'you mean? He's over there with the other staff.'

'Tell him to get all these people off the premises immediately, would you, sir? You might want to make overnight arrangements for them at one of the local hostelries. Try the Cross Hands, they're pretty good.'

'Right.' Ewan went loping off to do as he was bid.

Presently the mill premises began to empty. Some of those whose stay was at an end opted to make tracks for home immediately, rather than wait till morning. The new intake were happy to be removed with their luggage to the hotel. Soon the line of cars with their occupants went rumbling away into the night.

Beth and Glenys, each firmly holding a small boy by the hand, hovered uncertainly at the entrance to the tea-rooms-cum-gift-shop. Glenys flung an unhappy look over her shoulder at the shelves of gifts and books and other holiday souvenirs. 'All those things! Greg said to leave them, but you never know.'

'Best do as he says,' Beth replied. 'Oliver, will you please stop *fidgeting*!'

The boys, wide-eyed and silent for once, took in the scene

before them. 'My furniture and other things,' Beth said with an anxious glance at the cottage, which stood dangerously close to the trouble. 'We stand lose it all if the fire catches.'

'It won't,' Glenys replied. 'Look, the men are getting it under control.'

'I wonder how it started,' Beth said.

'It was the wheel,' Oliver chipped in. 'I saw smoke coming out of it.'

'I saw it first,' his older brother Sam put him right. 'Then the alarm went off and the red lights on the control board came on.'

'You didn't touch anything that you shouldn't have, did you?' their mother enquired anxiously.

'No Mum.' Vehemently the boys protested their innocence.

'Of course they didn't touch anything,' Glenys said in defence of the boys. Glenys had offered to put up the Marriotts for the night, and Beth had gratefully accepted. 'Beth. There's nothing more we can do here and Sam and Oliver look tired out. Let's go, shall we? Greg can come on afterwards, when they've finished.'

'All right,' agreed Beth, and slipped off to tell her husband they were leaving.

Much later, the blaze out and the firemen gone, the weary group of male and female staff stood mutely surveying the smoking wreckage. Starlight gleamed on the soot-blackened walls and gaping windows of what had once been the control room, and the pale crescent of a waning moon was reflected in the pools of murky hose water on the forecourt. The damaging and unprecedented end to what had been intended to be an enjoyable evening was hard to take in. All looked stunned.

Greg sniffed in the acrid smell of burning that hung on the air and grimaced. 'Well, that's that,' he said wearily. 'I suggest we all get some sleep and meet up again tomorrow. Ewan, you can't stop here. Have you got somewhere to stay?'

'Mam's just called me on my mobile,' Catrin said, her voice hoarse and strained. 'She said to bring anyone short of a bed back to Brynteg.'

'Thanks,' Ewan accepted.

'Right, let's get off, then.' Greg bent to adjust the protective tarpaulin the firemen had thrown over the piles of equipment. 'See you all tomorrow. Around noon?'

Over in the east, the sky was beginning to lighten a fraction. Somewhere in the forested slopes of the hills a blackbird tried out a first sleepy phrase of notes to bring in the day. Tiredly, the group split up and began to make their individual ways home.

Catrin and Ewan took Catrin's car and were soon drawing into the Brynteg yard. In the farmhouse kitchen, Bron waited up with sandwiches under cling-film and the kettle singing. 'I'm off to bed now,' she said as they subsided wearily down on the shabby old sofa by the range. 'Just wanted to make sure you were all right. I've put Ewan in the room over the porch, Catrin. I shouldn't be in too much of a hurry to get up in the morning. Get what rest you can. You look as if you need it.' She placed the tea and food to hand, bid them goodnight and left.

Catrin took a sandwich and toyed with it listlessly. Suddenly it was all too much. 'What a thing to happen,' she said, choked. 'Another fire, just like before. Makes you wonder if the mill is fated.'

'Nonsense,' Ewan snorted. 'There'll be a perfectly rational explanation for what's happened. Fate doesn't come into it.' His reply was probably sharper than he intended and Catrin's face immediately crumpled. 'Oh, come on,' he said in quite a different tone, and putting his tea-mug down on the floor he took her weeping in his arms and drew her to him. Cradled in the comforting warmth of his embrace, Catrin found she was able to master her emotions.

'Sorry,' she said, raising drowned eyes to his. 'It was just … oh, everything!'

'I know.' He smiled down at her, his rugged, soot-streaked face full of kindly understanding and concern. Next moment he had dropped a swift, very tender kiss upon her mouth.

Brief though it was, the wave of emotion that engulfed her when his lips met hers was terrifying. She thought of Will and guilt tore through her. She made to draw back, but the traumas of the night weighed heavily upon her and instead she smiled up at him uncertainly and allowed herself instead to relax once more against him. They sat on, her head on his shoulder, his arm around her, and slowly the quiet of the old farmhouse enveloped them, lending a perilous intimacy.

'If anyone's to blame for the fire, it's me,' Ewan said abruptly into the silence.

Catrin turned to him, seeing in the flickering light of the range the anxiety in his face. 'What d'you mean?'

'I've had my suspicions about the wheel all along. I should have argued the point with Heritage, instead of giving in the way I did.'

'But the final decision was theirs, not yours. If anyone is responsible for what's happened, it's them.'

Ewan twisted his lips wryly. 'Try telling Heritage that! Come on, we'd best polish off this supper your mother was good enough to prepare, or I'll have Bron to account to as well in the morning, and that'll never do!'

'I'm too shattered to eat a thing. I'm going up,' Catrin said, seeing the first fingers of dawn sneaking in through the window. She explained to Ewan where his room was, said goodnight and went yawning off to bed.

The dream was upon Catrin the moment she sank into sleep.

'Fire!' Hywel burst out of the cottage, dragging on his jacket as he went. 'The mill's on fire! Quick, Marged, put the babe somewhere safe and get what you can out of the house. Where's John? John, man? He was finishing off that order. Dear God, he's never trapped inside?'

He raced towards the blazing building, but the heat from the flames forced him back. 'Can't get near! An inferno it is! We've got to put it out!' Seizing two heavy wooden pails from outside the cottage door, he ran to the river for water.

Beyond, concealed in the bushes, the army recruit kept his eyes glued on the rear entrance to the building. No one could stop in there for long. Any moment now John Caradoc would make a run for safety, and then he'd jump. The tinder box and empty cache that had contained the gunpowder to fuel the flames lay forgotten at the soldier's feet. Sure enough, the door flung open and Caradoc rocketed out and came sprinting up the slope, practically into the path of his pursuer.

'Got you, Caradoc!'

'What the ...? Damn you, fellow! Let go of me!'

A short fight ensued. John Caradoc, the stronger of the two and spurred by desperation, bunched his fist and landed his captor a blow that momentarily felled him. Then he was off, sprinting up the track through the trees and away. Cursing and gasping, the soldier heaved himself to his feet and staggered off in pursuit.

Below, Hywel and Marged were trying in vain to put out the fire. Unhappily, a breeze had got up, fanning the flames closer and closer to the cottage. A spark caught the dry thatch of the roof and within seconds the whole lot was alight. From a clump of reeds along the riverbank where Marged had left her, the baby wailed in terror.

Shouting heralded the approach of neighbours. Snaking up the hillside came a hurried line of men and women bearing pails and any other container they could lay hands on.

'It's too late,' Hywel said brokenly, his gaze flitting in despair from the blazing ruin of the mill that was his livelihood, to the house that had sheltered them all their married years. 'Come away, Marged girl. It's too late.'

'Too late,' Catrin murmured, stirring in the bed. Voices and the slamming of the back door brought her eyes fluttering open. The smell of scorched timbers and burning was still there in her nostrils. In panic she reared up, disorientated, her mind a confusion of leaping flames and rampaging clouds of thick black smoke. And then comprehension dawned and she fell back again in relief against the pillows. She was not trapped near the blazing mill but safe in her bedroom at the farm. The burnt aroma she could smell was the smoke from last night's fire that clung to her hair, which she had been too tired yesterday – or was it this morning? – to wash out prior to falling into bed.

Her head ached dully. Faintly, from downstairs, came the sound of voices. Catrin recognized Rissa's, and the low answering tones of Ewan.

Ewan. Catrin remembered last night, the way he had kissed her and how they had sat closely like lovers, and felt the hot colour rush to her cheeks. It had seemed natural, as if there was no reason at all why they should not be there together, commiserating with each other and grasping a little innocent mutual comfort. This morning though, in the bright clear light of the new day, it was a different tack altogether. Ewan had kissed her and she had not discouraged it. How on earth could she face him?

A healthy rumbling in her stomach reminded her of the missed meal of the previous day. Almost twenty-four hours had elapsed since she had last eaten. No wonder she felt jaded. She'd take a long soak in the bath and wash her hair, by which time Ewan might with any luck have left for the mill. Then she could go in search of breakfast. Pushing aside the covers, Catrin got up, pulled on her dark-blue chenille dressing gown and went padding off to the bathroom.

When she finally arrived downstairs, dressed, her wet hair bundled up in a towel, it was later than she realized – but Ewan had departed and only Rissa sat there, tucking into boiled eggs and toast as if there were no tomorrow. Bron stood at the cooker where pans bubbled and steamed. The tantalizing smell of fresh-brewed coffee filled the air.

'Hi,' Rissa said as Catrin came in. 'How d'you feel this morning? Like you've been run over by a bus, if it's anything like me! Some party that turned out!'

'True. Has Ewan gone?' Catrin tried to make her voice casual.

'Ages ago,' Rissa said. 'He couldn't have got more than a couple of hours' sleep. He's agonizing over that wretched wheel – you know what he's like. Couldn't wait to get over there and check something out. From what I saw of the way it was burning, he'll be lucky to find anything left.'

The long-cased clock on the wall opposite started to strike twelve. Catrin looked at it, horrified. 'Heavens, is that the time? We'd better get down there as well. Greg will be expecting us.'

'Food first,' said her mother, deftly ladling an egg into an eggcup and bringing it to the table, together with toast and a pot of coffee. 'No one can work on an empty stomach. Do you have Greg's mobile number handy?'

'It's on the telephone pad. I'll go and—'

'I'll see to it. You sit down and eat. I'll tell Greg you won't be along just yet. He'll understand.'

While they were breakfasting, Llew came in from the farm for his lunch. Bron whipped a plate of home-cured ham and a bowl of salad out of the fridge and put it in front of him, announcing ruefully that she had a party of trekkers waiting, and she'd better go and attend to them before they all upped and left for home!

Catrin, her meal consumed and feeling the better for it, went back upstairs to blow-dry her hair and get ready for whatever awaited them at the mill.

The kitchen had suddenly emptied. Rissa found herself alone with Llew. Suddenly ill at ease, and seized with the urgent need to be busy, she rose and began to stack the dirty dishes into the dishwasher.

'You don't have to do that, girl,' Llew said, helping himself to a home-grown tomato from the dish. 'You folks must all be worn out after that hubbub last night. What a thing to happen! News was all over the village this morning. Leave it, Rissa. Sit down and rest.'

'It's really no problem.' Rissa put in detergent and started the machine, and was glad of the responding gush of water that filled the silence. Here she knew was the opportunity she had been waiting for. She had Llew all to herself to ask about her mother. Somehow though, she could not get her head round it. Long-ago dates and the odd anecdote her mother had let slip jiggled in an incomprehensible tangle in her mind, fading to nothing as other, more urgent issues honed in. Her summer which had looked so promising and clear-cut was now drastically altered. No mill, no holiday job. So much was obvious.

And without her job she no longer qualified for the Ty Coch cottage. She sighed. She liked the job, loved the cottage, liked its closeness to Will Meredith and his mother, Kate, whom she looked upon as a friend.

Then again, she had her father to consider. Geoffrey Birch was not in the best of health. When she had rung this morning to tell him what had happened, he had sounded distracted, as if he had not taken it in. It was so unlike his usual quick response that Rissa had asked what was wrong. Typically, Dad had said he was fine, after which he had become irritated and told her to stop fussing. Rissa knew that tone of old. When Dad got ruffled, he was not feeling at his best. Maybe she had better cut her losses and go home.

That said, it would do no harm to lightly question Llew. At least it would give her something to mull over for the future.

Rissa was pondering how best to broach the subject when there was a light tread on the stairs and Catrin appeared again. She wore a lightweight pink sweater over her serviceable jeans and shirt, and comfortable trainers on her feet. Her newly-shampooed hair was restrained by a gauzy scarf and hung in a glossy rope down her back. She looked fresh and eager and ready to tackle whatever lay ahead.

'Shall we walk there instead of taking the car?' she said with a glance through the window at the sun-filled farmyard. 'It's a lovely day, and I wouldn't mind some fresh air.'

'If you like.' Rissa fought back a spurt of irritation. Catrin *would* come bursting in on them, just as she was about to take the plunge.

They set off down the rutted drive and took the lane to the mill. Sun-warmed scents of clover and hawthorn blossom rose to meet them as they walked along. Birds squabbled in the hedgerow at either side and from somewhere came the drone of a tractor and silage machine. For once Rissa was oblivious to her surroundings. Lost opportunity and self-recrimination seethed in her mind. Why hadn't she grasped the chance to confront Llew while she could? It wasn't like her to chicken out. But then there were a lot of considerations to make, she excused herself with all honesty. She had come to like the people involved, very much indeed. Above all, she did not want any of them to be hurt. And for the life of her she could not see how she could avoid it. If Catrin had not appeared as she had, maybe she could have asked Llew enough to satisfy her suspicions and left it at that.

Rissa plodded on at Catrin's side, her steps dragging a little as sheer physical tiredness bore down on her. All this on top of a disturbed night was too much.

'Had another dream last night,' she said suddenly.

Catrin looked at her swiftly. 'Really? So did I.'

'The fire must have triggered it off. I dreamed about that other fire.'

'Same here,' Catrin said, and without waiting to hear any more she plunged into telling Rissa precisely what had happened. 'It was more real than ever,' she finished, shuddering. 'Something woke me up in the middle of it – I think it was the back door slamming – so I don't know what happened in the end. I could hear voices and smell burning. I truly believed for one horrible moment that I was still there. It was really frightening.'

'Yes, it would be,' Rissa commented dryly.

'What's that supposed to mean?' said Catrin, stung.

'Nothing. I think you're over-reacting a tad, that's all. You're not the only one to have been affected by what's happened. Think of Greg and the others. They could be in danger of losing their jobs and all that goes with it for all we know. You'll be all right. You'll be getting married.'

'I am thinking of them,' Catrin said quietly. 'That wasn't my point. I was just telling you how I felt. There's no need to get huffy about it.'

'Wasn't,' Rissa snapped. 'Why did you oversleep anyway? I left the mill the same time as you, and I was up more or less at my usual hour.'

'Ewan and I sat up for a while. We were talking,' Catrin said haltingly.

'Huh, fine for some. All I've got to listen to me is the wall!' There's Will, reminded that inner voice. Will had taken to dropping in at the cottage for a cup of tea. She knew he liked her company, and the very fact was a boost to the confidence as well as overcoming the loneliness problem. Remembering Will's admiring dark gaze and the way she could always make him laugh, Rissa felt some or her antagonism drain away. She said, more rationally, 'Do you want to know what happened to John Caradoc?'

'Of course I do.'

'Well, the recruit caught up with Caradoc and they had another fight. They were right on the cliff edge, and the soldier lost his footing and fell.'

'To his death?'

'Not quite. A band of mounted militia came along and found him. He was in a bad way, but before he died he managed to form the name of the man he claimed was responsible for what had happened – John Caradoc.'

'Heavens! He'd have been held guilty of murder, then. I bet the army were laughing. It was just what they wanted, to have a valid reason for getting John in their clutches. So what happened next?'

Rissa shrugged. 'How should I know! The dream petered out the way they do and I woke up feeling shattered. At a guess

Caradoc went back to the mill to see if he could help put out the fire. He wouldn't have, obviously. The mill was gutted, and so was the cottage – those thatched roofs they had in those days were lethal. One spark was all it would have taken for them to go up. He'd have rounded up his in-laws and baby daughter and made a run for it.'

'But where would he have gone? That's what we need to find out. I know it's all in the past, only I can't help feeling that those earlier events have a bearing on the present.' Catrin broke off. 'Just had a thought. Will didn't call round. I was certain he'd look in to see how I was.'

'Oh, I saw Will earlier. He was going past with the dogs and stopped for a cup of tea. Don't worry, I filled him in on the details. Told him everything was under control and that you were all right.'

'I still think he could have come and seen for himself,' Catrin said reproachfully. 'You'd think he didn't care.'

'Well, you can hardly blame him for keeping his distance. Will probably doesn't know where he stands any more in your affections. It's always Ewan this, Ewan that. Can't think why Will puts up with it. How d'you think he'd feel if he knew you and Ewan had been sitting up half the night ... talking.' Rissa sent a look that said it all, and didn't miss the swift colour that touched Catrin's cheekbones.

'So what if I did?' Catrin pulled to a stop, glowering at the other girl. 'Where's the difference between that and you and Will having your little get-togethers at the cottage? Cups of tea indeed! Do I get all jealous and start making comments?'

'No, but only because you didn't know until now,' Rissa said triumphantly.

'What nonsense. What is it, Rissa? Why so stroppy all of a sudden?'

'I'm not. I'm just pointing out the facts. If you don't like it, then tough!'

'I never said—'

'Look, are we due at Capel Mair Mill or not?' Rissa said. 'Because if we are we'd better get a move on before Greg goes ballistic and comes looking for us. Or you. I'm only a minor here. You're supposed to be part of the main act.'

They walked on in affronted silence, not looking to right or left, both eager for the mile and a half trek to be over.

In fact the mill when they arrived did not look as bad as either of them had anticipated. The control room of course was the worst hit. Roof damaged, windows blown out, walls blackened. The water wheel, its ancient timbers seasoned by time and water to the durability of cast iron, remained virtually unchanged. Only the more recent repair work, undertaken during the renovations, had suffered. Catrin gazed in disbelief at the metal cogs reduced to shapeless masses by the heat, and the new wooden wheel buckets that had been carefully fashioned to match the old, now charred to cinder.

Ewan appeared from behind the wheel, wiping his grimy hands on a crumpled handkerchief. 'Hi, girls. You took your time getting here.'

'We walked,' Catrin replied. 'How are things? Where is everyone?'

'Inside, weighing up the likelihood of getting the mill going again. Greg was here first thing, going round the place with the officials. It's not all bad news. The main structure is unharmed. Smoke damage of course. Amazing, how soot sneaks in through every small crack. Every surface is covered in a sticky layer of goo. Not so bad in the barn and shop, though nothing's escaped totally. Fortunately for the Marriotts, the house is fine. It's just a bit whiffy in there. As to the rest, smoke damage is not irredeemable. A good scrubbing down and a dab of paint, and we should be as good as new.'

'And the control room?' Catrin asked with a doubtful glance in that direction. 'Doesn't look good to me.'

'No. The control room will have to be completely redone. Same goes for the wheel workings.' He went very quiet, his slate-grey eyes darkening. 'Don't like what I've seen of this. I mentioned how I'd told Heritage there was a risk if they cut corners, and how they wouldn't have it. Now let's see who gets the blame!'

'Not you,' Catrin said fiercely. 'The fire wasn't your fault. No one could accuse you of that.'

'Well, thanks for the vote of confidence, but I doubt Heritage will see it that way.' For the first time Ewan noticed a hint of restraint between the two girls. He looked them over carefully. 'Are you two all right?' he asked.

'Of course we are,' Rissa said shortly. 'I'm going inside to see what's to be done. Chances are I'll get my marching orders. You only need so many pairs of hands for cleaning up.'

They watched her go stomping off, bobbed hair bouncing. 'There goes a classic case of reaction,' Ewan commented perceptively. 'Shock takes people in different ways. I remember when my wife went off with my business partner, I wanted to hit out at everyone around me. Unfair, but there it was. I went to stay with my parents – well, it was a messy situation, took a lot of sorting out. I know I gave my mother and father a rather bad time in the process. Don't know how they put up with me.'

Catrin looked at him thoughtfully. This was only the second time Ewan had opened up to her about his background. The first had been oh, weeks ago, before the mill was officially opened. They had been chatting and he had mentioned his reason for moving here. To get away from the past, he'd said. A clean break. At the time she had privately and perhaps unworthily awarded him top marks for talking in clichés. It was only afterwards that she came to understand that this had been Ewan's way of cloaking a very deep hurt. Now, she knew the substance behind that hurt. He had lost everything. Wife, home, business; all that had spelled happiness and security for the future. Everything he had built up, gone.

She put her hand gently on his arm. 'Ewan, I'm so sorry. I didn't know.'

'No. Well, it isn't something you shout around, is it?' He smiled, and as his eyes met hers some of the bleakness left him. 'The others will be wondering where we are. Let's join them, shall we?'

Will was in the sheep barn, noisily dismantling some metal portable partitioning that ran the whole length of the building. A shadow fell across the wide doorway. He looked up to find Rissa standing there. She wore a baggy white shirt over cotton slacks in a sunny yellow colour, and her hair was damp from the shower and clung in a smooth bob to her head. She looked as scrubbed and glowing as a new day and Will's heart gave a lift of pleasure.

'Busy?' she said.

'Not especially.' He pulled down a bale of straw from the stack in the corner and threw it down for her to sit on. 'Make yourself at home.'

'Thanks.' Rissa subsided on to the bale and sat hugging her knees, watching him as he worked.

'What's the news from the mill, then?' he asked, raising his voice above the clattering and clanging. 'I take it you've been down there all day.'

'Right. I've been helping Beth wash down the walls in the tea-rooms – the smuts got everywhere! Catrin's home. Have you seen her?'

'Not yet. Thought I'd finish this job first, then get cleaned up and take her down to the pub for a bar snack.'

'You'll be lucky. They were talking about an evening session. Greg thinks they can get the mill up and running again quite quickly. I think this is a meeting to discuss how they go about it. I'm exempt, being a mere skivvy.'

He laughed. 'You're no skivvy.'

'Well, you know. Not a permanent member of staff. At least I'm being kept on for now, which is something. And actually, I'm glad not to be going back this evening. I feel shattered. Didn't sleep all that well last night.'

'I'm not surprised, considering.'

'Wasn't just that. Will, if I ask you something, would you promise not to scoff? It's serious.'

'I'll try. He threw down the final panel and straightened. 'Fire away.'

'Do you believe in psychic phenomena?'

He winced. 'That's a big word for the end of a hard day! If you mean second sight, then yes, I suppose I do. Mam's a bit fey.'

'Is she? Does she have dreams? Waking dreams, I think they're called. You can lapse into them whether you're awake or sleeping.'

'Don't know about that. Mam senses things before they happen. Premonition, you might call it. What's this all about anyway?'

'You won't think I'm off my head if I tell you? It's happened to Catrin as well. I don't suppose she's mentioned it?'

'No.' Will stared at her, mystified. All he ever got from Catrin was talk about the mill. 'You mean you're both experiencing one and the same thing?'

'Dreams, yes. It started on my first day here. I went for a walk along the mill leet and came across Catrin on the bank. She'd dozed off....'

Will listened, scarcely knowing what to make of it, as the story of the previous incumbents of the mill unfolded. He heard about John Caradoc's tragically brief marriage and his involvement with the Rebeccaite movement. And he heard about the fire that destroyed the miller's livelihood, and how it was brought about. 'It's fact, not fiction,' Rissa said defensively. 'We've checked it out as far as we could. Elin's buried in the churchyard here. And John Caradoc's name is mentioned in the books on local history in connection with the riots. What we don't know is what happened to the family after the fire – though there's time yet, I suppose. Will, stop staring at me like that. You're making me feel as if it's all make-believe and it isn't!'

'Sorry. I was just thinking. A bit ago I took Cattie to the summer festival celebrations at Lampeter. The history group were re-enacting a scene from the riots, and she had a funny turn then. I put it down to overwork – you know how she's been going all out with this job of hers. I can see now what it must have been. I don't know. I wish she'd told me.'

But she hadn't, and Will felt a huge chasm of doubt and disappointment opening up inside him. At one time he and Cattie had no secrets. Now, they lived two totally different lives. So much so that she had not felt fit to confide in him, no matter how worried or frightened she had felt.

Rissa blurted, 'Ewan thinks—'

'McInnes? She told *him*?'

'I—' Rissa bit her lip. 'I'm sorry. I didn't think. Perhaps I shouldn't have mentioned it. But Ewan believes that these things have a trigger. If we find out what that trigger is, the problem – dreams, timeslips, whatever – usually stops.'

'A trigger? How can there be!' Jealousy pounded through Will, threatening to overwhelm him. That Ewan McInnes! Coming down here with his clever ideas and smart talk. Taking his girl from under his very nose. Didn't someone mention he'd had his own architect's business and lost it? Will wasn't a bit surprised. The guy didn't strike him as being as nearly competent as he made out.

A hard knot of pain, raw and unwelcome, blossomed in his heart. Bleakly he gazed at Rissa, sitting there pink with mortification, and despite his own dark emotions he had it in him to feel sympathy for her. She wouldn't have made trouble deliberately, not Rissa. He liked her a lot. She was different, with her funny slimming diets and her inventive ideas on how to make his farm work! Not as pretty as Cattie, of course, but attractive all the same in a smooth, girl-about-town sort of way. And she knew how to make him laugh! Though at the moment, Will thought soberly, laughter had never seemed so far away.

'Fancy coming out for a drink?' he heard himself say.

'But I thought ... you said you were taking Catrin.'

'She's not around, is she? Give me ten minutes to wash and brush up, and I'll be right back. Have you ever been to Tregaron? There's a decent pub there. Food's good, and we could go on to the Red Kite Centre you once mentioned and take a look at the young birds they've reared. Bring your camera. You might get some good shots.'

Rissa managed a smile. 'Thanks, I'd love to come. There's something else I wouldn't mind talking over as well. It's connected with my past.'

'Skeletons jumping out of the cupboard?' Will made a huge

effort to be jovial and gave himself a mental pat on the head when Rissa responded with a chuckle. 'I can't wait. Go fetch that camera. I'll pick you up at the cottage in fifteen minutes.'

Over the next weeks, some sort of order was gradually brought to the mill. Rissa and the other staff got together and a massive clean-up was undertaken. Even given the seriousness of the situation, the hard and mucky work was lightened by moments of fun. Young Sam and Oliver insisted on offering their services. One day Catrin turned up to find the boys had 'cleaned' the gallery with gravy browning filched from the tea-room's kitchen. Beth had thrown a wobbler and the stuff had taken ages to clean off, but as they scrubbed down the pine panelling for a second time the smiles were in evidence.

Another time Greg was up a ladder whitening the ceiling, and accidentally tipped up the can of emulsion. Ewan happened to be passing underneath at that exact moment and received the full whack of it. His howl of surprised outrage reverberated round the mill. Everyone looked up to see Ewan's startled red face, liberally embellished with lashings of thick white one-coat.

'Look at him!' Glenys shrieked, subsiding into fits of laughter. 'Talk about strawberries and cream!'

The place fell to uproar, mops, dusters, brushes dropping to the floor, the whole company doubled over with mirth, whilst the victim hopped helplessly about trying to scrape the stuff off. Even now, a week later, Catrin giggled to think of it.

Temporary office quarters were made in the spare room of the cottage, which had – much to Beth's relief – suffered the least from the effects of the fire. Here Greg and Catrin struggled to cope with the tedious and often trying issues of insurance and locating a building company to undertake the repairs. As well, there was the distressing business of cancelling bookings and returning down-payments, not to mention the more serious wrangling with Heritage, who insisted on calling an inquiry as to why the fire started in the first place.

Quietly, the small boys were questioned.

'They both firmly deny having sneaked into the control room and played about with the switches,' Ewan said to Catrin over a lunchtime drink at the Drovers. They had taken to slipping down here at midday and found it good to take a break from the muddled and somewhat fraught tenure of their days. 'Imps though they are, they are not fibbers. I'm inclined to believe them.'

'Me too.' Catrin remembered her dream. 'It couldn't have been deliberate?'

'Arson?' Ewan put down his drink in surprise. 'Why d'you say that?'

She told him. She told him about the soldier and the desire for promotion that had ultimately cost him his life, and had robbed the good people of the mill of all they possessed.

'So now we know,' Ewan said, accepting her words without question. 'I don't see how arson could apply in this case. No one was against the mill venture going ahead in the first place, surely? No dark muttering in the village, was there?'

Catrin frowned in thought. 'Not that I recall. When the project was first broadcast it stirred a lot of interest in the village. Small businesses grow – at least, they do when they get the chance – and that means jobs for people. No one would want to destroy the chance of an income deliberately. I was thinking more of youngsters fooling around. The youth club went alight once. That turned out to be teenagers.'

'Playing with fire.' Ewan looked grim. 'Young idiots! I don't think that was the case here. My thoughts go back to those dicey workings on the wheel. I explained to you once before, it happened a lot with these old mills. Bit too much friction, and bingo! You've got trouble. With a tad more care and, admittedly, a good deal more money invested, the cause of the problem could have been modified and this would never have come about. Something overheated and damaged the electrics. The rest you know.'

'You've heard from Heritage, haven't you?' Struck by the bitterness in his tone, Catrin tried to frame the right words. 'It's not good, is it?'

'No,' Ewan replied heavily. 'It's as I predicted. The finger points at me. I'm the architect, I drew up the plans, therefore I'm to blame. Great, eh? I sometimes wonder if anything will ever go right for a change!'

'It's a bad patch, that's all,' Catrin encouraged.

Worse was to follow.

That night she and Will had arranged to go out. They went to try out a new hostelry up in the hills. Over the meal Catrin noticed that Will was rather quiet and put it down to the usual problems over the farm, or health of his mother, always a worrying issue. They left early and drove home through the dusk. It was a balmy evening, and they took the coffee Catrin made out on to the small private courtyard her mother had made attractive with tubs of flowers and clematis on the old stone walls.

She recalled how for once Will had not pressed her to leave the mill as he might once have done. Given the present circumstances, it would have made sense. It wasn't like Will and the fact left her feeling vaguely troubled and uncertain.

The scent of the pink clematis was sweet on the air. For the want of something better to talk about, Catrin started to enthuse about them. 'Will, what is it?' she asked when his mind was plainly not on her words. 'That's the second time I've asked you something and you haven't replied. What's wrong? Is it me? Something I've said?'

'No, it's not you.' Will's face looked grim in the starlight and for a moment Catrin was tempted to leave it. She had enough problems to contend with without inviting more. But Will was looking at her closely and she had no choice but to continue.

'What then?'

'It's McInnes.'

'Ewan? What do you mean?'

'There's talk. Apparently he was messing about with the old wheel workings before Heritage, or the insurance people for that matter, got there.'

'So? It's his job, Will. Naturally he'd be curious to find out what went wrong.'

'How d'you know he didn't tamper with anything?'

'What d'you mean? What for?'

'To make it look as if his work wasn't responsible for what happened. I was there on the night of the fire, Catrin. I saw him make a dive for the old water wheel. The place was ablaze by this time. It was a crazy move. Only someone damned desperate would have made it. He'd have been done for, no doubt about it, if it hadn't been for one of the men seeing him and stopping him.'

'That's ridiculous,' Catrin said. 'I don't believe Ewan would do anything so underhand.'

'Not even to save his own neck? I reckon McInnes knows more about the fire than he's letting on. He went back the next morning, didn't he? Couldn't wait to get there. I was up on the tops with the sheep. I saw him tinkering about with the damaged workings. It was early, before anyone else had got there.'

'Will, what are you suggesting?' Catrin felt horrified. Even if there had been something to hide, with the state the wheel was in after the fire there was no way anyone could have covered his tracks, was there? 'Ewan wouldn't,' she said, a hint of uncertainty in her voice. No sooner were the words out than she understood how hollow they sounded. Will remained silent and disbelieving in the rustic garden seat. He picked up his coffee spoon and began to play with it, flicking it in an irritating tattoo against the wooden table top. Catrin went on in a more controlled manner, 'Ewan McInnes is the most honest person ever. He knew the wheel was suspect. He made no secret of the fact. He even told Heritage but they wouldn't listen. You know what Heritage are? Restoration work having to follow the original exactly and all that palavar! Well, in this case it's rebounded on them. Ewan is blameless.'

The spoon continued its bothering rhythm. Tap-tap, tappity-tap, loud in the quiet of the night.

'Ewan wouldn't do anything underhand,' Catrin repeated. 'He's as concerned about what happened as anybody else – oh Will, do stop tapping that wretched spoon!'

'Hello? Anyone there?' called a voice from the far side of the garden wall. 'It's me, Rissa. Can I come in?'

Catrin mustered patience. Ever since the spat on the day following the fire, relations had never been quite the same between herself and Rissa. She struggled to inject a degree of welcome into her voice. 'Rissa, hello there. Yes, come in do.'

Rissa was there at once. She wore a loose jacket over smart trousers and had her leather bag over her shoulder. Her face was tense in the dimness. 'I've come to say goodbye,' she said hurriedly. 'Dad ... my father's been rushed to hospital and it doesn't sound too good. I've got to go home at once.'

Chapter Seven

Rissa left Catrin and Will in the courtyard and hurried across the bright halogen-lit farmyard to her car. The night was clear and silvered with stars. With luck she should be in London well before dawn. She'd go straight to the hospital. Their GP, when he had rung to inform her that her father had been taken ill, had said he didn't think there was any immediate cause for concern, and suggested Rissa travelled down in the morning. Rissa wasn't leaving anything to chance. Dad had had these attacks before. She knew how severe they could be.

She was fumbling in her floppy black sack-bag for her keys when the door of the calving box at the end of the row of farm buildings opened. She glanced up to see Llew coming out. 'Thought I heard a car,' he said. 'You off out, Rissa? It's a bit late, isn't it?'

'I've got to go back to London, Llew,' Rissa explained worriedly. 'It's my father. He's been taken into hospital.'

'Oh dear.' Llew was immediately all concern. 'Sorry to hear that. Is there anything we can do? They'll be expecting you at the mill in the morning. Want us to let them know where you are?'

'No, it's all right, thanks. I've just spoken to Catrin, so she'll put them in touch. Um … actually, Llew …' Rissa paused, her mind whirling. It could be some while before she returned to Capel Mair. Here was her last chance to quiz Llew about his past. Her past. The past that bound them inexorably together, but whose revelation she knew would have far-reaching consequences on the people she looked upon as her friends. Could she do it? Rissa bit her lip. Really, Dad was more important. She pictured the man who had brought her up and taught her so much – Geoffrey Birch, kindly, considerate, his intelligent grey eyes filled with pain as he coped courageously with his illness. This was her real father, not the man in the crumpled boiler suit and mucky Wellington boots who stood before her. In any case, was finding out about her past really so vital? Rissa didn't think so. It wasn't nearly as urgent as getting to Dad. 'Oh, it's nothing,' she blurted, choked with sudden tears. 'Must go, Llew. It's a four-hour drive to London. If I get off at once I should beat the first of the rush hour. Just hope Dad's going to be OK, that's all.'

Her fingers closed at last around her keys amongst the jumble of odds and ends in her bag. She pulled them out, not realizing in her haste that her mother's locket and chain, put there for safe keeping, had become entangled in them. It slipped unnoticed to the ground. Rissa unlocked the car, jumped in and wound down the window.

"Bye, Llew,' she called, fastening her seat belt and firing the engine.

'Cheerio then. Safe journey.' Llew stood back as the car shot off across the yard to the entrance, where the big double gates were not yet closed for the night. Llew's eyes fell at once on the locket. He snatched it up hastily and went after the car, gesturing to Rissa to stop. But Rissa, her mind on the journey ahead, was already through the gateway and off, bumping along the rough-made drive to the lane.

Llew stood there in the floodlit yard, the locket in his hand, listening to the car speeding away into the night. Drat. He'd have to keep it safe till she came back. It was a pretty thing. Old, he wouldn't mind betting. Curious, Llew opened the clasp and looked inside. Staring at the two portraits before him, the past came rushing remorselessly back and Llew went very still, hardly able to believe what he saw. Smiling out from one of the pictures was the girl he had known many, many years ago in Malta. Gabriella, that was it. Little Gabby, with her sweet face and laughing charm. And the sailor boy with the close navy crop in the other photo, sun-browned, grinning, was him!

Shocked, disbelieving, Llew glanced up towards the dark ribbon of road Rissa had just travelled. It couldn't be. There had to be another explanation. And yet the girl in the locket was Gabby all right. And when he thought about it, he could see in young Rissa a passing family resemblance. His mother, his grandmother too, daughter of the indomitable Anwen who was said to have had the Sight, all had been possessed of those same flashing dark eyes and head of thick blue-black hair. Catrin was the same. Bron laughingly called it the stamp of the Jenkinses.

Bron! Llew's thoughts flew to his wife of twenty-five years, whom he loved and who had worked so loyally and tirelessly at his side. Not always easy years either. If Bron got wind of this it would shatter her. Dear goodness, what was he to do!

Could he be jumping to conclusions? Llew felt a surge of hope, and then shook his grizzled head. He didn't think so. Rissa was as much his own flesh and blood as Catrin. They were half-sisters, God help him! What a pretty kettle of fish!

He couldn't go inside, not yet. Llew headed mechanically

back for the calving box out of which he had just emerged. The new mother turned her black and white head reproachfully at the interruption and turned back to the manger and her feed. Curled in the straw at her feet, her shiny-coated new little heifer calf rested. In the adjoining stall another cow and newborn calf shifted restlessly.

Llew subsided on to the straw bale where he had spent the best part of the past few hours and contemplated the locket, turning it over and over in his big work-roughened hand. Rissa had been going to say something, he was sure of it. If she hadn't been in such a panic to get off she might have done, and what could he have answered? There had been other times when he had thought she wanted to speak, but had seemed to change her mind. And no wonder!

Llew thought of Gabby, the quiet darkness of her, the way her eyes smiled when they were together. It had been a boy-girl romance, nothing like what he felt for Bron. Over the years their marriage had strengthened, the first heady flush of togetherness deepening into friendship and trust. He and Bron were two halves of the same whole, tree and leafy bough, sun and shining moon, soul mates. He could not imagine one without the other. But at the time he had loved Gabby with a fierce passion. He would have married her if he could.

They had arranged to meet outside the harbour café, where they served that strong coffee she liked so much. He had waited, consulting his watch impatiently from time to time, wondering where she was. Gabby had never turned up. It wasn't like her, and after a while he had gone on to the big white-fronted house in the secluded garden where she lived. All had been quiet, as if those within were expecting him to come. The front door had not even opened to his summons. He had lingered for a while, looking up at the windows, wondering if one of them was hers and if Gabby might send him a sign. None had come.

In the end he had given up and gone for a stroll alone along the harbour path, confused, annoyed, kicking irritably at small stones along the way and sending them spinning into the bay. The tide was high, he remembered. The sun shimmered on the water, making the sun-pennies dance and sparkle. When he had eventually got back to the ship he had avoided his two mates and made straight for his bunk. Llew had written Gabby a note asking what was wrong? It had been the first of many such missives.

Not one had been answered.

And no wonder, Llew thought now. Not by any means an imaginative man, he could nonetheless picture the situation. Gabby pregnant. The house in uproar, her father angry and accusing. They were a Catholic family, staunchly devout. Gabby was gently-reared, convent-educated, her father well-respected in the town. Of course he wouldn't want his only daughter married to a serviceman from some place in the back of beyond. So what would he do? Marry her off as speedily as possible to someone more suitable, possibly a business acquaintance in another land, far away from Malta where folks would count on their fingers and tongues might wag. It was to the man's favour and to Gabby's good fortune that the marriage, to all intents and purposes, had been a sound one. Rissa was a bright, well-balanced young woman. Llew recalled how on more than one occasion she had made him laugh at something she said. Of a sober outlook in the main, the spontaneous bursts of humour had made him feel good.

Not any more though! Where the blazes could he put the locket where no one was likely to find it? Llew thrust it for now into the small back pocket of his overalls and buttoned it up carefully. He'd find a safe hiding place later. Voices and soft laughter from the farmyard brought his head up. That would be Will leaving. He'd give them a minute or two to say goodnight and then follow her into the house.

Will shut the gate of the sheep-pen with a clang. It was early yet, the sun not up, mist still creeping around his feet. In the distance the cottage had already taken on an empty look. No Rissa waving to him from the kitchen, bringing him out a mug of tea, pausing for a chat before she tore off to work. Suddenly bleak, Will called the two dogs more sharply than he intended, then bent to pat them reassuringly when they came slinking up with their tails rammed between their legs.

In the Brynteg yard, Llew emerged from the calving box with two empty feed buckets. ''Morning, Llew,' Will called. 'Not a bad morning.'

'It's dry anyway. Promises rain later in the week, according to the forecast,' Llew said dourly, dumping the buckets down and coming across to the boundary wall, where he stood scanning the hillside with the view of the cottage. 'See your tenant's had to leave in a hurry.'

'That's right. Doesn't sound too good, does it? Rissa's very fond of her father. Pity she's had to go, all the same. They're going to miss her at Capel Mair.' He'd miss her too, Will thought, remembering her merry smile and the way her dark eyes brightened when she spoke of a subject especially important to her. She was certainly no empty head. She'd come up with some good ideas for the farm. He could kick himself now for not listening properly to her, the way Mam had. He always had been slow to accept another's point of view. 'I only hope she'll soon be back, but there you are.'

'Wouldn't hold your breath!' Llew muttered. 'These youngsters are all the same. Here today, gone tomorrow. You never know where you are with them.'

Will stared at him in surprise. What was biting him then? 'Come on!' he chivvied. 'Rissa had good reason to leave. What's up, Llew? Trouble with the calving?'

'No – everything went off fine. Couple of nice little heifer calves I've got.' Llew's eyes slid again towards the empty cottage, as if the fact bothered. 'Be letting it out to someone else now, will you?'

'No, I don't think so. This spot of bother with Rissa's father might well blow over. I'll keep it free for her for now.'

'It's throwing away good money to me,' Llew growled. 'But it's your cottage. It's up to you. Oh well, better get along. I've promised Bron a hand with the ponies. There's a fresh party of trekkers due at the weekend. Fully booked till the end of September, she is. She takes on far too much, what with the trekking and all she does in the house and around the farm. I've told her there's no need, but she won't listen! See you, Will.'

He went stomping off, clearly out of sorts, a maternal bellow from the calving box following him. Two healthy calves, Will thought with envy. He missed his dairy cattle; sheep weren't nearly as satisfying. Both heifers too, Llew had said. Some folks didn't know their own luck! Shaking his head in perplexity, he turned and made for home, the collies bounding on ahead.

'So there you are,' said his mother, looking up from the cooker with a smile. The kitchen smelled pleasingly of frying bacon. Will's mouth watered as he kicked off his boots by the door and went to scrub his hands. 'Rissa rang,' Kate Meredith went on, taking his meal from under the grill where it was keeping warm and placing on the table. 'You've only just missed her. I told her you'd call her back.'

Will's heart gave a leap. 'Did she say what she wanted?'

'Not really. I asked after her father. Did you know he's in a private hospital? They can't be short of a penny or two.'

'Well, they're business people, aren't they. Fingers in every pie. Her father's been pretty successful by all account. I expect that's where Rissa gets her ideas from.'

'True. I liked having her in the cottage. She kept it very spick and span, and I shall really miss her popping in for chats. I took her mobile number, by the way. It's on the phone-pad.'

'Thanks. Want me to give her a message?'

'Just tell her I hope everything will be all right, and that we're thinking of her.'

'Right.' Will sat down at the table. 'This looks good, Mam. Aren't you eating?'

'Oh, I'll maybe have a round of toast,' said Kate, whose appetite was still not good. 'How did you get on with the sheep? Have you finished the dipping?'

'Not quite. I'll do the rest later. After I've made that call,' Will said, spearing some bacon with his fork and eating it with relish.

Breakfast over, he went outside to ring Rissa.

'Hi, Will.' Her voice over the miles sounded strained. 'Thanks for ringing back so promptly. I wanted to tell you that I've spoken with the doctor. Will, Dad's not good. I've never seen him so poorly. As a rule he has a good sleep after one of these attacks, and then seems to pull round. But this time—' She broke off, clearly in some distress. 'Will, it doesn't look as if I'll be coming back to Wales in the foreseeable future. If you want to re-let the cottage—'

'Don't be daft,' Will said. 'Paid the three months' rental, haven't you. The cottage is yours till the end of August. Unless you wanted reimbursing?'

'Now who's being daft?' He caught the hint of a smile in her voice and the corners of his mouth tugged in response. 'Have you seen Catrin?' she went on.

'Not yet. Had a word with Llew, though. He's not in the best of humours. He'd been up most of the night calving – well, a broken night does tell on you and Llew's not as young as he was.'

'True – what did he get?'

'What? Oh, two heifers. Not bad, eh?'

'Not bad at all. You should get back into dairy yourself. Run the place as a working museum like I said. You couldn't go wrong.'

'I'll think about it. Promise.'

'Will you really? Heck! That's a turn up for the books!' There was a pause. 'Will, there's something I've been meaning to tell you. It's quite … well, personal. You know those weird dreams I told you about, the ones about Capel Mair when it was a proper working mill? Catrin gets them too. I think what I wanted to say could somehow be tied up with those. Can't really go into details over the phone. It's all too complicated.'

'Sounds serious. Is Cattie in on whatever it is?'

'She's involved. All the family are. I really can't go into it now.'

'Right. Where are you? At home?'

'No. I'm still at the hospital. It's awful just sitting here waiting. I feel so useless. Dad was in a private place at first, but he's been moved now to the heart unit at Richmond. I might pop home afterwards for a shower and something to eat. Don't want to be away too long though. You never quite know what to do for the best.'

'Well, remember we're all thinking of you. Mam sends her best wishes, by the way. She says she misses you already. We all do. Rissa, you will keep in touch?'

'Of course.'

'Quiet here, without you bossing us around,' he added. He wanted to add more, but couldn't.

'Bossy yourself,' Rissa said. ''Bye Will. Love to Kate and everyone. Big pat for the dogs.'

She rang off. Frowning, Will tucked the phone away in his pocket. He wondered what it was Rissa wanted to impart. He might have a word with Catrin when she got home, see if she could throw any light on the mystery. He sighed, seized by a sudden misgiving. Catrin hadn't been exactly pleased last night over that business with McInnes and the mill wheel. He wished now he had not opened his mouth. It had sounded as if he were accusing the guy, which was not the case at all. True, it had struck him as odd on the morning after the fire, when he had seen Ewan inspecting the damage. Anyone watching the man's deep preoccupation with the wheel, seeing his set face, would have reacted the same.

Will riffled his fingers edgily through his crop of curling dark hair. He might have mentioned something about it in the pub when he had called in for a quick pint. He hoped not, but there you are. Will understood that his jealousy had got the better of him, but it had been nothing but Ewan with Catrin for weeks now, and a fellow could only take so much. All right, so Catrin and Ewan worked in the same place, therefore the guy's name was bound to crop up from time to time. So long as that was all it was. Lunching together, calling for drinks after work, seemed to Will a tad too cosy for comfort.

He stretched slowly, flexing tired muscles, wondering again what it was that Rissa had wanted to say. The sun was up now, the mist gone, the sky a clear cornflower blue. It was the sort of day Rissa loved. He tried to imagine what it would be like in

London and failed utterly. He'd get Catrin to ring her this evening and cheer her up a bit. Rissa had not mentioned the boyfriend, Mike. Perhaps it was all off.

Will mentally tossed up whether to bring the new special breeds down for dipping first, or get on with creosoting the barn. The sheep won. Whistling up the dogs, he crossed the small farmyard, cut through the tangled orchard at the side of the house and headed off for the hills.

Catrin was in the weaving gallery. The loom had been assembled again following the fire, and she had spent the greater part of yesterday setting up her work. This morning, after dealing with the mail in the temporary office quarters in the mill cottage, she had slipped across to start the first section of pattern. Since this was all to do with fresh starts, she had opted for her Wedding Ring design for the throw she was making for the mill shop for when they reopened. It was good to be back at her weaving. The gallery was pleasantly cool after the stifling little room in the cottage, which was like an oven in spite of the two fans working on full power. Catrin hummed as she worked, a number with a heavy beat, keeping time with the rhythmic clatter and clang of the loom. She wandered if Elin had sung to herself as she stood in this self-same mill and wove her blanket, the one with the pattern so amazingly similar to Catrin's own.

Elin, who had lost her life at such a pitifully young age. Not for the first time Catrin tried to puzzle out what had happened to the sad little family after the old mill had perished. John Caradoc would have done his best for them, she was sure. There was no record of him having been captured and imprisoned. Chances were he had fled with his infant child and in-laws into England. London maybe, where he could take on a new name and lose himself amongst the multitudes that flocked there by the day.

Catrin kept watch over the pattern forming on the loom, her mind running on. Rissa had been gone over a week now. There had been no more dreams. Not for Rissa either, so she had said last night on the phone. What a strange thing. It was as if Rissa's appearance in the spring had triggered the dreams off.

She glanced up as the gallery door opened to admit Ewan, and gestured to his mail that lay on the table. There were several letters addressed to him. Ewan, nodding his thanks, riffled through them and ripped one open, glancing through it with a frown. After a moment he slammed the letter down. 'Damn!'

'What's wrong?' Catrin asked, her voice raised above the racket.

'Only what I've been expecting. This is from Heritage. They're questioning the feasibility of my design. There's to be an inquiry.'

Catrin stopped the loom. In the silence that followed she gazed in concern at Ewan across the expanse of deep blue and white cloth. 'But you know you're in the clear and that's the main thing,' she said at last. 'You pointed out the shortcomings of the old wheels to them right at the start. You even offered to modify the design. Heritage didn't want to know.'

'They still won't. They'll do what they did then and shout me down. Heritage are very good at looking after number one. It wouldn't surprise me one jot if the correspondence that went to and fro at the time has got conveniently lost – though that could be me being cussed.'

'Have you kept the letters they sent and copies of your own?'

'I did, though a lot of stuff got damaged during the fire – the men weren't fussy where they aimed those hoses! I'll have to look. What d'you bet the very ones I want have gone.'

'You won't have lost it all. Some will still be on the computer.'

'Good point.' He quirked his lips dolefully. 'I don't know, Catrin. I'm not at all optimistic over this. My chief worry is that it might hold up the building work on the new control room. I was speaking to Greg just now. Apparently, he's got the go-ahead from the insurance company.'

'I know. Isn't it great? And the builder's willing to come as soon as we give the word as well. No hanging around waiting for them to turn up. Greg got in touch with the man who did the previous construction work, so he already knows what it's all about. He doesn't think the repairs should take too long.'

'Greg said as much just now. It's just this.' Ewan stabbed his finger angrily at the letter on the table. 'They're so blasted high and mighty it makes you want to laugh. Except that it's no laughing matter.'

'Ewan, I'm sure it can be sorted,' Catrin said encouragingly. 'You're a top architect, for goodness' sake! Your word has to count for something! And we're all behind you in this, you know that, don't you?'

Ewan allowed himself a small smile. 'Yes, I know that.'

'There you are then. It will be fine. The mill will soon be up and running again. All this trouble will die a death and we can get on with what we're supposed to be doing, instead of all this messing about. What with doing the paperwork and every-thing else too, I don't know whether I'm on my head or my heels. I'm missing Rissa in more ways than one. She was good on the office side of things.'

'She's got the right background. Have you heard any more from her?'

'Yes, we speak most nights. It's still not good with her father. He sounds very poorly indeed. Rissa's gutted about it. She's split up with her man too. He's found someone else, apparently.'

'Huh, that'll make her feel great!'

'I don't think she was all that bothered. They're still friends. It was one of those cases of the two of them having known one another forever. Rissa admitted to thinking on Mike more as a brother than a future husband. She's even talking of moving back here permanently, depending on how things go with Mr Birch of course. Be great if she's back in time for the new opening. We'll all be together again.'

'Not quite all,' Ewan said. 'I meant to mention this before. I might be leaving for pastures new. Been keeping an eye on the trade ads for some time now – well, my contract ends with the close of the season anyway. There's a job advertised this week that I wouldn't mind applying for.'

'Oh?' Catrin went very still. 'Is it round here?'

He shook his head. 'No. It's in New Zealand. South Island. It's a government scheme for improving the output of existing water mills. I've always wanted to go out there. Now's my chance.'

'Oh,' said Catrin again, more quietly. Other words trembled on her lips, but try as she might she could not bring herself to frame them. She was engaged to Will. His ring glittered on her finger. She shouldn't be thinking along these lines. Only one's head did not always agree with what the heart spoke of, did it?

Ewan said, 'Aren't you going to wish me luck? On second thoughts, perhaps not. The way my luck's going at present I won't get as far as an interview. Or if I do, they'll turn me down in favour of another person.'

'Oh, Ewan!' Catrin smiled in spite of herself. 'Listen to you!

Of course they wouldn't turn you down! Think of your qualifi-
cations and experience. And you've got the enthusiasm as well.
That counts for a lot. I should have thought you were made for
the job.'

'Thanks for the vote of confidence.' He smiled. 'Pity they
don't have you on the interviewing board.'

'Oh, I'd turn you down flat.'

'Huh, that's great! Any particular reason?'

'Yes. Because I don't want you to go away,' she replied,
feeling the telltale colour flooding her cheeks.

Ewan just looked at her. 'Chances are by then you'll be so
wrapped up in work you won't even notice I've gone. You'll be
making wedding plans. When is it to be? Have you and Will
named the date yet?'

'No, we haven't,' Catrin said stoutly. 'I wanted some career
space before I settled down. Will understood that.'

'Then he deserves a medal for patience!' Ewan paused.
Their gaze locked. Catrin felt her heart turn over. She gazed at
him with that extraordinary capacity of hers to concentrate
wholly on the situation before her. And she knew with sudden
illuminating clarity that it wasn't Will who claimed her heart
at all.

'Catrin—'

'Yes?'

'Nothing.' Ewan dragged his gaze away and picked up the
offending letter. 'I'd better answer this. Would you mind typing
it out for me once it's done?'

'Not at all.'

'Thanks. I'll leave you to get on then. Cloth looks good.
That's a very eye-catching pattern. Who wants office skills,
when they've got a talent like that? Oh, when Greg comes in,
Catrin, you might tell him the worst. He's not going to be

pleased, and I don't blame him. We've had enough trouble for one year. Time things sorted themselves out.'

'Yes,' said Catrin, repressively.

Ewan darted her a brief searching look, and without another word he picked up his mail and headed off for the office. Catrin looked at her watch. Almost twelve. She might knock off now for lunch. Somehow, the weaving had lost its magic. Putting the brake on the loom, she covered the work over with the clear plastic sheeting they used for keeping off the dust, picked up her bag containing the apple which was all she felt like eating, and left the office.

Outside, the heat was smothering. Catrin made for the river path where it was cooler. A joiner and his apprentice were working on the new footbridge – the only damaged area not affected by the insurance claim – and the sound of the saw and the blare of a local radio station from a portable wireless made her wince. Skirting the work area, Catrin walked lightly on along the path, the hem of her flimsy cotton dress swishing about her bare brown ankles.

Ewan, going. Leaving Capel Mair. The sheer hard fact of it hammered on her mind. She couldn't imagine Capel Mair without him. Throughout these long, difficult weeks it had been Ewan's steady presence that had calmed and reassured. Catrin fully understood how hard it must have been for him to keep cheerful, when all the time he obviously had worries of his own. And yet somehow he managed it. She remembered his concern and kindness when they had visited the English mill and she had suffered that strange waking dream. There'd been no, 'Oh, come on, Cattie! Snap out of it!' that would have been Will's response. Ewan had gently coaxed the details of what had happened from her and given a rational reason for it. She had felt all the better for knowing she wasn't losing her mind totally.

She had almost reached the bend in the river now. Not far ahead lay the grove with the touchstone. She wasn't up to facing any more trauma today, thank you. Turning, Catrin stood a moment to watch the river splashing onwards over the mossy grey stones of its bed. A kingfisher darted out from the willows on the opposite bank, a flash of blue and russet, and she remembered Ewan saying there was a nest there. Shaking her head wordlessly at the pure injustice of life, Catrin took the apple from her bag and started off back, crunching it as she went.

Back in the office she dealt with one or two phone calls and switched on the computer. She was printing out an order for stock when Greg arrived back. He looked glum. 'Just been talking to Ewan,' he said. 'You'll know about Heritage?'

Catrin nodded. 'They can't pin anything on him, can they?'

'Not sure. Ewan went about the submissions in entirely the right way. If anyone's to blame for what's happened it's Heritage for not listening to him in the first place. It seems to me they're looking for a scapegoat. Trouble is, they're a pretty powerful body. Not easy for one man to stand up to. Ewan's got my total support, he knows that. We shall have to all stick together in this.'

'Naturally,' Catrin said. 'I told him as much myself.'

Greg looked at her sharply. 'You like Ewan, don't you? Really like him. Tell me to get lost if you like, but I should have a care, Catrin. Ewan's not a chap to tie himself down. You probably know something of his history. Once bitten twice shy and all that. Wouldn't want you to get hurt.'

'I won't,' Catrin muttered. 'You're wrong in any case. I don't like injustice, that's all.' She shunted the mail towards him to indicate that the matter was closed. 'There's a letter from the firm who made the replacement parts for the old wheel.

They're willing to repeat the process whenever you like, and at the original price as well. They've sent their regrets about the fire. Oh, and there are a couple of generous donations too. One is from France. It's amazing how word gets around.'

'Yes, it is.' Greg brightened visibly. 'Just Heritage to sort out, and then it looks very much as if we're back in business!'

That afternoon, Catrin arrived back home to find her mother in tears. 'It's your father,' Bron said, mopping her eyes with a tissue. 'He's just snapped my head off, and for no reason at all. I only reminded him to fetch me some hay for the ponies – these big round bales are so awkward to separate. Give me the ordinary ones any day. You'd have thought he had to go all the way to the suppliers for it, instead of the barn!'

'Oh, I shouldn't make a thing of it, Mam. Maybe he forgot and was cross with himself.'

'That's no excuse. Llew's been in a funny humour all week. One minute he's berating me for working too hard, then when I ask for a hand he grumbles. I don't know where I am with him, I really don't.'

'I noticed he's been quiet lately,' Catrin said. 'Perhaps he's tired, Mam. He's been up a lot at night. First the lambing, then the calves. There's no let up, is there?'

'It's never bothered him before. Perhaps he's feeling his age. I know I do at times.' Bron smiled through her tears. 'Sorry, Catrin. What an old misery to come home to.'

'You're not at all. Want me to fetch the hay for you? Have you got a trek this evening?'

'If you wouldn't mind. Bring enough for tomorrow as well. And yes, just the novice ride left. I thought I'd do the woodland trail and come back along the main road. It only takes an hour or so.'

'I'll do it if you like. Will's busy with the dipping so I

wouldn't be seeing him tonight anyway. It'll give you a break and I feel like some fresh air.'

'All right then. Thank you. Don't know what I'll do when you and Will are married. There won't be anyone here then to fall back on.'

Catrin made a wry face. 'Everyone's trying to get me married off today. I can't think why. And in any case, Mam, I'll only be over at Ty Coch, not the other side of the world. Like Ewan,' she blurted.

'Ewan's leaving Capel Mair?'

'Seems so. He said he's considering a post in New Zealand. Keep it under your bonnet for now, Mam. It's early days yet and you know how these things get around. Ewan's Capel Mair contract finishes anyway at the end of October.' She paused, then added dolefully, 'I thought he liked it here. I thought he'd look for another mill in the area to restore. But he doesn't seem to even have considered it. He said he'd always fancied New Zealand.'

Bron sighed. 'Oh dear. Nothing stays the same, does it? I really like Ewan McInnes too. And of course I won't mention a thing. Maybe nothing will come of it.'

'Could be,' Catrin replied.

Feeling slightly less exhausted after the ride through the forest with the cheerful group of trekkers, Catrin went to bed early. Inevitably, perhaps, she dreamed of her wedding day. It was a happy dream. The sun was shining, and Mam in her wedding finery was fussing over the posies for the two small bridesmaids. She was going to the church in the pony trap. Dad had groomed the ponies until their coats were like burnished copper. They were trotting there in the sunshine, and she was looking at the familiar landmarks through the gauzy lace of her grandmother's wedding veil.

At the church, she saw Will's sturdy figure waiting at the altar. He looked oddly distant and unfamiliar in his dark-grey wedding suit. She went down the aisle on her father's arm, and it was only when she reached the altar and lifted her veil for the ceremony, that she realized that it wasn't Will beside her at all. This man was taller, more rangy, and the face when he turned to smile at her was—'

She woke up. The radio alarm clock had come on. Jamie Crick was playing a cheery Mozart quartet and rain fell against the window with a soft pattering sound. Catrin lay a moment, her eyes tight shut, trying to hold on to the shreds of her dream. But it had gone as dreams do. She yawned, stretching, and turned her thoughts to the day ahead. Deciding she'd substitute trousers for the skirts she had taken to wearing during the heat wave, she got up and headed for the shower.

Downstairs, Bron was making the breakfasts for the trekkers. 'I hope they're equipped with waterproofs, that's all! This rain looks as if it's in for the day. Take that mug of tea out to your father, would you, Catrin?' she asked, deftly flipping over rashers in the huge black frying pan on the Aga. 'There's another cow due. He'll be in the calving box.'

'Right-oh, Mam.'

Catrin picked up the tea and carried it out, dodging through the rain that was now sheeting down. She heard her father grumbling before she entered the buildings. He was forking up a fresh straw-bed for the new calves, cursing to himself when the golden sections of compressed straw refused to separate.

'Blasted stupid stuff! The baler must have been playing up when they did this load. It's far too tight-packed. Wait till I see those contractors. I'll tell them what to do with their blasted straw!'

'Dad! Whatever's wrong?' Catrin took the fork from her

father and handed him his tea. 'Here, drink this and I'll do it. There. There's nothing wrong with the straw. It's a new bale, that's all. These round bales always are a pain to begin with. Mam was only saying the same yesterday about the hay.'

Llew looked at her mutely, and the hand that held the mug began to shake, spilling the tea on to the floor. Catrin felt her insides quake. 'Dad, what is it? It's not the straw at all, is it? You've been iffy for some while. Mam was upset about it yesterday. There's got to be something worrying you. You're not ill?'

'No. I'm not ill.' Llew swallowed hard and moved to the door, glancing up and down the rain-swept farmyard to check there was no one within earshot. He pulled the door to, blinking as the calf box went substantially darker. 'Listen, Catrin. There's something I must tell you. Haven't said anything yet to your mother. God only knows how she's going to take it when I do.'

'Dad, what is it?' Catrin asked, alarmed. 'What's wrong?'

'It's to do with Rissa Birch. On the night she left, we had a chat. Nothing much. She was in a hurry and dropped something when she was getting her car keys out of her handbag. It was a locket. She'd gone before I could catch her. I opened it and came across something that shocked me speechless.' He stopped, his jaw working in distress.

'Go on,' Catrin said gently.

'Don't know how to say this. I'm not good with words, you know that. Farming's my life, not fancy talking. Anyhow. Catrin, have you ... did you ever spot any resemblance between Rissa Birch and yourself? Because if you did, it's no coincidence.'

Catrin felt herself go pale. 'What do you mean, Dad?' she whispered.

'It's a long story. Maybe we'd best sit down and I'll tell you from the beginning. I'm not proud of myself, and I'm not making any excuses for what happened. But you might as well know my side of things, before you go jumping to conclusions. It's like this....'

Chapter Eight

'Dad, I ... I can't get my head round it,' Catrin stammered. 'Rissa? My sister?'

'Half-sister,' Llew corrected. He rubbed his chin tiredly with his hand, and the rasping of work-callused flesh against overnight stubble was loud in the quiet of the calving-box. 'I'm sorry to spring it on you like this. Ever since I found the damned locket I haven't been able to think of anything else. Can't eat, can't sleep. I keep going over it in my head, wondering how to put it to your mother.'

Catrin made a huge effort to gather her reeling wits. 'But Dad, this all happened long before you and Mam were married. You were very young. Mam will understand.'

'Maybe. It's a different world now from when your mother and I were starting out together. You youngsters have different values and opinions. Oh, I know we've been lucky with you. It's been Will from the start and I thank God for it. You and Will ... well, it couldn't be more right.'

Catrin bit her lip. In fact, things couldn't be more wrong between them. It had been that way for some time now. Couldn't Dad see that?

'What I'm trying to say is we're a different generation and however much we pretend otherwise, old ways die hard,' Llew went on. 'I can't help feeling your mother will take this as a betrayal.'

'But it wasn't, Dad. You didn't know about the pregnancy, so how could it have been? This has come as much as a shock to you as anyone.'

'I should have told her about Gabriella.'

Catrin looked at her father in the dimness of the calf-box. 'Did you love her very much?' she asked softly.

'I thought so at the time. Enough to want to ask her to marry me, anyway. Afterwards, when I got back and settled down to life here at Brynteg, it all seemed like a dream. I barely gave the girl a thought, so it couldn't have been the sort of love that lasts. Nothing like the bond your mother and I have had all these years.'

'Then that's what you have to focus on,' Catrin said. 'Make sure and tell Mam how you feel and she'll come to terms.'

'Think so? It's young Rissa and what her intentions were that worries me. She came here set on finding out about her past, I'm certain of it.'

'Well, that's not unusual. Look at it from her point of view. It must have hit her hard to be told that the man she'd called father all her life actually wasn't. There'd have been new avenues needing to be explored. She'd want to find out who her natural father was and what he was like. Anybody would.'

'And perhaps risk opening up a can of worms?'

'But Rissa hasn't done. Look Dad, over the summer I've got to know Rissa Birch pretty well. She's not a vindictive person. My guess is she did her homework on the three Taffies, whittled them down to the one she wanted and then came to a full stop. She'd got chummy with us all. She liked us, anyone could see that. She wouldn't have wanted to cause any unhappiness. So she said nothing.'

'And what if she hadn't been called away so abruptly? What then?'

'I don't know. What I'm sure of is that Rissa wouldn't want to cause friction between us all.'

Catrin paused. Deep inside her a tiny pain was growing. She recognized it as hurt that Rissa had not trusted her enough to confide in her. What she had just learnt explained a great deal. The dreams, for one thing. Ewan had once said that other-world experiences generally had a trigger. In this case the blood contact must have set it off. Would Rissa have realized that? Catrin imagined she might. So why not be upfront and say?

In the straw, the little Welsh Black cow and her new calf shifted restlessly. Catrin saw her father glance at them, saw his face change and take on a look of satisfaction at a night's work well done. Animals and crops he could cope with. Human emotions were something different. When he broke his news to Mam, the words would not come easy.

She stood up. 'Dad, I'll have to go or I'll be late for work. Just one more thing. The locket. Do you have it handy?'

Without a word Llew undid the button of the small top pocket of his boiler suit and withdrew the locket and chain. 'Couldn't think where to put it for safety. It's a wonder Rissa hasn't missed it.'

'Rissa's had other things on her mind,' Catrin said. Opening the locket, she peered at the two faces within. The young Gabriella had that flower-like prettiness that sometimes fades with the years. Rissa, with her strong dark hair and those very dark eyes that give such an intensity of gaze, had taken more after the Jenkins side. Catrin sighed. How blind she had been not to have spotted the likeness before now.

Snapping the locket shut, she handed it back to her father. 'She was lovely. I can understand you falling for her. Any lad would. Dad, you'll have to explain things to Mam yourself, but you can leave approaching Rissa to me if you like.'

'Sure?' Relief spread obviously over Llew's blunt features.

'Sure I'm sure!' Catrin sent him a smile of pure affection. 'Stop worrying. It'll sort out.' She pushed open the top-door and glanced out. The sky was clearing and a watery sun slid through the cloud, drawing steamy moisture from the rain-washed cobbles of the yard. 'Rain's stopped. Maybe it's an omen. See you, Dad.'

She slipped out of the box and hastened back to the house, where her mother was dishing out breakfast to the small party of trekkers. Seizing a slice of toast from the rack, Catrin sent the chattering group a cheery nod and headed upstairs to get ready for work. Showering quickly, she pulled on a bright blue T-shirt and fastened a long cotton skirt about her waist. She twisted her hair deftly into a thick plait, securing it with a gauzy scarf. Satisfied with her image, she picked up the large patchwork sack-bag that Rissa had inspired her into buying and ran down the stairs, calling goodbye to her mother as she left.

At the mill, Ewan had some news of his own.

'I heard in the post this morning I've got an interview for that job I mentioned. The New Zealand project?'

His eyes shone and Catrin felt her spirits, already low, fall even further. 'Really?' she replied, trying to sound pleased for him. 'When?'

'Not until the end of the month. Let's hope this wretched business over the mill wheel will be sorted by then.'

'Have you heard anything from Heritage?'

'Not as such. Greg says if they come on heavy he's putting the matter in the hands of a solicitor. Hope it doesn't come to that. It'll mean more bother and time I don't have. You OK? You look hassled.'

'I'm fine,' Catrin fibbed, picking up the office mail as distraction and flipping unseeingly through it. Her father's bombshell still pressed on her mind. She wondered if he had plucked up the courage yet to tell Mam. Poor old Dad. Words never came all that easily to him and this was something that would have to be broached very sensitively indeed.

She realized that Ewan had poured her some coffee from the pot Beth had left for them and put it on the desk in front of her. 'Thanks,' she said abstractedly.

'Sugar?'

She looked up and found he was studying her intently, his head to one side a little, the beginnings of concern in the depths of his storm-grey eyes. As she gazed back, Catrin's heart began to thump. 'What is it?' Ewan asked gently. 'More dreams?'

'No, not dreams,' Catrin replied.

'Will, then. You've never had a tiff!'

Catrin lifted a shoulder in a shrug. 'Not that. I think it might be over between Will and me. Though I'd appreciate it if you'd keep this to yourself for now.'

'Of course. I'm sorry. Still, better now than after you're married.' Sympathy coupled with bitter understanding buzzed in his voice. He was still looking at her with that steady grey gaze she found so disconcerting. 'Want to talk?'

'Oh, Ewan,' Catrin replied shakily. 'There are a whole lot of issues I'd like to unload, though some of them aren't mine to tell.'

'Those that are then. Problem shared, problem halved and all that! How about coming out for a meal? Somewhere away from here. Doesn't have to be far. Say, Aberaeron? I could book a table at the Harbourmaster.'

Suddenly, there was nothing she wanted more than to be away from the mill and home and all the ensuing problems.

And she couldn't think of a better person to be with than Ewan. 'D'you know, I might take you up on that,' she said with a wobbly smile.

'Good. Let's call it settled. Tomorrow night? Want me to pick you up?'

Catrin thought rapidly. She didn't really want to be seen with Ewan. To all intents and purposes it would be construed as perfectly innocent – there had been many occasions when they had gone off together on mill business. This was different. Something had altered between them. Catrin needed space to think about it. 'Perhaps not. I'll get there under my own steam and meet you on the quayside. I expect there'll be somewhere to park.'

'Fine. I'll ring them now. See you, Catrin.'

He sent her one of his rare smiles and left the office. Catrin watched his tall figure passing the window, put down the pile of mail she found herself still clutching, and sat up. She was gratifyingly aware of having become more focused. At lunchtime she'd ring Rissa and ask her what the heck she'd been playing at – or words to that effect. And immediately after work she would call in at Ty Coch and speak to Will.

Talk about a day of reckoning! Turning on the computer, Catrin switched her mind to work mode, starting with a letter to the firm dealing with the millwheel refurbishment, accepting their terms and telling them to go ahead.

The morning went by in the usual muddled way since the disaster, with stints of office work interspersed by sessions at the weaving loom. Since the workshops which normally comprised the bulk of Catrin's time were currently on hold, she was keeping her hand in by making some items for sale in the shop. She was now halfway through a throw in royal blue and white woollen, a copy as close as she could remember to the design she had seen in her dream. Privately, she dubbed it the 'Elin' pattern, and wondered about registering it under the name. Because the water wheel was still out of action, the loom was powered by electricity, an alternative which Ewan had cleverly had the foresight to include in his original blueprint.

The main building had now reopened to the public, and from time to time a party of tourists or holidaymakers would drift in to have a look around. This morning Catrin put on an impromptu weaving demonstration for a group of Americans, who marvelled long and loud at the quaintness of the mill and surroundings. The shop and café were also open for business, and when Catrin had a spare moment she made a point of going across to help Beth with the serving.

All in all the time passed quickly, and Catrin was surprised when she glanced at her watch to find it was after twelve. Before joining Ewan and the others for some lunch, she slipped down to the riverbank where it was private to ring Rissa on her mobile. She had no idea how she was going to broach the subject of the locket, and decided to play it by ear. Taking out her phone, she noticed a text message from Rissa requesting her to get in touch.

Foreboding shivered down Catrin's spine as she tapped out the number. Rissa answered immediately. 'Oh, Catrin! It's not good news I'm afraid. Dad … he died this morning.'

Catrin swallowed. She had never met Geoffrey Birch personally, but from what Rissa had told her he had sounded a kindly, generous man, good to his family and a fair and sympathetic employer to his staff. She knew how attached to him Rissa had been. Now he was gone.

'I'm very sorry,' she said quietly. 'You must be feeling pretty grim. Is there anything I can do?'

'Not really. It's nice just talking. It was quite peaceful at the end. He just slipped away.'

Catrin found she was clenching the phone so that her knuckles whitened. This was not just a friend she was speaking to but her half-sister. Suddenly she wanted to know more about Rissa's life. What had her stepfather looked like? Was he fair or dark, tall or short? She remembered Rissa mentioning he was a Cotswold man by birth. Did he speak with a gentle brogue, or had his years in business in the city ironed all that out?

Rissa was saying, 'Knowing Dad, everything will be in order. He'd already made it clear that everything comes to me.'

'I see,' Catrin said lamely. She hadn't been left badly off, then. In fact by most standards she was quite an heiress.

'The shops – there are three altogether – are all under management, so I don't have to worry too much on that score. Then there's this flat. Might sell it, actually. There are too many memories here and … and oh, Catrin! It was such a shock him going like that! Even when I saw him looking so poorly, I didn't expect this. He'd had these attacks before and recovered.' The tears that had probably been held in check started to flow, and it was a moment or two before Rissa could speak again. 'I'm sorry. It's just so awful.'

'You've got nothing to be sorry for. You're upset. It's natural.' Catrin badly wanted to comfort as a sister should, but how could she, when Rissa had no idea that she knew about their mutual background? Into the silence Catrin said, 'Look, I shouldn't worry about selling the flat and all that just yet, Rissa. Get the next days over with first. Will it be a big funeral?'

'Fairly. Not so much family, but Dad had a great many friends and business acquaintances. I've spent the morning ringing through the list.'

'Not easy.'

'No. Mike's been a big help. Mike Wilson, you know.'

'Oh, that Mike. I thought you'd split up.'

'We're still friends. Always will be. I guess we're more like brother and sister really. Marriage between us would never have worked. Anyway, Mike's seeing someone else. It looks serious and I'm glad for him. Dad ... Dad liked Mike very much, you know. He was really gutted when I broke it off. He used to say Mike was the son he'd never had.'

He never had a daughter either, Catrin thought. Not really. Child of his flesh and all that. What sort of a guy was it who would marry to give a girl's unborn child a name? Had there been money involved? According to her father, Rissa's mother came from a well-to-do family. Maybe at the time a generous handout was exactly what Geoffrey Birch needed to set up his photography business. It was an added bonus that the marriage had turned out well. Catrin wanted, desperately, to learn more about Rissa's mother. She'd been so vital and attractive; the photo in the locket bore testimony to that. And Dad – had Gabriella called him Llew, or had she used the more usual 'Taffy'? – had looked so happy. He thought at the time he loved her, he had said.

'Catrin, you still there?' Rissa's voice effectively brought Catrin back to the present.

'What? Oh sorry, Rissa. I was just thinking how alone you must feel.'

'Well of course,' Rissa replied snappishly.

'I mean ... it's hard to see how it must be when you're like me and surrounded by family and relations.'

'Consider yourself lucky. My mother's folks cut her off when she came to live over here. She had two brothers and probably loads of cousins, but I wouldn't know them if I fell over them.

Her closest family didn't even come to the funeral and we sent an invite.'

'Oh. Well. Since you mention it, Rissa ...' The conversation was getting awkward and Catrin grasped the straw eagerly. 'Perhaps you'd let me know when your father's funeral will be? I'm sure Mam will want to send flowers.'

'Sure. I'll speak to you again.' Rissa paused, then said haltingly, 'How's everyone else? Has Ewan heard any more over that nonsense with the millwheel?'

'Not yet. He's got an interview for a job in New Zealand.'

'Heavens! He doesn't let the grass grow, does he? You'll miss having him around at Capel Mair.'

'Yes, very much so. As for the rest, they're all fine.' Catrin remembered with a touch of hysteria what she was going to ring about. She could hardly bring up the subject now. 'Mam sends her love as always. Want me to tell Will what's happened?'

'If you wouldn't mind. Thanks, Catrin.'

'No problem. I'd better let you get on with your calls. 'Bye, Rissa – and take care.'

She rang off, and found she was shaking. That had to have been the most difficult conversation ever! The incident earlier with her father washed over her afresh. To think that all these years she had had a half-sister and never known! Poor old Dad, having to carry the secret around with him these past weeks. What a burden of guilt he must have felt. And all because of a passing interlude a long way back. Or had it been more than that? If he and Gabriella had had more time together, would their love have blossomed into something more lasting? Catrin would never know. She found it hard to visualize her father young and impulsive. To her he was just Dad – steady, unimaginative, wrapped up in his land and his stock.

Finding her appetite had deserted her, instead of returning to the mill and lunch with the others, Catrin wandered on along the river path a little way. At the bend in the river she sat down with her back to a sun-warmed rock and let her mind drift. The work on the wooden bridge was finished at last, the joiner with his hammering and loud radio gone. From here, the stillness of the old millwheel was very obvious in the silence. The restless churning of water and the creaking of the wooden buckets had become an integral background to the day. Catrin had not thought how much she missed it until now.

Lifting her face to the late August sun, Catrin closed her eyes. Immediately, Will's swarthy, good-looking image infringed. How was she going to tell him what was in her heart? Biting her lip, Catrin banished the picture and thought instead of dining out with Ewan. She recalled the night of the fire and Ewan holding her in his arms, comforting her. The embrace had stirred emotions other than mere comfort. She had felt so right there. Locked in his arms, the world and its hardships had swiftly receded. She remembered thinking – impossibly, shockingly – that this was perhaps the man for her. That together they could face whatever life chose to throw at them and survive. The moment of intimacy had never been repeated, and yet she had sometimes caught Ewan looking at her, as if he wanted to say something but could not – or would not – bring himself to voice the words. Inevitably perhaps, her mind returned to the mill and the unhappy clash with Heritage.

At her feet the river splashed and gurgled – at full spate after the heavy rain overnight. Slowly, some of her tension subsided. Time seemed to hang. But the noise of the water was still there, becoming even louder, more forceful. Somewhere, a baby was wailing, the sound carried thin and muted on the breeze.

*

'Hush now, *cariad*,' Marged murmured, settling herself more securely on the hard, narrow berth in the cabin and cuddling her little granddaughter to her. The baby hiccupped and gnawed fretfully at her small fist. 'Teething, you are. Nuisance from start to finish, those old teeth!'

All around, the creaking of boat's timbers and the battering of the wind grew louder. Picturing the angry, restless sea on the other side of the wooden wall, Marged prayed for a safe voyage. Home, the green valley and forested slopes and the stone-built mill into which they had put so much labour, now seemed a world apart. Ahead lay a new life, they hoped. There had been moments during the past week when Marged felt she was destined to be in this ship forever, sailing back and forth on the surging ocean with the baby locked in her arms.

The ship juddered again, fording the crest of a wave then dipping with a sickening lurch into the deep trough between the breakers. Spray hurtled against the tiny porthole window and crashed on to the deck above. From the neighbouring berths issued a series of long, low groans as less hardy travellers than herself wrestled with the throes of sea-sickness.

At least she had no problem with sailing, thought Marged, always one to look on the bright side. She wondered how the menfolk fared aloft. Anxious not to break too deeply into their small stash of money, they had splurged out only on a berth for herself and the baby. Marged worried about Hywel and his bad chest. He'd never been totally well in the long damp winters back home. God willing, the climate where they were heading might suit him better.

As if her thoughts had conjured him up, the narrow door to

the upper deck slid open and Hywel's face appeared at the top of the steep stairway. 'All right, Marged girl?'

'Yes indeed,' Marged replied, her voice raised above the noise of weather and tide. 'What about yourselves? Wet up there, is it?'

'Aye, and cold as charity too.' Despite the admission Hywel looked and sounded remarkably cheerful. 'John's anxious for the baby. Poor little mite. There's young she is to have to face a journey like this.'

'No choice, was there? Tell him she's keeping her feed down and doesn't seem bothered by anything worse than her teeth coming through. Poor man, he must feeling the responsibility hard. But he would have us come with him, so there it is.'

'True enough. I tell you, Marged, I'm looking forward to staking our claim in Australia. I've got my patterns and we've enough saved to get by. Together we'll build up a bigger and better mill than ever we had at the old country.'

Uplifted by her man's optimism, Marged smiled into the dimness of the cabin. They had a long way to go yet, but she wasn't going to dampen his spirits by pointing it out. In her arms the baby stirred, whimpering. 'Hush now,' Marged soothed. 'Quiet, little Sian. Quiet.' She started to croon a lullaby, a gentle little song, piercingly reminiscent of home.

Catrin's eyes flicked open. What was the name Marged had murmured? Sarah? Siriol? Sian! That was it. Sian Caradoc. And they had headed for Australia, of all places! Now at last she had something positive to help her with her research.

Always supposing the little party had arrived there, chimed an inner voice that could not be dismissed. Catrin pressed her fingertips to her throbbing forehead. She recalled the buck and judder of the boat and the crashing of the storm, and thought how fraught with danger the sea lanes had been. Many a ship must have perished, many a life been lost on those long, arduous crossings. To have come through safely, Catrin accepted that the brave little family's chances had boded slim indeed.

From the kitchen window Will saw Catrin's car pull up in the farmyard. Catrin never called on her way home from work unless it was something very urgent. One look at her set expression, and Will told his mother not to wait supper and went out to greet her.

'Hi Cattie.'

'Hi.' She slid out of the car, her long thick plait swinging over her shoulder, and reached for the lightweight shawl she had taken to wearing instead of the more conventional cardigans his mother favoured. She looked suddenly remote, a stranger, and a sense of unease rippled through Will. He had a fleeting vision of the old Cattie, before she became involved with the Capel Mair development, a laughing girl in jeans and skimpy top, her mane of black hair always flying loose about her shoulders. He swallowed. 'You coming in? Or what.'

'Wouldn't mind some fresh air, actually. I've been cooped in that poky office all afternoon. You wouldn't believe the correspondence that flits back and forth when something like this happens. With hindsight, Greg should have put in for a trained secretary. She'd have been a lot quicker than me.'

'They're lucky to have you to see to it,' Will grunted, wondering what all this was leading up to.

'Maybe. I'm not really fond of office work. Will I be glad when we're back to normal.' She paused, avoiding his searching glance. 'Are you busy, or can you spare a few moments? Let's walk over to the wood.'

Without another word Will fell into step. They crossed the small farmyard, clambered over the stile and walked across the spiky grass of the field towards a small copse of silvery hazel and rowan where they had played as children.

'So what's this all about?' Will asked as they entered the trees.

Catrin drew the shawl about her bare arms, more as protection against nipping insects than the coolness offered by the approach of evening. 'I take it Rissa hasn't been in touch.'

'Wouldn't know. I've been up in the hills for the best part of the day. Forgot to take my mobile. Why d'you ask?'

'Rissa texted me to ring her. It's not the best of news. Will, I'm afraid Geoffrey Birch didn't make it.'

Will came to an abrupt stop by a stand of prickly gorse. 'Heck. Poor Rissa.'

'Yes. Won't be easy for her, will it? She seems to be OK financially, so that's something.'

'She'll miss him. Very fond of her father she was.' They walked on, Will thoughtful, until they reached the trees.

'Slow down a bit,' Catrin said, panting. 'My head's thumping as it is. I sat down by the river at lunchtime and dozed off. It was only for ten minutes or so but I had this dream. Haven't mentioned them much before. They always leave me with a stonking headache.'

'Waking dreams you mean? Like Rissa's?'

'She told you? Heavens! Will, there's a fallen tree over there. Could we sit down? There's something I have to say. Something serious.'

Without argument Will took off his denim jacket and spread it on the crumbling bark of the dead rowan for her to sit. He remained standing, his face serious in the greenish shade of the trees. 'It's us, isn't it? You want to finish. You don't have to give reasons, Cattie. I've seen it coming for a while.'

'You have? I must say you've been more astute than me. But then I've been—'

'Occupied with other things,' Will finished for her. A mixture of emotions were surging through him. Sadness – they'd been Will and Cattie since high school days. A pressing apprehension for the future. What of the farm? Which way would it go now, without the injection of Brynteg's more productive acreage? This in turn brought a measure of guilt, though even as he chided himself for having mercenary thoughts, he knew his fears were not for himself alone. There was his mother to consider. She had set her heart on seeing her grandchildren raised at Ty Coch. It was yet another dream shattered.

And he still loved Catrin. He gazed at her, not speaking, all his hopes in ashes. But somewhere, beyond the darkness of anguish and disappointment and whole new set of worries, Will was aware of a faint glimmer of light. She was setting him free; whatever that implied. He could not give it his full consideration just yet. He'd have to wait until later, when he was on his own, and think it through.

'I'm sorry, Will.'

He saw she was handing him the ring he had given her. He took it without a word, stowing it away in his polo shirt pocket. He shrugged his sturdy shoulders. 'Not a lot I can do, is there? I'm sorry too but like I said, I've seen it coming.'

'Yes. Well. We'll have to tell everyone. Mam, Dad. Your Mum. Will, it's not going to be easy is it? Not for either of us.'

'These things rarely are. I guess we'll cope. You know where I am should you need me. Not that you will. There's a new Cattie appeared this summer. You've grown away from us all.'

She shook her head frowningly. 'I haven't. I'm still here. I'm not planning to go anywhere else, Will.'

'Well, we'll see. All I can say is I wish you the very best.

Don't let's talk any more, eh? It won't do any good. I'll walk you back to the house. Then I'd best tell Mam. Don't look so upset. Mam's tougher than you think. Her health's been better too, lately. She seemed to buck up a lot when Rissa was at the cottage. Funny, that.'

'Yes,' Catrin said, getting up. A breeze fluttered the leaves of the trees and she shivered slightly, pulling the lightweight shawl closer though it was not cold. In silence, they started off along the path they had walked many times together, leaving the little wood and crossing the field to Ty Coch. Below in the valley, the grey-blue slated rooftop of the bigger farmhouse glimmered in the evening light. And beside the boundary wall was the squat stone cottage that even given the briefness of occupancy, had come to be known with affection as Rissa's.

'Still speaking?' Will said as Catrin opened her car door and scrambled in.

She smiled faintly, nodding. 'Still speaking.' Then she fired the engine and drove out of the farmyard.

Will stood listening to the sound of the motor growing fainter. It struck him, suddenly and unexpectedly, that if he wanted to he could visit Rissa and help her through the difficult days ahead. Will thought he did want to, very much indeed.

Bron pulled the final article of clothing out of the washing machine, tossed it into the laundry basket and straightened, pushing back a greying-brown strand of hair from her damp forehead. It had turned close again. What with the weather, the mill dilemma and family problems, she was beginning to wonder where it would all end. On the flagged floor of the old scullery, the laundry was sorted into piles. Bron was filling the machine with the next load when Llew appeared in the doorway.

What now, Bron thought, having taken advantage of a free morning to deal with the hundred and one jobs about the house. Llew said, 'Will's outside. He's going off to London for a few days and wants me to keep an eye on things for him at Ty Coch.'

'Will's going to London?' Bron said. 'What for?'

'Bit of a break, I suppose. Seems he's got some idea of looking Rissa up while he's there.'

Bron snorted. 'I don't know what's got into everyone. Catrin breaking off the engagement, and now Will decides to go and look Rissa up. I thought Rissa already had a boyfriend. How many guys does she need at her beck and call?'

Llew made no reply. 'And another thing,' Bron went on. 'I'm sure Catrin's seeing someone else. Twice lately she's gone out all dressed up. I bet it's Ewan McInnes, and I can't help feeling there's heartache ahead. I like Ewan very much, but he's not the settling kind. Wasn't there some talk of him applying for work abroad?'

A look of the impatience that was all too familiar lately crossed her husband's face. 'I wouldn't know. Look Bron, Will's outside waiting to show me the works. Kate's bound to ask me in for a brew afterwards. Can't go into someone's house reeking of the cattle shed. I'd better change my working togs.'

'There's a clean boiler suit in the cupboard. Bring that one down with you, please Llew. It can go in the wash with the others.'

'Right-oh then,' Llew said, and vanished up the back stair.

Bron switched on the machine, picked up the basket of washing and went out into the steamy warmth of the early September day. Midges jigged in the long grass of the orchard as she pegged out the clothes. She could see Llew and Will taking the hillside with practised strides, talking as they went, and felt a tug of loss at the sight. She had done her best to support Catrin in her decision to end the relationship, but her sadness at the event was very real. Why were young people so restless these days? Perhaps they weren't. Perhaps it was just her getting older. She was aware of a change in her daughter, though. Catrin had grown up – and it wasn't only the recent short hairstyle and trendy clothes that made Bron realize it. There was a new maturity about her girl that made Bron fear she was growing away from them.

The air shimmered with heat, but over in the west storm clouds were forming. Hoping it would keep off long enough for the washing to dry, Bron headed back to the house.

Typically, Llew had not brought the mucky overalls down as she had asked, and sliding the big black kettle on to the hotplate of the Aga for a cup of tea, Bron went to fetch them. She was emptying the pockets of bits of binder twine and grease-smudged tissues, an eye on the boiling kettle, when something jingled in the top pocket. Assuming it was small change, she unfastened the tiny button – and drew out a rather attractive silver locket and chain.

Curious, her heart starting an uneasy tattoo, Bron opened the clasp and was confronted with her husband's much younger face. The other photo was of a girl; dark, incredibly pretty, love-light shining in her smile.

Realization hit Bron with a force like a physical blow. So that was it, the reason for Llew's recent surliness and long bouts of silence. Somehow, somewhere, he had met up with an old love. 'No,' Bron whispered, sitting down on a chair with a thump. Not Llew. This was something that happened to other couples, not to them.

Whatever should she do?

Chapter Nine

'Llew, we need to talk,' Bron said.

Standing with her back to the Aga, she aimed a pointed nod at the flowers he had given her – the third bunch that week. The pink carnations, probably picked up at the garage when he called for diesel and already wilting from being on the floor of the pick-up, she had put immediately in water. They now resided with the others on the kitchen windowsill. 'It's generally accepted that when a man starts showering his wife with flowers home it's a sign of a guilty conscience. So what is it, Llew? What are you trying to appease?'

For a moment Llew gaped at her as if he could not believe what he was hearing. And then his blunt outdoor face contorted, and he pulled out a chair and sat down on it heavily at the big square kitchen table. He looked so upset that Bron, despite the welter of doubts and insecurities that boiled within her, felt her heart go out to him.

'Well?' she said, hardening her resolve.

'Oh, sit down, woman,' Llew mumbled, tetchily rubbing a work-roughened hand across his chin. He had not yet shaved and the sound of callused flesh against overnight stubble rasped loud in the quiet. 'How can anyone have a proper conversation with someone standing over him like it was a court of law?'

Bron sat. Her heart had begun an uneasy thumping. 'It's to do with the locket, isn't it? I found it in your boiler-suit pocket when I was doing the washing. I don't know how it came to be in your possession, but at a guess the girl in the photo was an old flame and she's turned up again. Is that it?'

'No! Well, in a way. I mean … oh, damn it, Bron. You're partly right.' Dipping into his top pocket, Llew drew out the locket and chain and put it down on the table in front of him. 'The girl in there – Gabriella, she was called – was someone I met years ago in Malta when I was in the navy. We had a bit of a fling. She hasn't showed up again though. She couldn't. She's no longer living. Not that her reappearance would have meant anything to me anyway, not in that sense.'

'Wouldn't it?'

'No, of course not. You're my wife, Bron. I love you. We've got a good life here at Brynteg, the two of us. We've been happy – still are, I hope. This … interlude, if you like, is just one of those pesky hiccups that crops up in folks' lives when they're least expecting it. A ghost from the past come back to haunt.'

'Then let's exorcise it once and for all. Come on, Llew. Spill.'

'All right, all right, stop rushing me.' He drew in a long breath. 'You'd better brace yourself, Bron. I'm afraid you're in for a bit of a shock. The locket belongs to Rissa Birch. She dropped it by mistake on the yard when she was in a panic to get away when her father was taken badly. It was her mother's.'

He paused significantly. The essence of what Llew was trying to impart hit Bron with all the force of a physical blow. 'This Gabriella and you … Rissa's your daughter, isn't she? Oh, Llew!'

'I'm sorry. Bron love, I wouldn't wittingly spring this on you for anything. You'll have to take it on trust that what I say is the simple truth. Gabby and I were very young and yes, we were in love – or thought we were. I didn't know about the baby. The fact that she might have been pregnant never entered my head at the time. The first I knew of it was when I found the locket a few weeks back. Didn't take much to put two and two together. When you think about it, there is a strong family likeness in young Rissa. My guess is her mother told her who her real father was in one of those deathbed confessions, getting the slate clean and so on, and Rissa came out here with the intention of finding him. Well, she was bound to, wasn't she?'

With an effort Bron swallowed down a rising surge of hysteria in her throat. Rissa, Llew's daughter! Catrin's half-sister! It was a scenario that was impossible to take in, and yet the facts were there for all to see. Llew was right. Thinking about it, Rissa did have a strong look of the Jenkinses. Dear Lord, what a shock! What on earth would people say when word got out, as it surely would! What others thought had never been an issue with Bron before, but then nothing remotely like this had ever happened to her. 'Does Catrin know?' she asked in a strangled voice.

Llew nodded. 'Catrin suspected something was wrong and wouldn't rest until I told her. She's not as patient as her mother.'

"Tisn't that. I've been hiding my head in the sand. I knew there was a problem but I was afraid to confront it.'

'And now?'

'I'm not sure.' She looked her husband straight in the eye. 'Would you have married Gabriella if you had known she was pregnant with your child?'

'Yes,' he replied forthrightly. 'Attitudes were different in our day, you know that. I'd have done the right thing by her. Fact is, I wasn't made aware of it. Evidently Gabby's parents found out and took the matter into their own hands. They were well-to-do people, highly respected. With hindsight, any offer of marriage from me would have been shunned anyway. They wouldn't have had their precious daughter throw herself away on a common sailor lad! As it was I tried several times to contact Gabby, but it was useless. Suddenly she wasn't available. I thought she'd gone off me, found someone else, whatever. Then the ship left port and that was the end to it. I never saw Gabby again. Never gave her another thought. Until now.'

The past returning to haunt.

Some past, thought Bron shakily. She lowered her eyes and started to fidget with the rings she wore on her fingers, anything rather than meet Llew's pleading gaze. She knew she should try and deal with what she had just heard from a rational, liberated point of view. It wasn't so easy when it affected you personally. Badly wanting to patch things up between them, but still horribly shaken, she snatched a glance up at him and said, 'I suppose … since Rissa's gone back to London, and taking into account what's happened to her, losing her father and coming into this inheritance and so on, it's unlikely we'll see her again.'

'It's a thought. Bron, you know how deeply I care about you. Don't want this matter to come between us. Catrin felt … she said you'd understand. It all happened a long time ago, before you and I got serious. There's never been anyone since and there never will be.'

'No. Well. It's the shock. You think you know everything about the person you live with, and when something like this turns up it rather knocks you sideways.'

'It had me floored, I can tell you! To think after all these years ...' Llew shook his head at the sheer incredulity of it, then gazed with mute appeal at his wife's downcast head of greying-brown curls. 'Glad this is out at last, Bron girl. It's a relief. I'm just gutted to have been the cause of so much upset. Both in the past and now.'

'Well, it happened.' Bron locked her hands together in her lap and made herself face him. 'What will you do with the locket?'

He shrugged. 'Parcel it up and send it back to her, I reckon. I ... Bron, this may be hard for you to take but I don't want Rissa to disappear from the scene. She's my daughter. From what I saw of her she's a great girl. I want to get to know her better. Can you understand that?'

Bron bit her lip. She might have known Llew wouldn't have let the matter go. 'Some,' she said, hesitantly. 'Well, yes. Of course I can. It's really up to you, Llew. You'll need to write a letter of explanation anyway to send with the locket. Funny Rissa hasn't missed it. Maybe with all the upset it slipped her mind.'

'Could be. I'll do that, then.' Llew picked up the locket and, swivelling round in his chair, he dropped it with the motley collection of odds and ends in a large blue-patterned bowl on the dresser. 'It'll be fine there for now. Bron, you are all right?'

'Think so. Just got to come to terms.'

Llew held out his hands, and with a tremulous smile she put hers into them. The warm, familiar strength of his grip was reassuring and they sat on for a few moments longer, the long-cased clock on the wall ticking its slow rhythm, until the clamour of hooves on the yard heralded the last few trekkers of the season returning from their early-morning ride, and Bron was forced to release herself gently from her husband's hold and go out to attend to them.

*

Catrin stared at herself in her dressing-table mirror. So Dad's confession was out! Her mother was rather subdued and a bit edgy, but that was to be expected. And now Dad was faced with returning the locket, together with an accompanying letter. Where would it all end? Catrin suspected that letter writing of this nature would not come easily for Llew. He'd probably put it off, and the locket would sit in the willow-pattern bowl where he had dumped it until Mam nagged him into doing something about it.

She longed to see Rissa and come clean about what she knew. Contact between them had dwindled a little of late, but only because Rissa had flown to Malta to stop with her great-aunt for a while. There had been an unexpected letter from the long-estranged relative, expressing a wish to meet. Rissa had taken up the offer gladly. Catrin appreciated that the break would do Rissa good. There had been a couple of postcards with the usual scrawled messages. Rissa had put 'hope to see you when I get back at the end of the month'. Did that mean she was thinking of coming to Wales? To see Will, maybe? Catrin smiled faintly; she hadn't been blind to the chemistry between them, and Will was now a free man. She only wished her father would get his act together and send that all-important letter, then everything would be made clear and issues could move on.

Ewan's car pulling into the farmyard below jerked Catrin out of her reverie. She ran a comb through her short crop of hair – all part of her new image – and checked her make-up. They were going for a drive and would stop off at a pub for something to eat.

'Catrin?' trilled her mother's voice from below, where Bron was washing the Sunday lunch things with a lot of unnecessary clatter.

'Coming,' Catrin called back, and seizing her bag she ran thankfully down the stairs and out, glad of the chance to be away from the house and its uneasy atmosphere.

Hazy late October sunlight bathed the farmyard. Ewan greeted her cheerfully and soon they were heading out towards the coast. After the long dry summer, the autumn this year was particularly vibrant with colour. Woodland and forestry tore past in a blaze of russet and gold, and everywhere Catrin looked the mountain slopes were daubed with bronze and purple. It was very beautiful and unaccountably poignant. Snatching a glimpse of Ewan's clear-cut profile beside her, Catrin was clutched with a distinct uncanny need to hang on to every precious second of their time together. When at length they pulled in at Aberporth, where they could watch the sun sink into the sea in a blaze of molten crimson and amber, the reason behind the foreboding was made clear.

'I heard from the New Zealand company this morning,' Ewan said. 'They've offered me the job and I've accepted.'

Catrin's heart turned over. So he really was going. Up till now she had deluded herself into thinking he might pull out of the job that would take him so far away. She had not let herself contemplate how she might feel were he actually to go. Now, the hard facts hit her cruelly. She mightn't ever see him again.

For his sake she tried to muster some enthusiasm. 'That's wonderful. I'm pleased for you, Ewan.'

'You might sound a bit more as if you meant it!' He turned to look at her. He was smiling, a small quizzical smile. 'I shall miss you.'

'Truly?'

'Truly.' And that was all he said. It was something but it wasn't enough. Catrin knew the reason lay with herself. Having only just broken with Will, how could she be expected to embark on another serious relationship so soon? How could Ewan condone it?

'When ... do you expect to leave?' she asked in a low voice.

'As soon as the formalities are sorted. There's quite a lot involved as you can imagine, but it'll probably be the end of November sometime. My contract at Capel Mair ends next week so that gives me some space to get on with things. Did Greg mention Heritage were climbing down?'

'No! Really? Oh, Ewan, I'm glad for you.'

'Well, don't let's talk too soon. Nothing's been finalized as yet, but we hope this is a certain U-turn. It's all due to Greg. He's been totally unwavering ever since this clash with Heritage blew up. His ploy was to reject everything they flung at him, and it appears to have worked.'

'Come on! Heritage never had a leg to stand on in the first place. It was obvious you knew what you were doing with regard to the wheel workings. Plus the fact that you'd got dated copies of some the early correspondence over the fuss they made over the cost. Typical, the very ones you needed getting lost after the fire! I expect they were amongst the batch that got water damaged and had to be ditched.' Catrin frowned. 'I suppose the originals never turned up? The ones Heritage claim to have mislaid?'

'I wouldn't know. All I know is they're backing off.'

'And I should think so too!' Catrin said vehemently.

'Such faith!' He laughed at her gently. 'Let's go and eat, shall we?'

Ewan reached across and opened the door for her. His nearness brought a spasm that was almost painful. Fixing a smile, Catrin slid nimbly out of the car, waited while he activated the security system and locked up, then accompanied him into the hotel that specialized in the sea food they both enjoyed. Behind them on the horizon the sun vanished in a spectacular burst of dark vermillion, leaving a seascape leeched of all colour, and dusk crept slowly over sea and land.

Towards the end of November he was gone. And with him it seemed, the heady brilliance of autumn faded to the drab browns and greys of approaching winter. Their parting embrace had told Catrin just how much he thought of her. Ewan had kissed her as if he could not bear to let her go, a long, dizzying kiss that even now to recall it made Catrin weak with longing. He had written regularly, long missives describing his job, which he liked very much indeed. And as to the surroundings:

'Spectacular!' he wrote. 'Similar to Wales but vaster and grander. Weather good so far. Plenty of opportunities here for those willing to knuckle down and work – and the farming community are great. It's sheep and more sheep, but you'll know that. Met a Welshman the other day who reminded me of Llew. Similar age and so on. He'd brought his entire family out here to farm and set up a textile business using all their own resources. That's some enterprise, eh?'

She answered with newsy letters punctuated by little anecdotes about the mill, and always ended by sending him best wishes from everyone and telling him how much he was missed. Sometimes her writing struck a more personal note.

Llew, following various futile attempts at writing to Rissa, had finally managed it after being told sharply by Bron to 'just get on with it, Llew. Tell Rissa how you came by the locket and what you've assumed by it. Say we all hope to see her again at the farm and leave it at that. The ball's in her court then.'

Tired with the nagging that had gone on and being caught up in the middle, Catrin had longed to unburden herself to someone. Once the locket had been sent and the matter brought more into the open, Catrin felt justified in confiding some of the details to Ewan. She knew he could be relied upon not to spread the word, and somehow the shared confidence seemed to bring them closer. Ewan's response was typically philosophical and broad-thinking – having a half-sister tucked away in the Big Smoke was no unusual event these days. Rissa Birch had plenty about her, was a sister to be proud of, and did Catrin realize she now had the trigger behind the dreams?

Catrin had, but after the histrionics and drama of the past weeks, Ewan's reassurance and no-nonsense approach was heart-warming in the extreme.

Missing his solid presence that had steadied and cheered, Catrin did the only thing she could and flung herself into work, and even here there were drawbacks. With the school holidays over and the weather closing in, the tourist season had slackened off considerably. Come mid-December, the mill would be closed until spring. Greg was having workmen in to make a few improvements. Catrin planned to use the winter months weaving items for selling in the mill shop, and of course there was always the office work to be done.

With her days effectively sorted, there still remained the problem of how to fill her leisure time. The trekking season had ended, the ponies turned away on the hillside for a well-earned rest, so there was no solace to be had from that quarter. Each night as soon as her head touched the pillow, her thoughts went to Ewan and what they might have been to one another. The inner turmoil took its toll. Along came another dream.

Sian Caradoc sat at her spinning wheel in the cool shade of a white-painted veranda that ran the whole length of the big clapboard house. Trim, very upright, her thick dark-brown hair tucked away under a starched linen cap, she hummed tunefully to the rhythm of the wheel as her deft fingers fed the wool from spindle to bobbin.

All around, the air shimmered with heat. Birds squawked and fluttered in the stand of blue gum trees along the paddock fence. The distant bleating of many hundreds of sheep was so much a background noise as to be ignored.

The sudden galloping of approaching hooves brought Sian's head up, her hands stilling over the wheel. The rider pulled to a stop amidst a cloud of reddish dust.

'Father?' Sian greeted cheerfully. 'Hello there.'

Dismounting, John Caradoc – older, his head of thick black hair grizzled, his face burned a leathery brown by the sun – tied the horse to the rails and mounted the veranda steps. 'How's my girl, then? Busy as ever?'

'I'm well, Father. I like to keep occupied.'

He sat down on the wooden bench of the veranda, smiling at her. 'There's like your mother, you look. It does my heart good to see you. If your Gran and Grandda could only see you too.'

'Maybe they can,' Sian said simply. 'I put flowers on the grave earlier. I take some every day. They'll never be forgotten.'

'Nor should they be. Courageous, they were. It must have cost them dear to leave the old country, but they never complained, not once.'

'Wales,' Sian murmured, her snapping brown eyes going darker, remote. 'I can't imagine it, Father. Tell me again what it's like.'

'Oh, very different from here, *cariad*. Wales is green and lush, with rushing rivers and wild flowers growing everywhere. Springtime is what I miss most, I think. You get the snowdrops first. They were a favourite of your Mam's. You couldn't put a pin between them in the woods behind our home. Same with the primroses and the bluebells that come later. It's like a garden that goes on forever.'

'And the winters? The short dark days, the everlasting rain?' She eyed him mischievously. 'Was that good too?'

He laughed a little ruefully. 'Well, some things I don't miss.'

Sian went suddenly serious. 'Father, if you loved it so much, then why did you move away?'

John Caradoc's lean dark face tightened. 'I've told you before. There are opportunities in Australia you'd never get in the old country. We've done well here, there's no denying that. Two mills, a few thousand head of sheep, this house. Who'd have thought it of a simple village lad?'

'Will you go back one day, just to visit?' Sian persisted.

Her father shook his head. 'It isn't likely. The people closest to me will all be gone now. My main regret is never visiting your Mother's grave ever again. Pray God she'll forgive me.'

Sadness was in his voice. Sian said quickly, 'You carry her memory in your heart. That's what a woman cherishes most.'

'Is that right?' He paused, then said, 'Sian, there's something I want to speak to you about. You know the Whitelys up by the Ridge? Ralph Whitely has approached me for your hand in marriage.'

Sian pulled a face. 'That one! He's a bore. He talks of nothing but himself.'

'Oh, come on! Ralph's all right, hard working, reliable. The Whitely spread is well established. You'd not lack for luxuries. You could do worse than take a rancher for your man.'

'What reply did you give?' Sian said warily.

'I told him I'd see how you felt about the idea. You're not yet eighteen. There's plenty of time – though I'd be glad to see you settled and mistress of your own household. Your happiness and wellbeing means everything to me, Sian.'

'Then please, Father, don't push this marriage,' Sian said. She lifted her jaw stubbornly. 'I'm happy as I am. I like keeping house for you. My day is my own to organize. I'm free to go riding or to visit my friends, whichever I choose. As a wife I'd be more restricted. And anyway, I don't love Ralph,' she finished with a defiant toss of her head.

The action provoked a frown. 'You'll have to wed sometime,' her father said. 'You wouldn't want to die an old maid. Besides, this is no country for a woman alone. Think about it, Sian. You couldn't do better than Ralph Whitely....'

Catrin awoke to rain hammering against the window. Another wet Sunday, she thought sleepily. Already the dream was beginning to fragment and fade. Catrin burrowed down under the covers and shut her eyes tight, willing a return to dazzling heat and the song of unfamiliar birds in unfamiliar trees. It didn't come of course. Yawning, stretching, she flopped on to her back and stared up at the ceiling, pondering on what the dream had revealed.

For some reason, Sian Caradoc's childhood and early teens had been skipped by. Sian was all grown up and seemingly a bit of a miss! From what Catrin could remember of Elin Caradoc, Sian bore a marked resemblance to her dead mother. She was more sturdy, perhaps, not nearly as pretty, with a suggestion of her father in her firm chin and low brow.

Catrin's thoughts flew to Rissa. Had she experienced the same sort of dream? When the subject had last cropped up, Rissa had said that since coming home her dream sequences had become less well defined and were often muddled up with other dreams. They had agreed that bereavement and its resulting trauma might have accounted for that. And, Catrin had added silently, there existed the other obvious reason of blood contact.

What, Catrin wondered, had happened to the sparky Sian? Had she married this guy despite her reservations? What was his name? Whitefield? Whitton? No, Whitely, that was it. Ralph Whitely.

Greg, who as a winter pastime was looking into tracing his family tree, had mentioned a fantastic method of finding names from the past on the Internet. That weekend Catrin had brought home one of the office laptops to do a spot of work. Since it looked very much as if the rain was set in for the day, she might as well make the most of her chance and follow up Greg's lead, she decided. All her other research had ended in a blank, and the same could be said for Rissa. This might throw up something more positive.

It was afternoon before she got round to it. The lunch things were washed and put away. Mam had settled herself in front of the television set in the kitchen and was engrossed in a Thomas Hardy video. Dad was pottering about outside in the rain. Catrin had lit the fire in the front room earlier and the room with its deep inglenook and casement windows was warm and welcoming. Drawing the sofa closer to the crackling logs, she first she attended to the work for the mill. That done, she logged on to the address of the Mormon website that Greg had given her.

She was scrolling through pages and pages of Ws in her search for Whitely when her father entered the room, bringing with him the chill of the damp inhospitable outdoors.

'You're never still at it?' he said, coming to warm himself by the fire. He was looking better, his face more relaxed, his smile more spontaneous ... his deep-brown eyes perhaps still a little guarded. 'They'll work you to the bone at that place!'

'Hark at the pot calling the kettle black,' Catrin parried with a smile. 'I was actually looking something up on the Net. Fiddly things, these laptops. They cost a lot more than the ordinary computers and they come in very handy, but I know which I prefer. Oh, here's a Whitely. No Ralph though. Maybe I should try the Cs for Caradoc. Might have more luck there.'

'Caradoc?' said Llew. 'You don't need a computer for that. Caradoc was your great-great-grandmother's maiden name.'

'What?' Catrin gaped at him in astonishment, the laptop almost slipping from her knee. She rescued it hastily. 'Are you sure?'

'Of course I am. She was Anwen Caradoc before she became Anwen Jenkins.'

'Was she? I knew that I was named after her: Anwen, then Teresa after my great-grandmother and Catrin after Mam's mother. I was nick-named Cattie at school. Will still calls me that.' She paused, frustration and disappointment homing in. Trust the given name to be wrong, and just as she thought she might be getting somewhere. And then Llew said:

'She came here all the way from Australia. Western Australia, I think it was. Ran away from home – the story goes she was being pressed to marry someone she didn't care for and wanted out, though I don't know how true it is. Quite a romantic voyage it turned out for her. She met your Great-Great-Grandfather Jenkins on the ship, and married him within weeks of setting foot in Wales.'

'Really? Heavens! I never knew that.' This had to be it, the lead she was looking for. The Australian connection was too much of a coincidence for it not to be. At a guess, Sian changed her name and began using the new one when she embarked on her new life here. It wasn't unusual. People did that sort of thing.

'It was a happy union, by all account.' Llew looked at her curiously. 'What's sparked all this off, anyway?'

On the verge of confiding in him, Catrin held back. Maybe later, when she had properly checked this out. 'Oh, just interested,' she said, keeping her tone casual. 'Have you any idea where Mam keeps the photo albums? Not the family snaps. I'm talking about that big heavy hard-backed one with the early portraits in it. I used to giggle over them when I was small.'

'It'll be upstairs in that oak coffer on the landing with the other stuff. You might try the family Bible as well. Anwen'll be in there as sure as nines.'

'Right. That old Bible used to give me the creeps. All those names in spidery writing. People long dead and gone. Spooky! Bit like the Touchstone!'

'Well, you're not the first to be spooked by that, nor the last.'

'No, I suppose not. '

'Do you know anything about Anwen?'

'She was said to have had the sight.'

It got deeper. Catrin's throat went dry.

'She'd cut herself off from everyone when she left home, by all account. There's no knowing what might have been behind it. Could be that her old man had arrived in the country via a convict ship. That's how many turned up in Australia. Happen she found out and didn't like the association. Must have been a rum place in very early times. Wonderful country nowadays, of course. Plenty of opportunities there. Isn't it Australia where McInnes has gone to?'

'No. Ewan's in New Zealand,' Catrin said in a low voice.

'Now there's a country I've always wanted to visit,' Llew went on, quite unaware how the drift of conversation had affected his daughter. 'Good and rural. Not overcrowded. Bit like here, only with a better climate, and possibly more going for it on the work front. Heard anything from him since he went?'

'Oh yes. He loves the job – and the place.'

'There you are, then. What did I tell you? If I had my time over again....'

Catrin dragged her thoughts back to the matter in hand. If her Great-Great-Grandmother Anwen alias Sian did turn out to be the Caradoc she was after, that made John Caradoc of Rebeccaite fame her great-great-great-grandfather! But why the big fall out? In the dream, father and daughter had appeared the best of friends. One could easily have imagined Sian twiddling her father round her little finger. And John Caradoc hadn't seemed the sort to bulldoze his daughter into an unwanted marriage. Perhaps she had simply wanted to seek her roots, and her father had resisted. Not surprisingly, when you considered his background.

'Was Anwen into spinning?' Catrin asked.

'I should say so. Weaving too. Well, all the women spun and wove in those days. There's some family stuff up in the attic. Some of it may be Anwen's work – where are you going?'

'Where d'you think?' Catrin had flung aside the laptop and was already halfway to the door. 'I'm going up to look.'

'Well switch off that contraption first, can't you? And don't be disappointed if the moths have had a bean-feast up there. Or the mice.'

They hadn't. Bron had made an excellent job of storage. A strong smell of camphor issued from the iron-banded wooden sea-chest when it was opened. Wonderingly Catrin lifted out the collection of shawls, quilts and coverlets that her great-great-grandmother had made during her long life here at Brynteg. None of them was what she sought, and a crushing disappointment overwhelmed her.

Right at the bottom of the chest were a few oddments of woven cloth. Without much hope, Catrin inspected them. And there, staring her in the face, was what looked like the subtle blue and white arrangement of Elin's wedding ring design. Worn and faded with the years, it was nothing much to go on. But it was enough.

Eagerly Catrin held it up to the light to study the weave for the part that had so eluded her. She had it at once; an extra small yet significant loop that linked the larger circles and made all the difference to the overall pattern. Excitement shot through her. This was it. The very design Hywel and Marged Rees had perpetuated in honour of their dead daughter.

Whisking through her mind went a range of soft furnishing in this eye-catching pattern. Not only would the 'Elin' design keep the weaver's memory alive, it could also be the boost required to lift Capel Mair out of the chancy realm of local craft and set it on the more lucrative road to commercialism. Tomorrow, she'd make a graph of the pattern and approach Greg with her idea.

Putting the rest of the things back into the chest, Catrin picked up the scrap of cloth and descended the steep flight of attic stairs to the landing, where a large carved black-oak coffer had stood ever since she could remember. In the family Bible, she ran a fingertip down the confusingly long list of names. And there it was; Sian Anwen Caradoc, the marriage to Llewelyn David Jenkins recorded in the slanting copperplate in faded violet-coloured ink that had so freaked her as a child. Her death many decades later was also recorded. Here the name Sian was omitted, as if time had erased that earlier person for good.

The musty stiff-backed photograph albums did not yield up their secrets quite so easily. Very few of the portraits of bewhiskered men and lace-capped women bore the posers' names. Catrin stopped at a sepia print of a young woman that most bore a resemblance to the now hazy recollection of the character in her dream. The woman wore a high-necked blouse with ruffles and pin-tucks. Her hair, puffed and curled on to the low brow, was bound up on the top of her head. The long, long exposure had put a glazed expression on the face that would have been animated. Catrin slipped the stiff-backed photograph out of the cardboard inset, and there on the back was written in faded blue ink was the name S A Caradoc. Probably taken as a betrothal study, this had to be the proof Catrin needed.

Her first thought was to ring Rissa and tell her what she had discovered. Rissa would be as delighted as she was. But then Catrin remembered that Rissa was still out of the country. It would have to wait until she got back.

Catrin slipped the photograph back into its sleeve and put the album away. Shivering on the chilly landing, she tucked the piece of woven cloth into her pocket and went back to the warmth of the sitting room and her computer.

'Sorry, Mam,' Will said, pushing aside his half-eaten dinner. 'Not all that hungry.'

Without a word Kate took the plate out to the lobby and scraped the meal she had taken such pains to prepare into the pig bin with the rest of the scraps. She poured tea into thick blue mugs, handing her son his and sitting down opposite him at the chipped Formica table. Considering her recent spate of ill-health, her movements were encouragingly brisk and purposeful. A new doctor to the local practice had changed the medication she had been taking for a suspected heart problem and the results were startling. Kate looked less tired, less world-weary, more the Kate she used to be before the growing problems over Ty Coch had started to get her down.

'Will, what's wrong?' she asked. 'Is it Catrin? You haven't been yourself since you two called it off.'

'Well, what do you expect?' Will replied edgily. 'Doesn't do much for the ego, being told you're no longer the shining light in someone's life, does it?'

'Naturally not. You and Catrin are still friends, though. Maybe she just wanted some space. Perhaps she'll see differently in a little while.'

'Cattie won't, and nor shall I. Don't get me wrong, Mam, but in some ways the split came as a relief. I'd seen it coming for quite some time. I would have said something myself to Cattie before now, but the thought of the knock-on effect it would have kept putting me off. Marrying Cattie wasn't only about the two of us starting life together, was it? It was about the joining of the two farms as well. That's fact and there's no getting away from it. Our breaking up has affected others, yourself in particular.'

Kate made a gesture of resignation with her hands. 'It's as it is.'

'Think I was waiting for a miracle that would save the farm. Ty Coch can't be run as a viable business for much longer. It needs a golden handshake at the very least. If I could afford to do up the milking parlour and go back into dairying, turn us back into a mixed farm again, we might stand a chance. There's a lot to be said these days for not specializing. Trouble is, the grants that used to be available for diversifying are no longer forthcoming.'

'What about the sheep you brought in for the fleeces?'

'That was a good move. As you know, these things take time

to establish. I'm not sure if Ty Coch has got that much time left.' Will drank deeply of his tea. 'It's not only the farm. It's me as well. I can't seem to settle to anything lately.'

Kate shot him a knowing look. 'You've been unsettled ever since you went to London. It wouldn't have anything to do with Rissa Birch?'

Will choked over his tea. 'We've kept in touch, yes. That reminds me. Rissa rang last night from Malta. Apparently she's mislaid a locket that belonged to her mother. It meant a lot to her, naturally. She wondered if she'd lost it in the cottage and wanted me to go and check.'

'A locket? I haven't seen one. I've gone to the cottage every week to dust and air the place. If it had been there I would have come across it,' Kate said.

'Of course you would.' Will paused, wrinkling his brow in thought. 'I'm sure I've seen something of the sort somewhere. Just can't think where....' He rammed his fist suddenly on to the table top, clattering the pots. 'Got it! It was at Brynteg. I'd called for a key to the cottage. I'd forgotten mine and remembered Bron keeps a spare in that blue bowl on the kitchen dresser. There was this heavy silver-type pendant and chain in the bowl with some other bits and pieces. I remember thinking it looked valuable and what a naff place it was to leave it. I bet that's what Rissa was going on about.'

'Goodness. You'd better get down there, Will, and speak to them.'

Will, thinking how pleased Rissa would be to have the problem solved, was already on his way.

He caught Catrin in the farmyard, about to get into her car. She looked excited, fired up over something. Her eyes were bright, her cheeks flushed. She flashed him a brilliant smile. 'Hi, Will.'

'Hi. You off to the mill? I thought it was closed for the winter.'

'You're right, but I'm working on a new design and you know how it is. I can't keep away. It's rather important and terribly complicated. Was it Dad you wanted?'

'Not especially.' Will told her about the locket.

'Yes, it was Rissa's,' Catrin said, nodding. 'I thought Dad had returned it. Maybe he's waiting till after she gets home from Malta at the weekend. Um ... Will.'

'Yes?'

'Why not go and see Rissa when she gets back? She ... well, I've a feeling she might need you. She'll certainly be glad to see you. Think about it, eh?'

She jumped into the car and drove off, leaving Will standing staring after her. Go to London and see Rissa? There was nothing he'd like more!

Rissa read the letter yet again. It had arrived that morning by registered mail, together with a small package with a West Wales postmark. Even before she opened it she knew what it contained. Recalling Will and the pleasure in his voice when he had relayed the good news that the missing item was found, she smiled mistily as her fingers dealt with the packaging. The locket now lay on the polished mahogany table in front of her. It was a relief to have it back. She had clipped it open to peer at the familiar faces in the photographs, wondering how Llew had felt when he first set eyes on them.

Frowning in concentration, she skimmed over the letter again and tried to read between the lines. It was very abrupt and rather stilted, not at all reminiscent of Llew's usual rumbling eloquence that often held a spark of humour.

She thought of him, kindly, hospitable, with the quiet dignity of the true countryman – but a farmer when all was said and done. It was a mode of life not always compatible with putting pen to paper. For such as he, the letter would not have been the easiest to write.

It contained, more or less, an account of how he and her mother had met. He kept pointing out how young and green he was, making it sound as if he were making excuses though Rissa was sure this was not the case. He explained how he had not known about the baby and then gone on to apologize. If this was how it happened then why say sorry, for pity's sake! At this point Rissa had begun to get irritated. And yet reading on, it became obvious that Llew really cared about her and was anxious to assure her of this. He wanted to know more about her and asked about her life as a child and if her mother had been happy living in England.

Rissa had to wonder at how many attempts there been at writing the missive before Llew had one that finally satisfied. Quite a few, she decided. And that would account for the ponderous drift. Scribbled along the bottom of the last page was a message that went straight to her heart.

'I always thought what a grand girl you were, Rissa. We all agree how greatly you resemble my side of the family. I'm proud to claim you as mine, and I hope to see a lot more of you in the future.'

He had signed himself formally Llewellyn Carter Jenkins. And then in brackets, that wicked humour winning through, 'Taffy.'

Tears gathered and the words blurred suddenly before her eyes. He cared about her. They all did. She wasn't alone in the world at all. The stay with her relative in Malta had been pleasant and rewarding, but Rissa had not felt the closeness that she had expected. This was something different. No wonder she had been so at home at the Ty Coch cottage. It was where she belonged.

The phone ringing abruptly made her start. Snuffling back the tears, Rissa picked up the receiver. 'Hi, Rissa,' said Will's voice.

'Will!' Her heart turned over. 'Oh, Will! I'm so glad it's you. Listen, I've had this letter from Llew and—'

'Save telling me till later. I'm coming down to London.'

'You are? Oh – wow! When do you expect to get here?'

'Soon as possible. Just got one or two things to sort out here first, then throw a few things into a bag, get cleaned up—'

'You can come as you are for all I care.'

'Don't think so. Not after a day with the sheep. Better run the hose over the vehicle as well. And Rissa?'

'Yes?'

'Nothing. It's best I tell you to your face. Can't wait to see you again.'

'Me neither. Love to Kate. 'Bye-ee.'

He'd already rung off. She pictured him in his farming boiler suit, organizing the care of the animals, hurrying indoors and telling his mother. Kate fussing, making sandwiches and a thermos of coffee for the journey....

Rissa hugged herself in glee. He was really, really coming, and to judge by his voice there was only one thing he wanted to tell her! Suddenly weak at the knees, Rissa flopped down on one of the big squashy sofas and gave herself up to blissful daydreams. She had only yesterday returned from Malta. Her bags still stood unpacked in her bedroom. She should really go and sort them out but instead she sat on, thinking of Will, knowing it was going to be all right.

It was very warm in the room with the heating full on. Lights twinkled beyond the window as the short winter's day thickened to dusk. Despite the comfort and the joyful anticipation, a shiver ran unexpectedly through Rissa. She bit her lip, frowning, wondering what it was. Then she shrugged. She was bombed out with travelling, that was all. Flying always did knock her up. A long soak in the bath would sort her out.

Getting up, she went to run the water, adding her favourite herbal essence. Afterwards, refreshed, she got into casual jeans and a soft pale pink mohair jumper. Gladly, she fastened the locket around her neck. She was brushing her hair when the doorbell rang. She rushed to answer its summons. 'Will! Oh, Will!' She flung herself into his arms.

'Hey! What a welcome!' Will stepped inside, pushed the door shut with his foot and gathering Rissa to him he tilted her face to his and pressed a long, tender kiss on her lips. 'Hi there,' he said, when they both finally surfaced. 'D'you know, all the way here I've been rehearsing what I was going to say, so I may as well say it.'

'Go on, then.'

'Rissa, I love you. I know it's a lot to ask, expecting you to leave all this ... this luxury, but ... d'you think you could bring yourself to be the wife of a struggling farmer?'

'Oh Will!' Rissa's face glowed. 'There's nothing I'd like better!'

'Love me?'

She nodded furiously, her eyes shining. 'Right from the word go, I think. Only there was Catrin and—'

'I know. That's all over now. Come here.'

This time the kisses went on for much longer, whilst outside the busy London scene took on its night-time face. 'We must go out and celebrate,' Will said at last. 'Tomorrow we'll choose a ring, yeah?'

'A meal will do for starters. I'm suddenly starving. And Will, there's loads I've got to tell you but it'll wait till we eat. Remember that wine bar we went to when you were here before? Let's see if we can get a table.'

'Fine by me,' Will said.

Over the meal Rissa told Will about the locket and its circumstances. She told him about the dreams. Thoughtfully Will questioned and encouraged, as if he were trying very hard to put himself in her place.

'You don't think I'm off my head?' she asked him tentatively when she had finished.

He reached across the table and squeezed her hand. 'No way. I used to wonder about Cattie. She'd never have owned up to me if I'd asked her, she'd have been too scared of a ribbing. What it boils down to is that you and Cattie have both got the Sight. Meeting up was the trigger – it'd be the blood tie. What I'm wondering is what the dreams are leading up to?'

'Come again?'

'Oh, I don't know. Mam's more into this sort of thing than I am. I think she'd say that waking dreams can be a form of prediction.'

Rissa stared at him, foreboding trickling down her spine. She remembered the same feeling earlier, as if a dark cloud hovered.

Will fixed her with his warm brown gaze and immediately the feeling receded. 'It's getting late,' he said. 'Let's go, eh?'

Later that night, the dream started. There was an explosion of flame and billowing clouds of thick black smoke. She was trapped. The choking heat was getting to her. She had to get help. Through the leaping tongues of fire and dense screen of smoke she searched for Caradoc, for Elin, anyone! They weren't there. In their place, screaming for help, was her own sister!

'Catrin!' Rissa bolted up in the bed. It was Catrin she was dreaming about. There was a fire and Catrin was in danger.

She had to get back. *Now*!

Chapter Ten

The journey out of the centre of London had been agonizingly slow, with traffic lights and roundabouts and the never-ceasing surge of city traffic holding them up, even though it was still the middle of a dismally wet winter's night. Once they had turned on to the M4, however, the going was decidedly better. Will put his foot down, pushing the four-by-four as it had never been used in all the time he had owned it.

'I never thought when I was driving down I'd be on my way back again within hours,' he said, darting Rissa a sideways glance, smiling a little. 'Hope this doesn't turn out to be a wild goose chase.'

'It won't be. I'll take over if you like. Give you a break.'

'No, it's OK. Want to pull in at Services? Give you a chance to try Brynteg again.'

They had rung before leaving, but had received no reply. They tried getting Catrin and her parents on their respective mobile phones. Neither one seemed to be working. 'I can't understand it,' Rissa said. 'Catrin was paranoid about having her mobile on her. And in my limited experience it was unlikely for Bron and Llew ever to leave the farm unattended for any length of time.'

'It was only just after midnight when we tried them. Bron

and Llew could have gone to Cardiff to the theatre. Andrea Bocelli's there on tour. Bron's a big fan.'

'Is she? Cardiff's a long way to go to see a show.'

'Llew could have got tickets as a surprise. He's done it before when there's been something special on. He's a country and western buff. He dragged Bron down there for a gig once. She wasn't impressed.'

'Can imagine.'

They exchanged a brief smile. Classics v lighter stuff was always a lively subject for debate at the farm. 'Wish we could have got hold of them,' Rissa said on a sigh. 'Dratted mobiles. They never work when you most need them.'

'Llew's always mislaying his. It could have been trilling away in the barn for all we know. Funny Catrin doesn't answer hers, though.'

There was a silence. Both stared ahead at the long ribbon of road. It had begun to rain heavily again. Will flicked on the wipers and dropped his speed slightly. He said, 'Cattie was on her way to the mill when I saw her last. She seemed excited. I think she'd had some idea about a special weave specific to Capel Mair – the way they did in the old days.'

'It'd be the wedding ring motif. Catrin did something similar for her finals at college. Then she saw it in the dream, only it was slightly different. It really bugged her, not knowing what it was. She was determined to get to the bottom of it.'

'That must have been it, then. Knowing Cattie, she'll be weaving the biggest blanket the loom can take! Maybe she was on her way home from the mill when we rang. She could have been working late.'

'In that case I wish now we'd gone ahead and rung Greg and Beth.'

'In the middle of the night? Get a grip, Rissa! What would

you have said to them? I've had this nightmare and wondered if the mill was on fire? Greg would think you'd truly lost it!'

'Kate, then. She might be able to throw some light as to where Llew and Bron have disappeared to. Let's pull in at the next Services and ring her.'

'No way. Mam'd be worried out of her mind. Don't want her poorly again. She's been so much better lately and that's how I'd rather keep it. Rain seems to be easing off a bit. Another couple of hours should see us at Carmarthen. Let's go for it, eh?'

They sped on in silence. Will was aware of Rissa falling into a doze beside him, her head resting comfortably against his shoulder. He could feel her warmth, smell the light flowery perfume she always wore, and despite the current anxiety his heart glowed to think she was his.

Reaching their exit at last, they left the motorway behind and Will sent the vehicle bowling along the familiar roads of home that dipped and soared through deep, tree-clad valleys that swam here and there with drenching mist. Rissa woke, stretching, peering out at dark, damp countryside. 'It looks different now it's winter,' she said. 'Sort of lost and mysterious. Oh, it's great to be back. I only wish it was in better circumstances.'

The headlamps picked up the road sign for the village of Capel Mair. 'Where first?' Will asked, turning off.

'The mill. Is this the right road?'

Will nodded. 'Short cut. Takes you through the forest and comes out on the other side of the bridge. Hope the river isn't up with all this rain. It's been a wet winter so far, but that's nothing new. Here's the forest road now.'

They sped through the blackness of trees. Rissa found she was holding her breath, expecting at any moment to catch the sudden horrifying sight of buildings gone up in flames through the lacework of branches. When they reached the mill though, all was intact and serene under a watery sky. The Marriotts' cottage was in darkness. Its white-painted walls and those of the mill and the barn accommodation glinted eerily in the misty darkness. Hanging mute for the winter months, the mill wheel was still and silent, with only the surging of the river and the endless pattering of rain to shake the peace.

'There was a fire!' Rissa hissed, defiant. 'It wasn't imagination.'

'No.' Doubt, for the first time, crept into Will's voice. 'Want to knock Greg up, ask him if there's been any trouble?'

'At five in the morning? Like you said before, he'd throw a wobbler. Let's go on to Brynteg. And drive slowly so I can have a proper look around. Mind if I keep the window down?'

'Of course not,' Will said, letting off the brake.

It was a three mile run from the mill to the farm, the road criss-crossing several times over the river via narrow stone bridges. At one point the road took a particularly sharp bend. They were right in the valley bottom now and the river, charged and querulous, overflowed its banks and formed a shallow lake across the way ahead. Driving cautiously through it, snatching quick glances to the left and right, Will forded the bridge and took the bend with the ease born of familiarity. The smell of burning metal and rubber reached both of them at once.

'Stop!' Rissa gasped, fumbling with her seat belt. 'Look! Over there in the bushes! Oh my God!'

Will yanked the car to a halt with a screech of brakes, leaving the headlamps directed at where Rissa indicated. 'Grab the torch. It's under the seat. Christ!'

Spears of rain lanced the yellow beams of light as they

jumped out, raced across the road and went plunging into the sodden undergrowth, the twiggy boughs catching and tearing their clothes, the ground soggy beneath their trampling feet. A short way into a small copse of trees, Catrin's blue Fiesta lay on its side, a barely recognizable burnt-out wreck, the metalwork still smouldering pungently in the cold wet air. 'Oh no!' Rissa whispered, clutching Will's arm. 'She's not … she can't be—'

'C … Cattie?' choked Will, equally stunned. Then louder in anguish. 'Cat … tie!'

His cry echoed, loud, impotent. Rissa gazed at the scene in horror. 'We … we'd better phone for the police. Will, I don't believe this. I just can't. Catrin can't be hurt. I'd *know* if she was. I'd get the vibes and – listen! What was that?'

'What?' Will shook off her restraining hand. 'I didn't hear anything.'

'I did. A sort of groaning. Shush a moment. There it is again.'

Faintly through the slap and drip of rain and roar of white water came a small yet distinct cry for help. 'It came from those rocks over there,' Rissa gasped, pointing. 'Catrin! Where are you? Hang on! We're coming.'

Calling, training the torch this way and that, they went pushing through the undergrowth in the opposite direction to the river. And there, huddled into the cleft of a rocky outcrop, wrapped up in what appeared to be a vast woven throw, the circlet of light picked up the huddled form of Catrin.

Will dropped to his knees beside her 'Cattie! Cattie, are you all right? What the blazes happened?'

Rissa bent over her, hands gently searching for sign of serious injury. 'Catrin, are you hurting anywhere?'

'Don't think so,' replied Catrin feebly. A deep cut on her ear was oozing ominously. Her knuckles that showed outside the woven cloth were skinned. 'Just … only scratches I think. Been here ages. There was a flood. Car went off the road. Couldn't control it. Managed to crawl out of the window and … it went up in flames. Oh, am I glad to see you….' Her voice wobbled to a stop.

'She's fainted,' Rissa said.

Will was already phoning for an ambulance. That done, he took off his quilted all-weather jacket and laid it gently over Catrin's still form. 'We'd best not try and move her. Heck, she feels cold. There's a rug in the car. I'll fetch it. Ambulance has got to come all the way from Carmarthen. It'll be a good twenty minutes yet. Christ, hope she's going to be all right.'

'She will be – now,' Rissa said. 'You might bring my coat for her as well. Drat this rain. She's getting soaked.' Wonderingly she fingered the patterned throw that Catrin had evidently had the foresight to drag out of the car with her. Woven in a pure woollen, it was thick and warm and had clearly saved the wearer from an untimely end. Darkened now with the wet, the blue and white motif was still discernable.

'The wedding ring pattern,' Rissa murmured. 'Well!'

Impatiently they waited, crouched close to Catrin to keep her warm, until flashing blue light and the strident blare of a siren heralded the approach of help. In record time the patient was borne away, and Will was phoning Brynteg to find its incumbents there at last and to inform them what had happened. After that, for Rissa, the rest of the night passed pretty much in a blur. She managed to bear up long enough to greet a very shell-shocked Llew and Bron in the accident and emergency unit at the sprawling hospital complex on the edge of the town, and to learn gratefully that apart from cuts and bruises and the obvious shock Catrin was unharmed, and then she seemed to fall apart and couldn't stem the tears that fell.

'Bed for you, my girl,' said Bron firmly. 'What a night! I shall never be able to hear Andrea again without being reminded!'

'Oh well, let's be thankful it wasn't any worse news.' Llew looked from Rissa to Will and shook his head. 'What you two were doing here at all defeats me. I thought you'd gone to London, Will.'

'Long story,' said Will. He and Rissa exchanged a telling glance.

'Oh, right.' Llew placed an arm protectively about each of his womenfolk's shoulders. 'Come on, you two. Let's go home.'

'Catrin's been in an accident, you say?' Ewan's voice came shocked and disbelieving over the many thousands of miles. 'Is she all right?'

'She actually seems fine,' Rissa said. 'We've just got back from the hospital. She was in a bit of a state last night when we found her, naturally. I didn't want to ring you until I'd seen her again.' They had found Catrin sitting up in bed, pale, battered, but smiling. 'No broken bones or other damage. She'd cut her head so she's got a few stitches, that's why they're keeping her in under observation for a day or two. Otherwise ... well, she's been lucky. You should see the car. It's a write-off.'

'I must send her some flowers. Have you got Catrin's hospital address?'

Rissa gave it to him and went on to explain how they had come across Catrin in the first place.

'The dreams,' Ewan said, a weight of understanding in his tone.

'I take it you knew about them. I suppose Catrin must have mentioned the wedding ring pattern?'

'Once or twice.' Now he was assured of Catrin's safety the wry humour so typical of him was back. 'So she owes her life to this plaid she wove. Ah.'

'What's that supposed to mean?'

'Well, there are those that have it that some waking dreams, as they're called, can be a form of premonition.'

'Will said as much and Kate agrees. Her theory is that the past reached out to form a link with the present in order to save Catrin's life. Seems hardly credible.'

'Oh, I don't know. Just accept it for what it is. This call's costing you a fortune, by the way. Want me to ring you back?'

'No, it's OK. I'm only too glad to have got in touch. Had to wheedle your number out of Catrin. She didn't want me to ring you. Said she was going to write and tell you what happened. But ... you know. In her situation I don't think I'd feel up to writing letters just yet.'

'Quite. Thanks for everything, Rissa. I appreciate it.' He paused. 'Tell me to push off if you like, but am I right in assuming that you and Will are an item?'

'Well actually ...' Rissa peered round the Brynteg kitchen to see if anyone was within earshot. Bron, giving a repeat performance of the Andrea concert in her passable soprano, issued from the utility room where she was loading the washing machine. Llew had changed into his working clothes the moment they had arrived back from Carmarthen and gone out to do the milking. No one was around to hear, but Rissa dropped her voice all the same. 'Will and I are getting married. We haven't announced it yet so keep it under your hat, eh?'

'Sure,' Ewan said. 'And many, many congratulations. I hope you'll both be very happy. Have you set the date?'

'Not yet. We're not hanging about. No point.'

'You sound very sure. That's great. Wish I wasn't so far away, then I could claim a congratulatory kiss!'

Laughing, Rissa said her goodbyes. She could hardly believe

her good fortune. Everything was working out splendidly. Her only sadness was that the man she had always known as her father was no longer here to share her joy. Then again, maybe he was. At one time she would have shunned any such notion as fanciful, but after what had happened since had come to Capel Mair last summer, she was prepared to keep an open mind on the matter.

Will's mother was the first to be told of the engagement.

'Oh, my, how wonderful!' Kate cried, kissing them both ecstatically. 'I wish you both every happiness.'

'Thank you,' Rissa said, beaming. 'We wanted you to know first. Then later on, when we go with Llew and Bron to visit Catrin again, we'll let them in on the news as well.'

'We should really go into town and buy a ring,' said Will. 'I want to do this properly. 'Tisn't an engagement without a ring.'

'Of course it is. We're promised, aren't we? I'd rather put all the pennies we can muster into the farm, to be honest.'

Will looked unconvinced. They talked on, Will persuading, Rissa laughingly sticking to her views. Neither of them noticed Kate getting up from her easy chair by the living room fire and going upstairs. Coming back, she dropped a small old-fashioned ring-box on to the coffee table in front of them. 'This was my grandmother's. She gave it to my mother on her engagement who in turn gave it to me. John and I never had a daughter and I'd thought the tradition to be ended but ... well, I'd like you to have it, Rissa. It's up to the two of you of course. If you'd rather go for a new ring, then I quite understand.'

She sent them both a smile and quietly left the room. Will opened the box. Inside was a sapphire and opal Victorian engagement ring in an ornate rose gold and platinum setting. A shaft of sunlight glancing in from the sash window struck blue fire off the central gem and set the tiny opals gleaming.

'O … oh!' Rissa swallowed, gazing mistily at Will as very solemnly he slipped the ring on her finger. 'Oh, Will, it's the most beautiful thing I've ever owned.'

It was a near perfect fit. Will stood up and pulled Rissa into his arms. There was no need for words. For a moment they stood clasped closely in the beamed and flagged room of the old farmhouse for which they had such plans, happily looking forward to the future, while the clock ticked away the minutes and Kate's little black cat purred in noisy contentment before the crackling wood fire.

Much later, after their return from the hospital, the champagne Will had taken with them consumed to the very last bubble, warmest best wishes still ringing in her ears, Llew drew Rissa to one side.

'Rissa girl. I'm not much one for speeches. You'll know that from my letter. Want you to know how proud we are to have you back with us. It's not been an easy time for any of us, but I thought Catrin seemed as pleased as anyone over the news. It would never have worked between her and Will. They're too much like brother and sister.'

'Kate said that too.'

'Kate's a wise woman. This'll put fresh life into her, you'll see. She's been a good neighbour to us over the years, and I know she thinks a lot of you. I'm only saddened to have been the cause of such distress for your mother. I loved Gabby at the time. Wouldn't have knowingly let her down.'

'But it's turned out all right in the end, Llew,' Rissa said. 'Mum and Dad – I'll always think of him as that – were very happy together and wonderful parents to me. And now I've got you and Bron, haven't I. And Kate. I'm really very fortunate.'

Llew pressed a bristly kiss on her cheek. 'Like I said, you're a fine girl. Will's a lucky chap.'

Within the week Catrin was home again, still pale and rather wobbly, but glad to be out of the hospital environment, even if she was struggling to consume the hearty servings of what her mother called nourishing food. Her appetite seemed to have deserted her. Catrin knew it was nothing to do with the accident, more to do with her state of mind.

She was glad for Will and Rissa. Of course she was. And yet seeing the ring glinting on Rissa's finger, her heart had twisted painfully. Her thoughts had flown to Ewan and that last, despairing kiss. Had it been final? At the time she had thought not. Now, she simply did not know what to think. Flowers had arrived for her – twelve crimson rosebuds that had opened quickly in the heat of the hospital ward. The accompanying card had told her little. 'All my love, Ewan,' could be construed any way one liked. After the flowers – nothing. No get well card, no letter to enquire how she was. Every time a phone call had come for her at the hospital Catrin had expected it to be Ewan. It never was. She told herself that he was busy and would be sure to get in touch when he could, but deep within her the disappointment was crushing.

Next week a party was planned to celebrate Rissa's and Will's engagement. How was she going to cope? It wasn't that she begrudged them their happiness. On the contrary, she couldn't have been more glad for them both. It was just this draining cloud of loneliness that enveloped her. To make matters worse, Christmas was bearing down on them fast. Over breakfast her mother had been making noises about puddings and the turkey. Normally Catrin would have joined in with enthusiasm. She loved Christmas and all it involved. This time she could not get fired up over it. Only twelve days to go, and she had never felt less festive.

The dreams had stopped. But her slumber was not easy, tossed as she was by visions of being trapped in the car as it skidded terrifyingly and shot off the road. Gingerly Catrin fingered the cut on her head. It was healing well and the pain had gone, but her head still felt muzzy. Maybe some fresh air would help.

Reaching for the thick, soft mohair shawl that had been Beth's get-well present from all of them, Catrin hugged it round her shoulders and let herself out into the frosty brightness of the December afternoon.

Crossing the cobbled courtyard where winter jasmine flamed yellow against the old stone walls, Catrin entered the farmyard and went to lean on the gate. Everywhere glistened under the cold red sun. Over to the right, the roof of the Ty Coch cottage was just visible, its squat stone chimney rising smokeless and barren above the stark black line of the hill. High above, a buzzard traced lazy circles in the sky, its plaintive cry and the bellow of a cow from the shippon breaking the silence of countryside in the grip of winter.

Movement down on the valley road caught her attention. Someone was striding along it between the shining drystone walls, turning into the track to Brynteg. Seeing the sun glint on reddish-brown hair, the familiar long-legged stride, Catrin's heart skipped a beat. It wasn't. It couldn't be....

'Ewan!' she gasped, and heedless of her semi-convalescent state Catrin wrenched open the heavy wooden farm-gate and went flying down the stony track to him, shawl streaming, short hair bobbing, shouting as she ran. 'Ewan! Ewan! Oh, is it really you?'

'Hey!' Abandoning his flight bag, he swept her into his arms and swung her round, placing her down again firmly and looking searchingly at her. 'Thought you were supposed to be an invalid?'

'I'm feeling heaps better now. Ewan, what are you doing here?'

'What do you think? Oh, Catrin. When Rissa rang and told me what had happened … well, all I could think was that I might have lost you for good. She said you were all right, but I had to come and check for myself I … oh, come here, woman.'

He cupped her chin in his hand, tilted her face to his and pressed a powerfully sweet kiss on to her lips. For a moment the world seemed to rock and reel about Catrin, and then she was in his arms and kissing him back in a way she had never dared to dream about. Released, breathless and gasping, she stole a vivid confused glance up at his face with its newly acquired tan. The eyes that met hers burned with emotion and a shiver of pure joy ran through her.

'You'll catch cold out here,' he said with concern. 'Let's go and see if your mother's got the coffee on.' Retrieving his bag, he put his free arm around her waist and ushered her back along the track, to where the smoke huffing from the chimneys of Brynteg spoke of comfort and welcome within.

After Ewan had been warmly greeted, Bron tactfully nudged Llew, who wanted to hear all about New Zealand, back to his work and left the couple alone together in the front room. It turned out it had taken most of the week for Ewan to make the necessary arrangements to get over here. 'I've got an extended compassionate leave but I don't want to take advantage. Means I'll be here over Christmas – depending. The flight over seemed to take forever, and then I had to stop off in Cardiff to enquire about a special license.'

'A … what?'

'For us to be married!'

'But you haven't asked me yet.'

'Oh, Catrin. Why d'you think I've travelled halfway round the world if not to say this to your face. I love you, can't function without you. I must have been crazy not to have been more open with you before I left. Tried to text you when I sent the flowers. The wretched thing wouldn't accept the message.'

'It couldn't. My mobile went up in flames with the car.'

'Grief! Don't tell me any more. Just say you'll marry me?'

'I will. Of course I will.'

'There's just one point that must be made and there's no easy way of saying it. Catrin, you know I'm tied to my job out there for the next five years. I like it very much in New Zealand. It's a great country.'

'What you're trying to say is you want to settle there. Permanently?'

'I'd like to, yes,' Ewan said. 'On the other hand I know how much your home, family and friends mean to you. There's your job at the mill too. If you feel you really can't tear yourself away—'

'I don't mind where I am so long as we're *us*. Ewan, I've been so miserable since you left. Rest assured, this time when you go whizzing off I shall be right there by your side!'

They kissed. Ewan said, 'Shall we go and tell them the glad tidings?'

'Yes, let's. Be prepared for the floodgates to open. Mam never could hear good news without bursting into tears!'

They were the speediest nuptial arrangements ever. Bron, once she rallied to the idea that her girl was being taken off to the furthest corner of the earth, pulled out all the stoppers. Enlisting the help of Kate and Beth Marriott, Bron set about organizing the sort of wedding she had always envisaged for Catrin.

The date was set for the last day of the old year. The venue – Brynteg.

'I can't think of anywhere nicer. The house will be decorated up for Christmas too,' Rissa enthused, having dragged Catrin into a wine bar for a lunchtime sandwich during a trek round town for a bridal gown. They had settled on ivory velvet, with dark rose for Rissa who was to be bridesmaid.

'Can you see the write-up in the paper?' Catrin said, ruefully. 'The bride wore her grandmother's veil of antique lace to hide the stitches in her head!'

Rissa spluttered over her coffee. 'Idiot! They'll have been removed by then. Just be glad they didn't have to shave your hair.'

'I am. Might grow it again, actually. It's such a bother having to keep it trimmed all the time and anyway, Ewan liked it long. That reminds me. Must make an appointment with the hair-dresser. Want me to book you in as well?'

'Please. Was that the wedding cake Bron was icing when we left?'

Catrin nodded, quirking her lips. 'I tried to talk her into making do with the Christmas cake. She's got enough on without all these extras. Mam wouldn't hear of it. Dear me no!'

'Well, that's Bron for you.'

'Fortunately she'd made three large fruit cakes in October like always, so it didn't mean a last minute bake and a panic over them needing to mature and so on. Poor Mam. This must be the first time ever that Christmas has had to take second place.'

'You've got to hand it to her though. She's been brilliant. D'you think she'll like the dresses?'

'Oh yes. Mam said to go for velvet if possible.' Catrin looked suddenly doubtful. 'You don't think I'm a bit pale for white?'

'Not a bit of it,' Rissa said firmly. 'You're looked less bombed-out with every day that passes. Good thing Ewan showed up when he did. I was getting worried.'

'I'd love to know what you said to bring him hot-footing all the way from New Zealand.'

'Probably no more than you said to Will when he turned up in London.'

They both laughed excitedly. Then Catrin sobered. 'Rissa, my one reservation is not being here for when you and Will get married. Have you decided when it's to be?'

'Not yet. We were going to go ahead regardless. You know me once my mind's made up. But there's so much to be done. Selling the flat, making arrangements about the businesses. You know how slow these things can be. And there's Ty Coch. A farm doesn't stop just because there's to be a wedding.'

'You sound like a farmer's wife already.'

'I feel like one. Kate wants us to have an August wedding and I must say I quite fancy the idea.'

'August? I wonder if we could make it back for then? Oh, heavens. Why does it all have to be so complicated?'

'It isn't really. The pieces will shake together, the way it did over the dreams.' Rissa took a bite of ham and cheese baguette and chewed thoughtfully. 'You know, I think it's sad the way Sian deserted her father after all that had happened. 'Tisn't what one would have expected. Wonder what happened to him.'

'Well actually,' Catrin said, 'Ewan's been doing some research on our behalf. John Caradoc didn't exactly sit around brooding. Ewan found out that he married again. An Australian girl, quite well set up. Apparently they had four sons. And Sian was grown up when she left, after all.'

'So she was. Well. What a story to tell the grandchildren, aye? Have you finished your lunch? Only we've got the going away outfit to find yet. Unless you feel like breaking with tradition and wearing jeans!'

When Catrin finally arrived home with her parcels, more exhausted than she cared to admit, her father had a surprise in store. Llew called her through to the sitting room, where Ewan stood with his back to the fire and Bron sat pink-cheeked and flustered looking, a faint powdering of icing sugar in her hair mute witness to recent activities. They'd opened a bottle of red wine, Catrin saw with surprise. Ewan poured her a glass and gestured her to the sofa to sit beside her mother. A smile hovered about his lips. His dark-grey eyes held a secretive gleam.

'Your mother and I have been talking,' Llew said, once Catrin was comfortably seated. 'What would you say if we moved out to New Zealand as well? Wouldn't be immediately, of course. There'd be the farm to sort out first.'

'Sell Brynteg?' Catrin nearly dropped her glass in shock. 'You're joking!'

'Well, only to the right buyer,' Llew said.

'Think about it, Catrin,' said Ewan. 'Who desperately needs the extra acreage if they've got any hope of surviving as a farm? And has got the capital to invest.'

She had it at once. 'Rissa and Will? But—'

'Listen,' Llew said. 'New Zealand for me has always been something of a shining star. Told you once how much I'd wanted to go there. It was a sort of longing, one I thought would never be realized. Well, here's my chance. And your mother's not against the idea. We're both fit and able for a good few years yet, God willing. Frankly, I relish the prospect of getting away from all the red tape and bureaucratic rigmarole we have to put up with here in farming nowadays, and starting afresh in a new country.'

'Can't guarantee there won't be any red tape and rigmarole there as well,' Ewan put in, but he was smiling.

'Never mind. We'll cope. And the bottom line is we'll all be together.'

Bron spoke for the first time. 'Catrin love. What do you think?'

'Me? I think it sounds very much as if it's settled. I think it's a splendid idea.'

'It'll be a wrench leaving Brynteg,' Llew confessed. 'Old place had been in the family for a good many generations. But if Will and Rissa do take up the offer, and I've no reason to think they won't, then we couldn't be leaving the farm in better hands. And Rissa does have a vested interest after all.' He coughed and looked away, faintly embarrassed.

Ewan said, 'You know you can rely on us to make all the enquiries necessary for starting up over there. Catrin can be in charge of the search for a farm. I wouldn't have a clue.'

Bron put down her wine on the low table in front of her and clapped her hands together in glee. 'Oh my, on top of everything else this really is too much. I'm so excited I can't think! I have to pinch myself to know it's all happening, and I won't suddenly come round to finding it's all an illusion.' She stopped. 'Just had a thought. What about my ponies?'

'Well, we're not taking them with us,' said Llew in mild exasperation. Catrin took her mother's hand. 'I think we can safely leave them in Rissa's care. Oh, Mam. Imagine. It'll be all so different. So new. A real challenge.'

'It'll be fine,' her father said, smiling. 'Rissa can bring her children up here. We'll be the New Zealand branch of the family. Great, eh?'

'I think we can all drink to that,' Ewan said, his eyes meeting Catrin's over his wine. Glasses were replenished, a toast drunk. It was the first of many over the days that followed.

On the afternoon before they were due to leave, Catrin stole away to be on her own for a while. Goodbyes had already been made at the mill and in the small greystone village where she had been born and raised. One place remained where Catrin felt she needed to visit alone. All over Christmas the weather had been kind to them, keeping clear and dry, and frost crisped the short, sheep-nibbled hillside turf as she made her way across fields and woodland to the path that led to the druid's grove.

Brilliant winter sunlight glinted on the circlet of gold that Ewan had placed on her finger only days before. They had spent their first weekend together at a small coastal hotel at the pretty resort of Aberaeron, for which they both had a fondness. Now they were back at Brynteg for Catrin to undertake the packing of her clothes and other items.

Reaching the place with its holy well and famous touch-stone, Catrin paused and looked around her. Every twig, every blade of grass and mossy hollow, she wanted to imprint on her memory so that she could store it away like a treasured picture, and take it out and look at it whenever she needed to.

It was very still. Close by, the river chuckled on its course over the smooth brown stones of its ancient bed. The spring of clear water that had its source deep in the maw of the earth and never went dry, made a soft trickling sound as it flowed from a fissure in the touchstone rock into the pool below. Coins glinted there, tossed by unknown hands. Catrin had brought no silver, no posies or other offering. What she had brought was accept-ance. All her life she had been uneasy in this place that was sacred to the old gods. Now, as she reached out and reverently touched the stone that was said to have superhuman properties, all she felt was an overwhelming peace.

A light step behind her made her turn. 'Thought I'd find you here,' Ewan said. 'No more waking dreams?'

She shook her head, smiling at him. 'None whatsoever.'

He came and placed his hands on her shoulders and dropped a kiss very tenderly on her lips. 'Love you, Catrin.'

'Love you,' she replied.

They linked hands and walked away from the place, heading for a future and the promise of a bright new life. Together.